Salvation

A Small Town Second Chance Romance

Kelsee Warrick

Contents

Author's Note

This story holds a very dear spot in my heart. It's the first of many, and I truly hope every one of you who reads this falls in love with it as much as I did. I hope you take whatever lesson you need to learn from it and apply it to the world you experience every day. Dreams are only dreams if we let them stay that way.

There were times where I'd lose my motivation to write. Months would go by without me writing a word, and during those times I'd feel like a failure. This is your sign to keep forging ahead. Your happy ending is waiting for you, you just need to fight for it.

Content Warnings

This story contains content/themes that may be distressing to some readers, including the use of strong language, depictions of physical abuse, child abuse, alcohol abuse, mentions of drug abuse, and explicit sexual scenes. Please read at your own discretion.

This is a work of fiction. All characters and events in this book are products of the author's imagination. Any resemblance to actual persons, living or dead, is purely coincidental.

"To those who leave to find themselves, and to those who wait, hoping they will return."

Elise's House
Ana's House
Clover Hills Diner
Jake's Quick-Stop
Belle's Coffee
Buddie's Bar
Maurice's Antiques
BENSON'S
Clovers' Vet
Buddie's Ranch
Wesley's House
Blake's House
Town of
CLOVER HILLS

Chapter 1

BLAKE

Click-clack. Click-clack. Click-clack.

I attempt to focus on the sound of my rose-colored heels clacking against the marble flooring instead of the roaring panic bubbling in my chest, which accelerates with each step toward the ornate elevator doors. Today is the day. Today is the day I *finally* crawl my way out of Managing Editor and into the position of Chief Editor.

Chief Editor has been a dream since I set foot in New York City, and the dream became all too real just last week when Sarah Abrams left Ingrid's office with a ginormous box of tissues and red-rimmed eyes. I should feel remorse for Sarah. I should even feel a little terrified about her sudden departure, but all I can focus on is the sheer excitement coursing through my veins, knowing that all the endless coffee runs, the late nights, the boring as-shit meetings, and the back-bending hard work was finally paying off.

I *need* it to pay off. Otherwise, it will all have been for nothing.

Entering the elevator, I turn to the floor-to-ceiling mirrors and make quick work of checking my teeth, reapplying some gloss, and straightening my blazer that perfectly matches the new pumps Marshall gifted to me. I check my phone once more, hoping to have finally heard back from him since I let him know about the potentially life-changing news, but still no answer. He's probably just sleeping in, he warned me he had a late night in the office tonight. The doors chime, signaling my arrival to the top floor, and I tuck my phone back into my mini purse. Plastering on my most charming smile, I exit the doors and immediately spot Ingrid's glossy black hair draped over the back of her white office chair. I chirp a "Good Morning!" as I cross the room to place her iced coffee on the desk, only for a startled gasp to escape my lips.

All *three* of our lips.

I watch in horror as the coffee cup slips from my fingers and crashes to the floor, staining my heels with thick droplets of dark brown liquid. "Oh my god!" A hand flies up to cover my mouth as my brain works to catch up to what I'm seeing. A man is between Ingrid's legs.

Not just any man...Marshall. My Marshall.

Between...her legs. Ingrid's legs. Between *my* boss's legs.

Oh. My. God.

The glee I had at the possibilities of where this morning would take me was immediately replaced with nausea. I'm frozen to the spot, my feet like cement blocks as I watch the two before me scramble to get dressed.

"Blake?" They both ask, their voices laced with disbelief.

"This isn't what it looks like!" Marshall quickly adds, his words rushing out.

Ingrid ducks under her desk in an attempt to cover her naked form, but the image of her flushed cheeks and bare skin is forever engraved in my mind. Her manicured hand shoots out to steal one of their shirts, and I take that moment to close my eyes. The noise in my head rises to a crescendo as my brain finally catches up, and the utter horror that I just felt is gone in an instant, replaced by icy, cold anger that I so rarely let make an appearance. I abruptly jerk away from the desk, knocking over the hideous spider plant *she* made me buy last month to 'freshen up' her workspace.

"How long?" I grit out between my clenched teeth, forcing myself to look Marshall in the eyes.

I'd be damned if this man made me look like an even bigger fool than I already do.

"S-since you introduced us." He stutters, wincing when Ingrid shoots him an angry look of disbelief.

I suck in a breath as Ingrid hops up from where she was hiding beneath her overly large desk, talking as she hurriedly buttons her shirt. I see and register her mouth moving but can't seem to hear a single word that leaves her lips.

Over a *year*. Over a *year* of sharing the same bed with this man only for him to be fucking my boss. 4 years. 4 *years* of hard work and dedication went down the drain in less than a minute. I blink, and without thinking, I blurt out, "I quit."

I don't acknowledge Marshall, who's currently hopping after me with one shoe off. No, I'm already spinning on my heels and racing for the same doors I was so excited to enter just mere seconds ago. "You – you can't quit!" Ingrid's nasally, high-pitched voice echoes after me. I ignore her continued spiel, ignore Marshall's pleading, ignore that discarded plant now littering the perfectly polished floor, and ignore that familiar burn creeping up my nose, begging to be cut loose.

"Should have thought about that before choosing to whore yourself out to the first man to pay you any attention." I spit the venomous words from my mouth but feel little to no shame as they hit their mark. They both flinch and just to be petty in the only way I know how I whip back around and bend down to pick up the half-emptied coffee cup.

"And pick up your own damn coffee!" I yell, launching the cup at the two of them, savoring the shock rippling their features.

***

I outwardly cringe at the influx of texts pouring onto my small and cracked phone screen. I had been meaning to get it replaced for months now but haven't had the motivation or time. I scroll through the various other texts I've gotten from him over the past few hours, choosing to ignore them *again* and block the unknown number. Love bombing and gaslighting seem to be his new favorite trick.

This is the third phone number he's texted me from, and I'm at the point where I'll need to change my number if I can even begin to hope for a moment of peace. Probably, moving out of the country is more like it. I throw the phone behind me, sighing as it hits the plush pillow at the top of my bed. I rub my hands over my face, not surprised to find no tears littering my warm cheeks.

We had been together for quite some time, so I suppose I should feel a little more distraught. But I can't bring myself to feel anything other than pure annoyance. I liked Marshall, but I didn't love him. He came from a good home and family. He made me laugh, he was smart, and the sex was fine. He bought me overly lavish gifts and took me out to dinner twice a week. He's the type of man any woman would be happy to have. It indeed was a shock to find out he'd been sleeping with my boss for the entirety of our relationship.

I introduced them at a Christmas party, blissfully unaware of the way they had studied each other and how they took a rather large interest in what the other did. I was naïve enough to think it was great. That it would get me a foot in the door when it came to growing my relationship with Ingrid, but clearly, that was not the case. It did the opposite.

Now I'm here. Jobless, single, and a failure. All accomplished in the past 24 hours.

It hurts, of course. Because trusting someone and having them break that trust will gut anyone's soul. But it doesn't hurt in the way I had thought it would. I'm not heartbroken, just disappointed. Disappointed that I settled for a man so *boring*. And for what? In hopes of proving something to myself? That I could move on? Heal?

I wish I could go back and shake some sense into my-self. Save myself a year, nearly two, of my life. Over the time I've been living in New York, I've gone on multiple dates with gorgeous men, and even brought many of them home, but something had always been *missing*. It rarely felt right, and I know deep in my bones that I had only ever been settling for Marshall. I had always thought his nose was a little too straight, his smile a little too perfect, and his hands a little too soft. I think I loved the idea of him more than anything. What he could give me, and what he was offering me. A distrac-tion, a home, a purpose.

I was not a woman without her flaws, but I sure as hell spent my time picking out everyone else's.

I rub the bridge of my nose in hopes of encouraging at least one single tear to fall free, but it never comes. Just like that promotion. Just like that hope of creating and holding onto something that was so selfishly for myself.

I choose to glare at the box filled with office supplies resting on my dining room table instead, and then at the empty duffle bag I pulled out the minute I set foot in my apartment.

"I'm so, so sorry, babe. They never deserved you," Vivienne says as she hugs me for what must be the tenth time.

I had immediately texted her as I left the office, and she'd shown up in less than twenty minutes with an armful of goodies she deemed essential for this kind of heartbreak. It's one of the many reasons I love Vivienne. She's sickeningly sweet, but she'll always go to bat for the ones she loves.

"I know. It's just-" I drop my head into my hands, pushing them through my hair. "I've been working towards this for years. *Years.* What the hell am I supposed to do now?"

Vivienne and I met when we were both eighteen, courtesy of her older sister, Whitney. We became fast friends when she welcomed me with open arms into her tiny studio apartment. I had nowhere else to go when I landed in New York, and despite the fact that I was a stranger, she was more than happy to take me under her wing and treat me as her own. I finally stopped freeloading when I saved up enough to attend college and live on campus. I tried more than once to pay her back in full for all the money she had spent keeping both of us afloat, but she never accepted it. Funnily enough, a few months after I moved out, she ended up transferring to the same school as me, where we became roommates once again. In our last year of college, though, we unfortunately weren't able to stay in the same part of campus due to our different career paths. We got stuck with roommates we admittedly complained about more often than we should have, and Vivienne soon became that type of friend that you didn't need to see every day or even every few weeks. When we came back together, it always felt as if no time had passed. Despite that, our busy lives still took a toll on our friendship. So, after graduation, we decided to remedy that in the best way possible.

By buying an apartment together.

It wasn't a hard decision to make, considering we already knew what it was like to be housemates. We were more like sisters than anything else. She was one of the very few people who knew everything about me. And I knew that regardless of anything that happened, she'd always be the one consistent thing in my life, and I'd always be hers.

"This is going to sound terribly cliché of me but shit like this happens for a reason, right? Maybe this job wasn't what you needed right now. That man was *definitely not* what you needed right now. It sucks, but maybe you can use this as an opportunity to explore *you* a little bit more? You've always wanted to write a book, so why not take a couple of months and give that a try?" She pauses when I look back up at her. "You've been working non-stop since you got to the city. You have enough saved up to take a break. So, maybe it's time for a change in pace? Maybe even scenery?" She gives me a knowing look as I mull over her words, letting the air fill with silence.

"I have to get back to work," Vivienne says as she reaches forward to give my hand a tight squeeze. "But I promise we'll watch all the chick flicks, eat all the snacks, and drink all the wine the minute I get home." She's one of the best Veterinary Technicians in the city. She loves her job more than probably deemed healthy, but I could not help beaming with pride every time she talks about it. It makes me so happy to know just how hardworking she is and that she scored the job she's been dreaming of since she was a little girl. She no doubt deserves it and more.

"Sounds good," I sigh. She leans over, kisses my cheek, and gives me a small smile. Sauntering away, she calls out over her shoulder, "Don't you dare open that merlot without me!" And then she's gone as quickly as she came, and I'm utterly alone with all my unwanted thoughts.

New York is home. It's been home for the past six years. I *made* it home when I needed it the most. But maybe Vivienne is right. Have I been a fool for thinking I could so easily run away from my past and start anew? Maybe it's time to head back to my roots and face everything that's led me to *this*. I dwell on that line of thinking while I pop open that forbidden bottle of merlot, and once it's finished later that night, Vivienne walks back in the door with another one as if she already knew what to expect when she got back home.

Chapter 2

BLAKE

"**I** said shut up, you little bitch!" My father barked, bringing the back of his palm across my face, striking hard.

"You're just fucking like her!"Again, and again, and again.

It didn't matter that cry after cry tore its way out of my already swollen and bruised throat. His hands are merciless in their assault, and I know well enough that he'll only stop when he's satisfied. If he even chooses to stop.

I'm usually so careful when he's drinking. Knowing when to retreat to my room, when to lock the door, when to keep my mouth shut. And it's never this bad. Never physically, at least. He usually doesn't leave bruises where anyone will see them. But tonight, something inside me snapped. I was angry at myself for letting this go on, at *him for his brutal assaults, at my mother for being gone, and at everyone else around me for not seeming to notice his unchecked anger. I could no longer stomach the hits, the harsh words, or anything else from the man that holds no resemblance to the father that was once the center of my entire universe.*

"This is why she left you!" I screamed, spitting in his face. I screamed as loud as I possibly could, as if someone could hear. As if anyone could hear.

Again, and again, and again.

Maybe this time will be it. Maybe I won't wake up this time. Maybe this will be the last time he can hurt me.

Again, and again, and again.

But that line of thinking only forces me to see the faces of everyone who will miss me. And I promise myself that if I survive this, I'll tell Mama. I will tell her everything. Maybe Wes, too. If only I survive.

Again, and again, and – "Again, thank you for flying with us today, and welcome to Clover-Hills."

I jolt awake, the pilot's voice cutting through the overhead speakers. I murmur an apology to the older gentleman I spooked and try to blink the sleep from my eyes and steady my breathing. My neck is drenched with sweat, and my palms are clammy with nerves. I must have slept the entirety of the flight, which I no doubt can thank my hangover for. I sigh as I open the window, pressing my pounding head to the cool glass, willing the pain to fade.

I can still hear that crack from his hand, the sound rattling in my bones and echoing in my heart. I haven't been home in years. Which means I haven't had a dream in at least the past three, yet the minute I sense where I am, all the progress I've made seems to fly out the window. Rubbing my temples, I recall the moments that led up to such a ridiculous decision. The last thing I've ever wanted to do was return to this crappy little town, but after leaving my job, boyfriend, and getting roaring drunk with Vivienne, I woke up to a packed bag (courtesy of my best friend) and a non-refundable one-way plane ticket to my hometown that I must have purchased after the second bottle of wine. Or maybe the third.

"Ma'am, did you need help with your bags?"

I pull my face from the window as a petite blonde dressed in a deep, blue uniform leans over the row of seats before me.

"Uh, sorry?" I say, blinking hard and trying to shake off that dream.

"Everyone else has deboarded. Did you need help?" she asks again.

"Oh, no. Sorry. I guess I'm still waking up," I respond quickly, embarrassment flooding my system. The flight attendant gives me a weird look but nods and walks back down the aisle without another word. I gather all my things and follow. I'm certain that if anyone was standing close enough, they could hear the booming thud of my heart against my ribcage. I clutch my bag tighter and force myself to step off the plane and back into Clover-Hills.

Chapter 3

WESLEY

Closing out the text from my brother, I slam the door of my old, rusted truck shut. I watch as blue paint chips crumble to the dirt road beneath my feet.

"You know you can afford something new. Why bother with that old shit-wagon?" My mom chirps from her rocker on the front porch, sipping what I can only assume is her 'homemade' lemonade. Which means vodka with a dash of lemon.

I shake my head as I near the old yellow steps of my childhood home. I don't linger on the fact that she's right, I can afford something new – another truck or car that I wouldn't have to constantly fix and worry about breaking down on the side of the road. I inherited the old Ford the year my dad passed and avoided it like the plague for quite some time. The idea of riding around in it without him was always too painful.

Over a year ago, I was feeling sentimental and lonely enough that I dug it out of the garage. Somehow, it's still a long way from being anything but an eyesore. I don't have the heart to scrap it or sell it just to buy something pretty and polished. So, I'll keep reviving it as long as it'll let me.

"We've already talked about this," I said, nodding toward the drink in her hand, hoping to steer the conversation in a new direction, "and don't you think it's a bit early in the day?"

"You know what they say," she winks and swishes around her drink, "it's 5 o'clock somewhere."

Raising my eyebrows and forcing back the smirk creeping up my lips, I glance at my watch, knowing I want to work on a few things before heading to the bar. I have a knack for never telling my mom no, which is exactly why I showed up in the first place. Helping Wyatt get the loose cattle back where they belong took up the majority of my day and I need to get a move on.

"What did you need me for?" I ask, maybe a little too bluntly.

"Such a charmer, my boy," she sighs as she sets down her glass and shuffles out of her chair. "I need you to take some stuff to El's."

El, or Elise, is her best and possibly *only* friend. The two are as thick as thieves. I can't remember a time when they weren't attached at the hip. I've known El for as long as I've known my mother, which easily makes her just as hard to say no to. I follow my mom inside, and the smell of baked goods immediately hits my nose, filling me with a comfort that can only come from the woman in front of me. Early-morning baking and running around in the yard with her are some of my fondest memories. While I no doubt inherited her skills in the kitchen, mine have never tasted as good as hers. I reach to snag a muffin off the table.

"Oh, you shouldn't ha-" But she slaps it from my hand before I have a chance to stuff the freshly baked muffin into my mouth.

"No, you neanderthal! This is all for Elise," she grumbles. She adds something under her breath about how I *"haven't changed a bit"* and then begins loading a tower of dishes into my hands.

"*Why* exactly does she need fifty different flavors of muffins?" I mutter, rubbing my temple with a free hand.

The last time she baked this much was after my father's funeral. And when Elise served her husband divorce papers.

"You ask too many questions. And it's a hundred, not fifty. Now get going. They'll only stay fresh for so long," she says, shooing me out of the kitchen.

She's slamming the door on my ass before I can ask any more questions, and I'm left with the sinking feeling that my mother's up to another one of her schemes. One that I want *no* part in.

Chapter 4

BLAKE

I step out of the car, slinging one of my bags over my shoulder.

"Thanks," I say to the driver, slipping him a tip.

The man gives me a nod in return, and I watch as the red car peels down the road, kicking up dirt and rocks as it goes, before eventually disappearing from view. I watch, as if I can track it long enough to delay taking in what awaits behind me.

Clover-Hills still smells and looks exactly as it did the day I left. It's fresh, quiet, and peaceful. There are mountain ranges, trees, and fields that stretch for miles. A few updates have been made to accommodate the town but most of the land has been left in its natural state. It's a small town consisting of mainly the necessities with few family-owned businesses scattered throughout.

Such a stark contrast to the bustle of New York City.

Anxiety, fear, and a little nostalgia course through me as I turn and take in the little white house with green shutters before me. So many happy memories. But so many painful memories, too.

How can something be so terrifying yet so comforting at the same time?

The all-too-familiar creek of the screen door draws my attention. As it slams open, my eyes lock on the blonde mop of curls and brown eyes that so fiercely resemble mine, standing frozen in the doorway.

"Hi, Mama," I choke out.

When I speak those two words, I finally let the burning in my nose that's been building for days wash over me. I let the tears fall as my mom rushes toward me, reaching for me as if I'm a lifeline. Hugging me as if I'm as fragile as I look. As fragile as I *feel* being back in my hometown and so far away from what I thought was the right space to piece myself back together.

Chapter 5

BLAKE

"You haven't changed a thing," I comment, looking around the place I once called home.

Booking a plane back to New York City is my first and only thought the minute I step into my old bedroom. It's as small as I remember it being. My old vanity is consumed with little trinkets I hoarded in my early years. Posters of my favorite bands cling to the baby-pink walls. The twin bed still houses a pristine white comforter that my mom replaced dozens of times due to my clumsy habits. The dark ebony dresser is tucked neatly underneath the little window in the room, and its matching nightstand is still to the left of the bed. No dust or wear and tear, as if it's been upkept since I've left.

"Didn't feel right," my mom says, leaning against the doorway. "Do you want to talk about it?

"No," I shake my head. "Just – just not yet."

"Baby, you haven't visited in years, and I wasn't all there when you left. I have no idea why you're suddenly home, and aside from a few texts or calls, I have no idea – "

"Mom, please." I cut her off with a pleading look. "I promise we'll talk about it. About everything. Just not right now."

She sighs, clearly not happy with me avoiding the subject.

"Alright. Well, get some rest and then take a shower. You stink," she teases, shooting me a wink and grin as she shuts the door, leaving me alone in a room that feels far too small and suffocating.

***

"I'll be back, baby. I promise. I'll be gone for just a little while, okay? And then you and I will have all the time in the world. It's best for all of us if I go." My mom places a warm hand on my face before pulling me in close, hugging tight.

I knew this, but it didn't mean that it hurt any less. After my parents finalized the divorce, my mother spiraled. The anxiety meds became all too easy to abuse. She quickly understood that she needed help and wasn't scared to ask for it regardless of how hard of a decision it was. I deserved a mother who was whole, not bits and pieces of one, and that's why it was the best decision for my mom to make.

Ana could see what was happening with her friend early on, and despite their joint efforts to get her to quit naturally, it wasn't working. So, Ana helped guide her into the right hands, and my mom was off to a rehab center until she made progress in turning around her addiction. It could be just mere weeks, or it could be months, but either way, my heart hurt at the idea of not seeing her every day and of being with my father 24/7, who had become far more distant from me than he had ever been. "I know. I know, Mama. I love you."

I hug her tighter and let a few tears roll down my already red cheeks.

"I'll see you soon, okay?" My mom reassures me. She looks over my shoulder to where Ana waits behind me and nods her head in a way that says, 'Take care of our girl.'

"Always," Ana replies.

Ana and I spend the next few minutes hugging each other, watching as my mom steps into the passenger side of a black car and pulls onto the only road out of town.

"Ready to go, kid? I promised your dad you'd be there soon," Ana asks, breaking the silence.

I nod, pure heartache filling my chest from the whirlwind of today. I wipe my cheeks before following Ana back to her car.

Chapter 6

BLAKE

After taking a shower and getting little to no sleep due to the unease of being back home, I quietly make my way downstairs.

As much as I'd love to stay cooped up in a bed all day, my old bedroom does little to bring me any comfort. My therapist back in the city often told me how important it was to just *get out*, and it's something I do my best to stick by. Going for a walk, reading a book in the park, grabbing a coffee, whatever it may be, it keeps you busy and reminds you *to live*, not just survive.

Plus, avoiding town and all its close-knit people will be nearly impossible to accomplish, so why not dive in headfirst?

I made a note on the drive through town to stop in at Bell's and to surprise Whitney, so I might as well start there. "Mom, I think I'm going to-"

I pause in the doorway of the kitchen when I see that my mom is not alone.

"Hun, Wes is here!" My mom exclaims, sounding way too chipper.

Dive in headfirst indeed.

My mind must be short-circuiting because that is *not* the Wesley I remember.

Long, thick nose on his stupidly symmetrical face. Cropped chestnut hair. Broad, tan shoulders that fill out his crisp white t-shirt. Black ink of all shapes and sizes runs up one of his arms and peeks up over his shoulder blade. Light stubble litters his strong jawline, and I can almost feel the slight burn it would leave between my–

Nope. Not going there.

The only thing I recognize before me are those cerulean blue eyes, but what I last remember as a pimply, scrawny teenage boy now screams pure *man*.

Not a hint of that little boy I grew up with.

Not the boy who used to chase me around with dead garden snakes and wads of mud he'd meticulously use to paint my bright, blonde strands a muddy brown.

Not the teenager who held me under the stars the night before I left him and everything else in this town behind.

I'd be lying if I said I hadn't thought about running into Wes, but I wasn't expecting it to be so soon. I was hoping I'd have more time. And a plan, to sort out everything

I need and want to say. Heart slamming in my chest, I squeak out a, "Hi."

He flashes me a smile that's anything but warm.

God, even his teeth are perfect.

"Blake." Just one word, but it's low and slips out with a breath he doesn't mean to give me. The way his jaw ticks, tight like he's just swallowed something sour, makes my stomach twist.

"I didn't realize you were back in town," he adds, letting his gaze rake over my body.

"I-I didn't tell anyone," I say, crossing my arms and pushing down the urge to squirm under his hard stare. "Wasn't planning on coming back, I guess."

He responds with a short nod and a clipped, "Well, then. I better get going. Just wanted to drop those off."

My eyes land on the muffins taking up half of our kitchen counter. Who the hell needs *that* many muffins?

"Oh, yes! The bar. Blake, why don't you go with? You have to see what he's done with the place," Mom interjects.

Brown eyes meet blue.

"Buddies' Bar?" I ask, feeling a wave of nostalgia I wasn't prepared for.

Another nod.

"I didn't realize he left it to you," I respond, unsure of what else to say.

He shrugs, "Can't imagine you would've heard about it in New York City."

Ouch. *Okay.* Suppose I deserved that.

Buddies' is his dad's bar. *Was* his dad's bar. Ben asked us one day what he should call it, so we had picked Buddie, and it just stuck. I can't remember why we agreed on that one, but he loved it. And soon, it became the town's nickname for Ben. Everyone called him Buddie, and he even named the family ranch after it.

We often spent hours at the bar when we were younger, playing pool or helping clean-up for free ice cream that his dad would bribe us with (without telling our moms, of course). My heart cracks a little at the memories.

Hell-bent on breaking the growing tension, my mom claps her hands together, "On that note, you two should *really* get going. Don't wanna piss off the regulars by keeping them waiting!"

Screw this. My therapist was wrong. I'm definitely better off staying in bed. "Mom, I don't think that's a good idea –"

"Nonsense." She cut me off. "I need to run some errands anyways, and I'm sure Wesley will be more than happy to have you tag along. It'll be just like old times. I'll pick you up before dinner. Maybe it'll give you a chance to explore the rest of the town, too."

I go to protest, but one look from her has me snapping my mouth shut. I should have known, even before landing in this godforsaken town, that my mother would meddle with something so broken. I internally berate myself for not getting a rental car the minute the plane touched down.

I don't look at Wesley, but with a gesture of my hand, I say, "Lead the way."

Chapter 7

WESLEY

I wasn't planning on coming back.

Don't I know it.

Why is she here, then? Why, of all times, did she decide to come home *now*? I shove off those questions and all the restless memories that come with them. I tried and failed to focus on placing one foot in front of the other and not on the blonde bombshell trailing behind me. It doesn't matter what Blake's doing in town, not anymore.

Blake. She's exactly the same as I remember, yet so different.

Still devastatingly beautiful, and still the only person who can so easily crawl under my skin after just a few words. With full, plump pink lips, and big honey-brown eyes, her thick hair is tied back in a high pony that cascades down her back. She has perfectly arched eye-brows and dark, long eyelashes. A button nose that's still a host to the tiny scar she gained from the time she fell off her bike in my mom's driveway. Tight jeans and a white tank do little to hide her ample curves. It's as if the devil himself crafted Blake Warner just to *spite* me.

As I swing open her door and motion for her to hop in, my eyes lock on another scar that runs along her fore-arm, one I don't recognize. She does so, hopping in and completely avoiding my gaze. Slamming the door shut, I clench my fist at my side and walk around the back of the truck, hoping to prolong the awkward as-shit encounter that's inevitably about to happen. Thankfully, it's silent for the first few moments. Until her mom's house is fully out of view.

"I'm surprised you managed to get this thing up and running," Blake says, filling the silence.

I watch from the corner of my eye as she runs her pink manicured nails across the dash. Something about it has me squeezing the steering wheel and tearing my gaze away. I don't respond, still a little shocked that she's sitting in *my* truck. But leave it to Blake to prod the silence once more. For whatever reason, she never could stand it.

There's a teasing tone in her voice once we hit the one-way dirt road into town. "Bar owner *and* mechanic, huh?"

"Yup," I answer, not willing to elaborate.

She hums, "Hmmm. Long way from future astronaut."

I loosen my tight grip on the steering wheel and refrain from shooting her a look.

"I was ten when I said that," I say, keeping my eyes on the road.

"Oh, please. You said that all throughout high school. You *even* begged your parents to send you to space camp."

"If I remember correctly, you're the one who wanted to be a ballerina when you clearly only have two left feet," I retort.

"Whatever. At least *mine* was realistic," she says with a snort.

"You broke your ankle five minutes into the warm-up," I say, making Blake gasp.

"You promised you'd never mention that out loud!"

"You started it," I say, knowing it's a childish come-back. But she relinquishes.

"Fair enough," She sighs and crosses her arms over her chest, leaning back into her seat. "At least writing turned out well enough for me."

"If that was the case, you wouldn't be back in Clover-Hills," I bite back. The words are out before I can stop them, and they leave a bitter taste in my mouth.

For someone who prides themselves on being so calm and collected, that all goes out the window when it comes to Blake. We may have been apart for six years, but going back to our bickering ways makes it feel like we haven't been apart for even a day. But I took it too far, like I always do, and I don't have to look at her to know my words hit their mark.

"I didn't mean-" I start.

"Let's forget it." She whispers, interrupting me.

I snap my mouth shut at her broken tone. This is going to be a very, very long day.

Chapter 8

BLAKE

In Clover-Hills, everyone knows everyone. Even the ones who have been gone for the past six years. Little change happens in a town this small, and as I take in the bar, all I can feel is undiluted anxiety at even the thought of stepping inside.

I can tell it's been updated, but Wesley kept it the same for the most part. It's small, specifically when compared to those in the city. An old wooden sign swings above the door with "Buddies" in bold black letters, some of the lettering peeling from natural wear and tear. A few small windows litter the brick building. A red neon 'we're open!' sign buzzes in what looks to be a newly installed glass door. Where there was nothing before, now sits a small patio jutting out onto the sidewalk on either side of the main entrance. Metal tables, chairs, and black string lights hang from the wood pillars above. It's the perfect setup for a late-night drink with friends.

There are far too many memories that I've spent years forgetting inside that bar. The outside is different, but what if the inside looks the same?

Can I handle that? What if I see someone I know? What if they ask *why* I chose to come back? What the hell do I tell them?

"Ah, yes. I left this shit town because my father used to beat me and my mother was a druggie, but hey! I got cheated on, so I quit my dream job after four years, and here I am!"

I can't handle the pitying glances or small talk. Fear has me stuck to the seat of Wesley's truck like glue, and I don't even realize we're parked until he's swinging open my door with a scowl. "Gonna sit in there all day?"

I huff out a breath, ignoring his awaiting hand to help me down and hop out of the truck. The door slams with a thump, making me jump a little. His brows shoot up and he asks, "Something wrong?"

"No." I snap back.

His face tells me he can smell my bullshit a mile away, but he chooses to leave it alone and strides to the bar without another glance in my direction.

Good, the less he prods, the less complicated this will be.

I practically run to keep up with his long strides, but I falter once more as we grow closer to the doors. The smell of fries and burgers makes my stomach growl embarrassingly loud as we near. Buddies' may be a bar, but it has always had the best food in town.

The closer we get, the smaller the world around me feels. The simple act of breathing feels even harder, and before I can think twice, I'm swiveling on my heels and booking it down the street. Thankfully, it's still early enough in the day that not many people are out.

"Where the hell are you going?" I don't need to turn around to know it's Wesley's voice hollering after me. I call over my shoulder, deciding to throw his earlier jab back in his face, "Let's just *pretend* that the writing did work out, and I'm *not* back."

I can hear him calling my name, cursing, and maybe even taking a few steps to follow, but I'm gone and turning around a corner before he even gets the chance.

Blake screeched and pumped her arms faster, her long blonde strands swaying behind her as Wesley chased her through the tall grass with a glob of mud in his hands.

"I'm gonna get you back!" he screamed.

Blake had just pushed him into the mud baths the pigs love to roll in, and he was covered head to toe.

"It was an accident!" she screamed behind her.

Their mothers were watching from the porch, while Wyatt was sitting criss-crossed on the floor, a book propped on his knees and headphones covering his ears.

It was Sunday, and the two women always met each other for coffee on the porch while the kids burned off energy. Elise looked to Ana, who was covering her face with her hands and shaking her head.

"Oh, it'll wash off! Let them be kids," Elise says, nudging Ana with an elbow, earning a glare in return. One look at her best friend has Ana breaking out into a giggle.

"He's probably going to spend his entire life chasing after that girl," Ana says, trying to cover her growing smile with her hand.

Soon, Elise is joining her in a fit of giggles. They both begin to laugh so hard that tears spring to their eyes, and they have to hold onto each other as they double over and gasp for breath.

"Yeah," Elise laughs as they both look out beyond the porch and at the two running through the field. "Yeah, I think he will."

Chapter 9

BLAKE

The tiny gold bells above the coffee shop door ring as I step into the space. It's nothing like I remember. I left just a few weeks after Whitney had bought the space, and sadly, I missed out on the majority of the renovations. It was once home to an antique shop and is easily the largest space on the street. The perfect size for what she decided to do with it.

One half of the shop consists of towering walls of books, and the other half is a café. The wall of mugs dangling from old horseshoes is what separates the two sides. The marble countertops lying along the long black coffee bar are littered with everything coffee. I could smell the mouth-watering baked goods the minute I walked in. But the huge vintage mint-green espresso machine is what immediately catches my eye. Vivienne had found it in a thrift shop and anonymously mailed it to her sister's front steps. Whitney had called me, thinking I was the one who had sent it. The second I had tried to deny it over the phone, Vivienne had reached over and squeezed my arm so hard I thought it'd fall off. I never could understand why the two pretended to not care about the other, or why there was this weird bridge between them that they'd never cross. It was sad, knowing that they both so obviously yearned for a relationship with the other. I'm an only child, though, so what do I know?

Mismatched furniture and tables for working, reading, or a cozy breakfast are scattered throughout. The walls not covered by books, mirrors, or local art are old, rustic brick. The regal white ceiling is still gorgeously intact and is home to a huge crystal chandelier right in the middle of the space, but most of the light within the shop streams in from the glass windows taking up the front of the coffee house. Other adorable details are scattered throughout. Plush pillows, vases of flowers, an old wooden coat rack that's being used to hold even more battered horseshoes, bits, worn cowboy boots and hats, and lassos. Somehow, it's both chic and country. Something only Whitney's artistic eye could make look so charming. I immediately feel like grabbing a cup of coffee and a book to cuddle up with on the floral settee stuffed in the far-left corner.

"Oh, my god!" A girly shriek pierces the air. "Blake? Is that really you?"

Raven-black hair and hazel eyes appear, pulling me away from taking in the shop. It always shocks me just how alike Whitney and her sister look, no doubt sharing their mother's features. The only difference is their eyes. While Whitney's are more green than brown, Vivienne's are a brown so dark they're nearly black.

"Whitney!" I throw myself at her, hugging her until my arms start to cramp, only pulling back so we can take each other in. "It's so good to see you." Another bone-breaking hug.

"What the hell are you doing home? Why didn't you call? You look amazing!"

"It's nice to see you, too, Whit. The shop...It looks *amazing. You* look amazing!"

She beams at me, a glint of pride and excitement coating her beautiful features. "It's come a long way, that's for sure." She nods toward a booth by the window. "Take a seat and let me make you a coffee. We clearly have a lot to catch up on."

"Lavender and honey with oat milk, right?" She asks as she points a finger in my direction.

"That would be perfect," I answer with a smile.

Some time passes, and as I sit in the window seat of Bell's, I watch as people pass on the street outside. It's so quiet compared to the city, and for some reason, I find myself missing all the noise. It gave me something to focus on rather than the never-ending anxiety floating through my head.

Whitney comes around the table, using her foot to kick out a chair, and sits across from me, two coffees in hand.

"So? What's new? What are you in town for?" She questions, sliding my glass towards me.

"I lost my job. Well," I pause, nervously biting my lip. "I quit."

"Oh, B," No pity on her face, just pure curiosity and worry. "What the hell happened?"

So, I tell her everything that's happened since I've left. I tell her about college, I give her updates on Vivienne (without her asking, of course), what the city was like, and how exactly I ended up back in town.

She slumps back in her chair and crosses her arms. "Fuck them. I knew I didn't like that bitch. And Marshall? What the fuck kind of name is *Marshall*?" She seethes.

I can't help but laugh, something Whitney has never failed to make me do. My heart tightens, realizing just how much I've missed her. We kept in touch throughout the years, but with us both being so busy, it was hard to update each other on every aspect of life. I have her to thank for ever getting out of this town. She's the sole reason I even got a fresh start. I take a sip of my coffee, savoring the taste of lavender on my tongue. A beat of silence, and then Whitney's face lights up like it's Christmas morning.

Her grin widens as she says, "Funny enough, I've been looking for some extra help."

"Oh, no. No. I couldn't. I appreciate-"

"Blake," She cuts me off, holding up her hand. "We're practically family. And aside from that, you're one of my favorite people. This will benefit you just as much as me. I get to see you more, and maybe get a little free time for myself with an extra pair of hands around. Do this, maybe stay in town for a little, and then go from there? Maybe it'll give you some time to figure things out and clear your head."

Her words of wisdom sound oddly similar to Vivienne's, and before I can voice anything else, she sets down her coffee cup and grabs my hand that's resting on the table between us.

"Speaking of family...how do you feel about becoming a godmother?" She asks then she glances down, and I follow her gaze to the hand resting on her belly.

A noise I'm quite certain I've never made before escapes my lips.

"Oh my – you're pregnant!?" I lunge forward, nearly knocking my coffee over. "Why didn't you *tell* me?" Then another thought hits me, and my eyes widen. "Who-"

"Shh!!" She looks around, but thankfully, there's no one in here save for an elderly woman reading in the corner. "Quiet! Not many people know yet. I just found out."

"Does Viv know?" My brows scrunch, and I speak in a much quieter tone this time.

"No." She shakes her head. "And I'd like to keep it a secret for a little while longer."

"Hey," I squeeze her hand back, "I understand." My smile turns wicked, and I fail at keeping my features neutral. "My god baby is going to be one spoiled son of a bitch."

She laughs deeply in return, a watery smile of her own greeting mine. She goes to open her mouth once more, but the bell chimes again. Signaling someone else had joined our space. Whitney abruptly stands, nearly knocking over her chair from the force, and lets out a breathless greeting, "Hey."

"Hey," A deep voice echoes from behind us.

I don't get the chance to question her behavior or the odd tension radiating in the air because when I turn, a familiar blue gaze lands on me.

"Holy shit. Little Lake?" The man wastes no time in coming around and scooping me up in a bear hug.

I try my best not to roll my eyes at the old nickname. "I've missed you too, Wyatt," I say, squeezing him back.

Wyatt Conway is Wesley's older brother. Age has only made him more handsome. His eyes are the same blue as Wesley's, but the curly hair that now falls to his shoulders is a few shades darker. It makes me a bit envious that a man was gifted with something most women pray for. The two brothers could pass as twins if you weren't around them so often, the smallest features telling the two apart. Wyatt has always looked more like Ana, whereas Wesley looks like his father. We grew up together as well but were never nearly as close as Wesley and I were. He treated me like a little sister. He often was just in the background, off working or helping his mom where it was needed around the house. After his dad passed, he rarely ever spent any time at home. As soon as he turned of age, he moved out and took over the family ranch.

He sets me down, holding me at arm's length. "Mom didn't say anything about you coming home."

"She didn't know," I explain.

His brows raise at that, but one look from Whitney lets him know it's best not to question anything. Instead, he pivots the conversation, "Give me a call in the morning tomorrow. You've got to come see the ranch. I'm meeting someone now, but I just wanted to stop in for a coffee."

With that, Whitney comes back into view and hands him a cardboard cup.

"On the house," she says, not meeting his eyes.

Their exchange is tense, and it feels as if she's just trying to get him out as soon as possible.

He huffs, sliding a bill into her hands. "Keep the change."

Wyatt's always been one grumpy motherfucker too, especially after their dad passed. But if you've known him for as long as I have, you know just how cuddly and warm he is on the inside. Seems Whitney is one of the few he chooses to tolerate, whether she knows it or not. After he leaves, I face Whitney.

"That was...weird?"

The nerves she had when he was here vanished, replaced by something I can only read as annoyance.

She huffs out a laugh before flipping the open sign to close and locking the door. "Don't even get me started on Wyatt Conway."

Chapter 10

WESLEY

Blake and I sit at one of the booths in the bar. It's the middle of the afternoon, so business is slow. Just a few regulars pouring in for lunch. Everyone knows my dad makes the best burgers in town, so we often decide to show up on the weekends when we are both free. Blake and I just turned 15, and now we're in our first year of high school. I had asked her to help with my English homework, even though it wasn't hard by any means, and I truly didn't need the tutoring.

I just...wanted to see her. And to get her out of the house. Her parents were constantly fighting, and Blake didn't like to talk about it much, but I could tell it was taking a toll on her. So, I did it, and often. For both my sake and hers, even if she spent half the time yelling at me for barely paying attention to her instructions.

I hate to admit it, but I loved to get a rise out of her, to make her face flush in frustration. I have never looked at her the way I do now, but one day, something just sparked and never went away. She had met me early for breakfast one random morning so we could walk to school together, and I decided then and there she was the prettiest thing I've ever seen. It's as if she'd transformed overnight. Pretty really didn't even begin to cover Blake's features. All the guys at school saw it too, and as much as I hated it, I understood why it was so easy to lose all train of thought when around the girl sitting right in front of me. She was oblivious to it all of course, because Blake didn't see anything she didn't want to, and because she truly had more going on in her life than the average teenager should have to deal with.

Dad interrupted our bickering as he set down Blake's burger and fries for us to share. "You can try Blake, but you'll never be able to replicate that brain of yours."

She beamed back up at him, playing into the teasing tone. "I wouldn't dare."

He reaches forward to ruffle her hair before shooting me a wink and spinning around to return to the kitchen.

"Thanks, Ben." She hollers back, and she gets a wave of his hand in return before smirking at me as she pops a fry into her mouth. "I'm his favorite, you know that, right?"

I roll my eyes. "The whole town knows it."

I reach forward and snatch her burger from the plate before taking a ridiculously large bite out of it. "Hey!"

She smacks my hand, which only causes me to laugh in return.

"Now hurry up, I want ice cream after this." I grin through a mouthful.

She rolls her eyes, throwing a fry at me. "You're so gross." But a small smile curves the corners of her lips, and she picks up the flashcards she made. "Okay, so..."

***

My eyes are locked on the booth in the corner of my bar. The table that Blake and I always sat at on the days we'd hang out here. Its once spotless green seats are now worn, and the tabletop showcases marks that have accumulated over the years. It's the only seat in this bar that I haven't replaced. Everything else is pristine and up to date, but not that booth. I turn away, no longer able to stomach the memories we made there. It was her favorite because we could see the entire bar from that corner. She loved to people-watch, and once we deemed it our spot in the bar, nobody else touched it. It's not a seat many people would choose for comfort, anyway.

The sight of Blake walking away from me outside of the bar irritated me more than it probably should have. Regardless of what she said, I could see how uncomfortable she was once she saw the bar, and I can't say I'm surprised she tucked her tail and ran. It seems to be a habit of hers. A part of me is glad she didn't come in, so I didn't have to share this space with her again. Another part wishes I would have thrown her over my shoulder and dragged her in. I can't help but wonder if her memories from this place plague her just as much as they plague me.

"Hey, Boss." Harper, one of my employees, greets as she walks out from the back. My best employee. Always showing up on time, picking up extra shifts, or staying late when we need it. She came to town out of the blue last year and came in to ask if we were hiring, bags still in hand. I don't know much about her story save for the fact that she's saving for college and obviously on the run from something. As much as I've grown to care for her, it's not my business to pry. She'll talk when she's ready.

And as much as I'd like to hide away in my office, I give myself a few beats of silence to reign in my off-kilter demeanor. She doesn't need that shit from me, especially not in her workplace. "Harper." I flash her a grin as I set my keys on the bar top. It feels forced. "Closing go okay last night?"

"Aside from Haden's usual habits? Just fine." She lays down the rag she's using to polish some of the glasses and faces me with hands on her hips. Her southern accent is thick as she says, "I think you should hire him."

My eyebrows shoot up, and I can do little to hide my shock. Haden is an old friend and a retired war hero. He's the town flirt, to put it lightly. Mix that with a bit of a drinking habit, a short fuse, and a loudmouth, and he's a downright grade-A troublemaker. It's gotten him more busted lips than I can count on my two hands. Granted, he's been through a lot, so I tend to cut him some slack when he's in my bar. He's respectful, just an asshole to the assholes that tend to roll in when passing through town, and a sleaze to anything that has boobs.

"Hire him?" I ask, making sure I heard her correctly. Most of the time, she can't stand him. Although he seems to have an unusually soft spot for my bartender.

"He needs a job. A purpose. I think it'd do him some good. Plus, Tim quit last night, so we're shorthanded." With that, she hands me what I assume is Tim's letter of resignation. I curse. The bastard never could hold a job. I knew that when I hired him, so I suppose that one's on me.

"Yup. So? Haden?" she pushes.

"I'll think about it." She gives me a stern look. "Fine." I raise my hands in mock surrender. "*Fine*. I'll talk to him tonight. Deal?"

"Deal. Now, what's got your panties in a twist?"

"Excuse me?" I'm so taken aback by the sharp turn in conversation that I have no idea what else to say.

The door to the bar dings as someone walks in, but I don't bother turning as Harper greets them with a wicked smile. I have a feeling I know exactly who it is. Harper turns her attention back to me. "You're pissed off about something."

Pinching the bridge of my nose, I say, "No. I'm not." My brother chooses that moment to cut into our conversation. A teasing tone that makes me grit my teeth in annoyance. "Sure it's got nothing to do with a pretty blonde who's made her way back into town?"

"Ah. Dear mom told you before she told me, huh?" I don't hide my irritated tone, knowing damn well it's something my mother would do.

"Nope. Just saw her at Bell's." he says, staring at me, but I don't give him anything else. There's nothing I can say. I should have known she'd try to see Whitney first thing. She's adored her since they were kids.

"Wanna talk about it?" Wyatt presses.

"There's nothing to talk about," I respond firmly, wanting this conversation to end. Blake and I have a complicated history. Our mothers are best friends and had us so close together that we had no choice but to grow up side-by-side. From preschool to kindergarten, all the way to high school. We were two peas in a pod. Granted, once we hit puberty, the way we interacted changed. The way we viewed each other changed. Of course, we dated other people, and we acted like we hated each other when others were around, but there was always this understanding that something more laid beneath all those years of friendship. We understood each other in a way nobody else did. We both felt it. Or I thought we did. Until she turned eighteen and left this town and my life quicker than she came into it. And when she left, she took a piece of me with her. One that I'm not sure I'll ever get back or ever give freely to someone again if I do.

"He's lying." Wyatt, Harper, and even Mr. Sander's sitting at the end with a coffee in his hand, all say at the exact same time. Disbelief covers my features. What the fuck is this? An Intervention? She's been in town for less than 48 hours.

"Refill, Mr. Sanders?" Harper chirps, turning around to grab the pot of coffee from where it sits on the counter. "Yes, ma'am." I choose then to tune out the rest of their conversation and turn back to Wyatt, who's staring at me with an unreadable expression on his face. I sigh, knowing he's not going to let this go.

"Why is she back?" He asks.

"Your guess is as good as mine."

He swings back behind the bar before grabbing two bottles of wine from the shelf. "You hate red." I point out.

"It's not for me."

My brows scrunch. "Do you have a date?

The idea was almost laughable. Not that I'm much different. I've been on a few dates over the years and have had a few flings, but none that truly ever came out of the bedroom. We shared a mutual understanding of what we wanted from each other, and that was that. I had no interest in committing to a relationship anytime soon. But Wyatt? Wyatt didn't date. At all. The only thing he's ever made time for is the ranch or my mom and I, but even family time has its limits.

"I know that's a weird concept for you, brother, but yes, I have a date," he quips.

"With who?" He answers me with a look that says *I'm not telling you.*

"I'll tell Mom."

That causes his head to snap up. "You wouldn't."

I'm not above snitching on my big brother, even as adults, but I won't. It's just too good of an opportunity not to get a rise out of him. Our mother has a habit of trying to set us up with every girl in Clover-Hills, and she'd probably have a heart attack or gossip about it to the whole town if she heard that one of her boys was finally dating.

"I won't pry if you won't pry," I suggest.

With that, he shrugs as if to say, *"Fair enough,"* and turns on his heels, heading for the door.

"You have to pay for that," I tease, because why not take the chance to annoy him a little more? He doesn't pay, because I wouldn't let him even if he tried, but again, I can't resist.

"Payment is my silence, asshat." He flips me the middle finger and strolls out the door, my laughter following him.

Chapter 11

BLAKE

After catching up with Whitney, talking about the job and agreeing I would start on Monday, as well as promising to make plans to hang out, I decided to walk the town. One of the things I've always adored about Clover-Hills is that you can see the whole town's layout from wherever you're standing. It's open, shops wrapping around the town square in a circle. A walking path circles all around, with tall black lanterns and trees spaced every couple of feet. Street parking is available in front of almost every shop. A large white gazebo is placed in the center of town with a clock tower directly behind it, attached to the only church in town. Various benches and perfectly manicured bushes are scattered throughout the square.

It's cloudy overhead, making the beating sun far less intimidating. It's currently creeping towards the end of

July, and it's typically unbearably hot around this time, so I'm grateful for the reprieve. As I stroll, I bask in the feeling of the light that touches my exposed skin, glad that I chose to wear jeans and comfortable shoes while I take in the familiar buildings. The Clover-Hills Diner, Jake's Quick-Stop and Convenience, Clovers' Vet Services, Dusty Layne Boutique, Benson's Motor Shop, the Clover-Hills police and fire station attached to the town's local news station, and Maurice's Antiques.

As I pass Maurice's, I pause in the window, my eyes catching on the various glass figurines gleaming from the afternoon glow. So many glass turtles; it's borderline scary.

There's a little one with giant glasses holding what looks like a joint, and I can't stop myself from outright giggling at how ridiculous it is. Vivienne and I both smoked for the first time together in college and while we decided it wasn't something we wanted or needed to relive, it was easily one of the funniest nights we've ever spent together. I just know she'd get a kick out of this, and the thought of her makes me want to crawl back into bed and cry because of how far away I am from my best friend.

She has always had a weird obsession with sea turtles, even though she's quite literally never left the confines of New York to see one. I feel a smile creeping onto my lips at the reminder, so I snap a picture of the figurine and send it to her. I'll be wrapping it up and mailing it to her, but I'll keep that a surprise.

Viv:

OMG!!

That reminds me of the night we got stoned, and I forced you to watch a live aquarium cam with me

I would book a flight just to see that

And you, of course

I miss you ⊠

> I miss you too. Call you later?

I almost debated on telling her about Whitney's current situation, but I know it's not my place. She'll tell her when she's ready.

Yes, please! I think I'll start to break out into hives if we don't talk soon

I laugh at my phone before tucking it into the back pocket of my jeans and swinging open the door to the shop. I silently thank the gods above that I don't recognize the young girl scrolling through her phone and smacking on bubblegum behind the cash register.

"Welcome in." She murmurs from where she's seated, not even glancing up from her phone. "Hi." I mutter back, pivoting to grab Vivienne's turtle before bringing it to the checkout counter. The store is crowded with all sorts of random items, and I'm extra careful not to bump into anything. The young girl places her phone down after typing furiously on it. Her eyes light up when she sees what I've set down, but then scrunches into a look of surprise when she sees me.

"You smoke a lot of weed or something?"

A laugh bubbles up in my chest, and I cover my mouth, completely shocked by her question. "What? No," I respond, still teetering between shock and laughter. She glances down at the turtle with raised brows.

"It's for a friend."

"She smokes a lot of weed, then." This kid is hilarious. But I don't say that.

"Er-no...aren't you like twelve?" I crane my neck around the store to see if there's anyone taller roaming around. "Why do you know what weed looks like?"

"I'm seventeen." she deadpans, and I try not to wince at the look she's giving me.

"...Right. Well, just this please."

"That'll be five dollars," she says, smacking her gum. As I go to hand her cash, I catch a glimpse of a nasty bruise marring her wrist and slipping out from her long-sleeve shirt.

"Ouch. How'd you get that?" I nod towards her arm, and she rips it back, tugging the sleeve down to conceal what I've already seen and sitting up straighter in her chair. "I fell," she snaps.

My brows shoot up at her quick answer. Before I can say anything else, a soft voice from beside us calls out, "Elain, why didn't you say we had a customer?" An older lady, probably in her mid to late 40s, hobbles into view. Her hair is the same light brown as Elain's, and it's easy to place that it's her mom.

"I was just finishing up. Your daughter was super helpful in helping me pick out a gift." I wiggle the small white bag that houses the turtle after Elain pushes it towards me on the counter. I shoot a playful wink her way, causing her to look at me oddly before glancing behind her mother as if checking for someone.

"Well, I have to run some more errands. Thanks for the help." I chirp. My phone buzzes, and I nearly bump into a shelf on the way out because of it.

Mom:

> Can you pick up some toothpaste before I grab you later? I forgot it when I went grocery shopping.

> Sure

> Hope you're having fun with Wesley. I have to help Ana with something, so I'll pick you up in about an hour

> Or two

I roll my eyes, but her texts remind me that I need to get a car. The deafening sound of thunder looms overhead as I type my response.

I narrow my eyes at the text, like I can somehow manifest that she sees it. Of course there is, and of course she would hide that little detail so I couldn't protest going with Wesley or *at least* take a separate freaking vehicle. She may be getting older, but she's not senile enough to fool me. She knew about it before and deliberately didn't tell me. I'm not paying attention to where I'm walking, so I find myself barreling into a hard wall and nearly falling flat on my ass. My phone tumbles away, landing so hard on the concrete I'm sure it's cracked even worse than it already has. "Oh, sorry, Hun. I didn't see you there."

Not a wall. A man. A man I *know*. He bends down to pick up my phone, stretching out his hand to give it back to me. His eyes light up with recognition as he finally looks at me, and I wince. I was hoping he wouldn't.

"Blake Warner! That's so funny. I was just headed out of town to see your father today," he says, oblivious to the mental turmoil he's fueling with every word.

Nausea bubbles in my stomach, and fear lances through me. Jason. One of my father's closest friends. Probably the *only* friend my father has. I should have known he'd still see him, even if it's behind a glass wall.

He's going to tell him that he *saw me*. He's going to tell him that I'm *home*.

I do the only thing I can think of. Lie my ass off, and hope it works. I feign confusion, taking my phone back like I'm completely weirded out. "I'm sorry. My name's not Blake."

"Oh," he laughs nervously, rubbing the back of his neck. "You just look so much like this kid I know."

"Sorry. Have a nice day." I turn back the way I came. Trying and failing to make it look casual. Once I turn a corner, I allow my steps to slow. I place my hand on my forehead as I lean against a cool, hard wall. *I'm being crazy.*

I'm being crazy.

I have to tell myself that a couple more times in order to calm my heart rate enough to peel myself away from the wall. I break into a walk that probably looks much more like a sprint to the others on the street as I head towards Buddies'.

Chapter 12

WESLEY

I rub my forehead as I stare down at the pile of papers covering the entirety of my desk. While I love the bar and all the work that comes with it, the endless paperwork is one thing I always dread and always try to push off, leaving me with mounds of work to catch up on when I do come in.

I'm writing down a couple of dates I need to remember when commotion from outside my door draws my attention. I hear shouting from Harper, and then a flash of blonde enters my vision as Blake comes busting through my office door, looking disheveled.

Harper trails in after her, looking slightly concerned. "Sorry Wes, I have no idea who she is-"

"Harper, it's fine," I wave her off with a hand. "I know her." Her eyes widen, and she looks at Blake, putting two and two together.

"Why the hell didn't you just say that?" Harper questions quietly, raising her brows. When Blake doesn't respond, Harper shakes her head and leaves, closing the door behind her while muttering under her breath. My eyes land back on Blake, her large chest bouncing as she breathes heavily. Slightly damp from the onset of rain outside. I try not to dwell on how erotic it looks in her tiny white tank top and flushed pink cheeks.

Did she *run* here?

"Look who decided to come crawling back. Get lost?" I quirk an eyebrow before looking back down at my papers, not really seeing anything. I scribble a couple of random numbers on my notepad. It's easier than looking at what's right in front of me.

"I didn't get lost." She snaps. Her breathing slows just a bit, but her chest is still rising and falling faster than what's probably considered normal, so I stand and go to take a step around the desk, but seeing my intent, she takes one step back, causing me to halt.

"What the hell is wrong?" She looks at me, and for just a moment, all I see is raw emotion pooling in her brown eyes. Maybe even fear? I swear they begin to swell with tears, but they're gone in a blink. A look of feigned indifference covers her pretty features.

"Nothing." She shakes her head like she's trying to physically remove the thoughts from them. "Can you take me back to my mom's?"

The way she says it wraps around my heart like a vice. She sounds so small, so similar to when we were just children. Not sure what to say, I nod and just stand there. Pushing her will only cause her to run, and I stopped playing the cat-and-mouse game a long, long time ago. "Okay. Let me find my keys."

This girl gives me whiplash unlike anything I've ever seen. I don't know what's going through her head, and it bothers the hell out of me. But I do know something shook her, and I'm not so cruel that I wouldn't offer to take her home. The fact that she asked me for a ride in the first place tells me everything I need to know.

***

I pull into Elise's driveway as the sky settles into an array of vibrant reds and oranges. I had texted Elise before leaving the bar, letting her know that I would bring Blake home. The winky face she sent back did little to ease my sour mood. Blake didn't talk to me the entire drive. I even attempted to talk to her about her visit with Whitney, but she didn't say much other than that she starts at Bell's on Monday. I can see she's calmed down, but the idea that something is gripping her thoughts so tightly makes me want to reach over and shake them out of her. I know when something's rattled Blake, and she *was* rattled. She begrudgingly mumbles a "thanks" before trying to scramble out of the car, but I reach over her, grabbing the door and slamming it back shut.

"What the hell?" She shouts. I'd find the expression of shock on her face cute if it weren't for how irritated I was.

"Are you going to talk about what happened earlier or not?"

"Nothing happened." She snaps back, but I know this girl as well as I know myself, and she's full of it. So I push, "You came barreling into my office after avoiding the entire building like the plague. Don't bullshit me."

She shakes her head and stares ahead, refusing to budge on the topic. Yes, she came running into the bar, but she refused to take in any of the surroundings, even on the way out. It's not something that went unnoticed. I grit my teeth and swing open my door, walking around until I'm yanking her own open, admittedly more aggressively than I had planned. The sprinkle that started when she arrived at my office turned into a downpour on the drive here. My shirt begins to cling to my skin. I take a breath and then offer my hand, signaling for her to hop out. A beat passes, and then she's laying her fingers in my palm, my hand burning from the small touch.

"Stop opening my door." She says once she's on solid ground. She has to tilt her head up to look at me, her chin just barely meeting my collarbone. Rain consumes us as I try not to focus on how close we are, but it's damn near impossible. "It's weird when you're a gentleman." She's breathless, breath catching on the last word, and I realize she's still holding my hand.

"Not a chance, sweetheart." I smirk. Reveling in the fact that she's not as unaffected by my presence as she makes herself out to be. She rolls her eyes at the nickname and yanks her hand away like I've burned her before hurrying towards the steps of the home. I stand there, unsure of why I'm standing in the rain and haven't just turned around and gotten right back in my truck yet. Before I can stop myself, I'm calling out to her. "Blake."

She pauses as her hand touches the doorknob, but she doesn't turn around. "Yes?"

"Why are you home?" It wasn't harsh, just genuine curiosity, despite how badly I want to scream at her, interrogate her and ask her all the reasons she left in the first place. It's been years, and yet a part of me still wants answers. I'm more than sure her reaction back at the bar has something to do with it, and I vow that I'll figure it out sooner or later. My playful tone from a moment ago is gone, and it causes her to turn around and meet my gaze.

"I-I don't know." She shrugs and looks past me as if she's seeing something I'm not. "I was chasing...I don't know what I was chasing in New York, but I didn't find it."

"Are you staying?"

"I don't know that either."

I nod, and we stare at each other for a few more seconds, unspoken words we have no desire to touch hanging in the air between us. After a couple of minutes, she whispers, "Goodnight, Wesley."

"Goodnight." I watch as she walks into the house and I wait until the door closes with a click before rubbing a hand down my face and turning back to the truck.

I hate her for making me even ask. For caring that she's back and wanting to know everything that's happened since she's been gone. Did she still have a boyfriend back in New York? What happened to her big fancy job? What was college like? Did she still only take lavender in her coffee? Did her face still light up like a Christmas tree at the smallest amount of embarrassment? I hate that I don't know every little detail about her like I used to. I hate that she's probably not even the same girl who left six years ago. But most of all I hate her for driving me so goddamn crazy in such a short amount of time.

Chapter 13

BLAKE

I forgot just how hot it gets here towards the end of summer. Sweat coats my skin, causing my grey tank to stick to me like honey. My feet pad against the ground as I nod my head to the music blasting through my headphones. I didn't sleep well last night, my brain moving a million miles a minute, and once the sun finally rose, I decided it was best if I got out of the house and did something to occupy my mind. Panting, I try to tell myself, "In through the nose, out through the mouth," but it quite literally doesn't help the fact that my body is protesting at pushing it so hard. I'm unbelievably out of shape, and it's borderline embarrassing. It's something I truly wish I hadn't let slip while living in the city.

Yes, I hate it, because let's be honest, who *enjoys* running? What I do love is that sheer adrenaline that courses through you when you're done. The burn in your arms, legs, and chest. There's no greater high.

I slow my steps before stopping completely as I reach a dead end, gasping in as much air as my lungs will let me. Doubling over and checking my watch, I see I've only made it two miles. I left the house half an hour ago.

I know I shouldn't be so hard on myself, but I could easily run twice that distance without breaking a sweat when I kept up with my exercise. Sighing, I look up from my watch and take in the surrounding area, finally catching my breath. Thankfully, I'm not completely lost as I remember where I came from. There's the dead end straight ahead, but to my left, there's a gravel road leading uphill that I don't recognize.

I pivot my body toward the way I came with intentions of returning to the house and calling it a day, but for some reason, I have this nagging feeling to explore, so I turn onto the unfamiliar road and begin my hike up.

***

After a couple of minutes of walking, I'm panting once again, but mainly from the uphill slope and nerves that make little-to-no sense. The road goes deep and has begun to curve, with trees on either side of me. Somehow, it feels louder out here than it does in town. The wind rustling the trees, birds chirping, and sounds of machinery way off in the distance.

I stumble upon the first building on my left, still walking but taking it in as I go. There's a long driveway that leads to a small farm-style house with white paneling, a black roof, and brick steps that open up to the wide wrap-around porch framed by wooden beams. Floor-to-ceiling windows surround all sides of the house, and there's a little matching shed to the right.

It's cute. A dream, really. Living in a perfect white house where you can watch the dogs run around from the kitchen window, a backyard with a fire pit and a spot to host a family BBQ, a garden so full and bright you look forward to seeing it every morning. A porch with a swing to drink coffee in while the rain comes crashing down all around you. It's the kind of peaceful life you admire from afar when you're young and daydream of when you're an adult. It's the life I would have loved to see with Marshall. It's unfortunate that the one time I pitched the idea of moving somewhere more rural, he laughed in my face. But I suppose it's even more unfortunate that he enjoyed my boss's company far more than mine.

After a few more minutes, I start to wonder if that's the only house on this road until I catch sight of a little blue mailbox. Drawing closer, I peek down the open dirt road and scrunch my eyebrows. It's surrounded by more trees, and you wouldn't even know there was something here if it weren't for the mailbox. Shrugging my shoulders, I turn to continue my walk, but my eye catches the sign leaning against the wooden post, causing me to stop.

"For Sale" in big red letters. I glance over my shoulder, but curiosity gets the better of me, and I follow the road until it narrows into a cobblestone walkway. I walk along the cobblestones until it flows open into a lush green oasis with a home nestled right in the center.

Immediately, I can see it needs a little TLC, but otherwise, it's *gorgeous*. The garden is overflowing and crawls up the small frame of the house. So much so that it has even started to wrap around the porch railing. Flowers in shades of pinks, yellows, and whites are scattered all over the greenery. Its roof consists of the same grey cobblestone as the walkway with a matching chimney, and the walls that can be seen peeking through the overgrowth are a deep blue. I creep closer up the walkway, intent on checking out the porch, and spot a small pond nestled in the far-left corner behind the house. The lowering sun casts a beautiful glow over the water, and an old wooden dock that can't hold more than two people starts at the edge of the pond. Something about it feels so *familiar*, and the sight makes my chest ache.

I cup my hands and try to peek in one of the dusty windows, hoping to glimpse what the inside looks like. I'm so engrossed in exploring that I don't even notice I'm not alone until a voice asks from behind, "Gorgeous, isn't it?" I let out a startled scream, spinning around and then proceeding to trip over one of the white rocking chairs on the porch, causing me to faceplant on the ground. "Oh god! Are you okay?"

I groan and push up onto my arms to roll onto my back. "Yup!" I cover my face with both hands. "Fine. Just – just unusually clumsy." I force myself to pry open my fingers and peek up at the voice. An older woman with short brown hair kneels over me, checking me for any injuries. She lends me a hand once she deems me fine, and I refrain from throwing myself back on the wooden deck with how sore my limbs feel. I dust myself off. "I'm so sorry. I didn't realize anyone lived here. I saw the sign at the end of the road, and I thought –"

"No worries, Hun. You thought right. It was my mom's house; I was just coming by to pick up a few things. My name's Jane." She extends her hand to me in offering.

"Blake." I reply.

"Nice to meet you, Blake." She gives me a warm smile. "Were you interested in seeing the inside?"

"Um–" I consider saying no. It's not like I have any intentions on buying the place, but once again, my mouth betrays my brain, so I settle on, "Why not?" Another smile and she begins making her way to the door, so I take that as a cue to follow her. We step inside, and I feel my breath whoosh out of me all over again. It's not big by any means. It's an open floor plan, and you can see pretty much the entire house from the doorway. A kitchen to the left flows into a small dining area on the right. In front of that is a living room with a *real* fireplace. I haven't seen one of those in years.

It's fully furnished. A dining table with chairs, a couch, and an armchair. All a little outdated, but well-kept. Three closed doors are on the right that must lead to bathrooms or bedrooms.

The kitchen is possibly the most charming part of the house. The cabinets are the same blue as the outside of the house, and the countertops are made of butcher block. A matching island is in the center of the space, a rack of pots and pans swinging above. There's a large window over the sink that you can see the pond from, and wooden shelves that match the butcher block litter the faded brick walls. The natural lighting lights up the entire house. I don't know what it is, but something in my head just keeps screaming, *yes, yes, yes!*

"There's one bedroom, one bath, and a decently sized basement below. The basement's always been used for storage, but it would be beautiful if someone wanted to do some work. And there's only two other people on this road, with a ranch about another mile down."

"Who could possibly want to leave this place?" I blurt out before I can stop myself, running my hands along the back of the couch. It's private but not isolated. There's a story here, one you can see in the upkeep of this home. Someone lived here, loved here, and clearly, hadn't wanted to leave here. Something in my heart cracks at the thought, and I have the urge to give this house back its life.

"No one." She says with a little smile, and her tone tells me that maybe this house means more to her than I originally thought.

"It was your mom's, you said. You don't want to keep it for yourself? Or...in the family, I guess?" Maybe I was prying, and maybe it was an inappropriate question to ask, but I had to know.

"I could keep it, but I don't need to. And I think she would have loved for someone new to create a life here." She didn't sound sad, maybe a little mournful, some relief hidden in her expression at the prospect of the home being in capable hands. A comfortable silence fills the space as we both look around, contemplating. We spend the next half hour discussing prices, more about the area, a possible move-in date, and everything else house-related. I don't ask any more questions about her mom or the situation, and she doesn't pry about how I stumbled upon the house. "We haven't had any offers. We were even considering putting it up for auction, but it's yours if you want it. So, you can take a few days and-"

"I'll take it." I'm saying the words before I can even comprehend my own decision. But I have enough for a down payment saved up from my time in the city, and with a steady income from the coffee shop I should be able to handle monthly payments...

What's back in New York City for me, anyways? I tried that job I so desperately craved, I tried the man. It didn't work, and clearly, it wasn't ever going to work. I have

Viv, of course. But I can visit, and so can she. I had no plans of staying here, let alone buying a damn house, but I think consciously I knew my plans were changing the minute I saw that "*For Sale*" sign. Maybe even the minute I got on that plane when I truly didn't *have* to.

Is this insane? Yes.

Am I going to do it anyway? Also, yes.

"Let's get some papers drawn up, then."

Nerves from both excitement and fear course through me as I hear the familiar sound of a rock bouncing off the window. I jump from my bed, flinging it open and peering down. "You coming down, or what?" Wesley whisper-shouts, hands cupped around his mouth.

I roll my eyes and flip him a finger before crawling through the open bedroom window, careful to make as little noise as possible. I could have sworn I heard a light snicker slip from his lips. I can't imagine how my mother would react if she caught me climbing through a window at this hour. It's not that either of our mothers were very strict, but asking to leave the house this late at night would simply lead to too many questions.

And this little ritual had become something that was solely ours. I couldn't even remember when it started, or how, but I cherished the moments Wesley would show up to sweep me away for just a few hours under the stars. We didn't want to share it with anyone else, not yet at least. I drop to the ground in a crouch, wincing at the noise it makes. Wesley's now the one to roll his eyes at my paranoia. "Come on, I want to show you a new spot I found earlier." He reaches for my hand, and I take it, following. My cheeks burn at the contact, and I'm thankful for the darkness covering my features.

About a half hour later of walking through woods in silence, we come upon a clearing. As we walk, it opens to tall grass, with a pond nestled in the very center. Looking up, you can see the night sky so clearly, it's breathtaking. So secluded and quiet save for the sound of the night's creatures and their footsteps. I walk ahead of Wesley, spinning to take it in. I can feel him watching me.

"How did you find this?"

"You like it?" He asks quietly.

"It's perfect." I stop spinning, and we stare at each other, untouchable and unidentifiable emotions swirling in the air between us. Does he understand how much this means to me? These little moments? The ones where we could be away from the everyday chaos of our lives. Where I could forget the disaster of my family and just live in this bubble with him?

I hope he does.

Instead of acknowledging those feelings, or speaking about what I felt growing between us, we just took each other's hands and walked to the pond, where we dipped our toes into the cold water and talked all night about *anything and everything. That spot became one that the two of us visited every single night.*

Chapter 14

WESLEY

I've never wanted a dog of my own. Always been a fan of the idea, but never thought it'd be fair to get one when I'm not even home most days. The bar calls for long days and late nights, and it's never a steady schedule, so it has never logically made sense.

Benji though? He always makes me question that. He's awesome. Makes the lonely nights not seem so lonely, and I bask in the fact that it pisses my brother off to know his dog loves me more than him. I've tried on more than one occasion to convince Wyatt to just give him to me, but no luck. He loves the damn stray too much. Can't blame him.

We're going for a walk now, since he was waiting on my steps like a door-to-door salesman the minute I pulled in the driveway. He sometimes wanders down to my place when he's bored. So, basically, every day.

He's an off-leash dog, always has been. He's not the type to stray away. Always stays close and listens. So, now he walks just a few feet ahead of me, his butt swaying back and forth, stopping every so often to sniff at some invisible object on the gravel road. He pauses suddenly, nose pointing in the air before him like he just caught whiff of something new, and he fucking *bolts*.

"Benji!" I shout. "What the hell?" I break into a jog after him, scanning the area to see if I missed maybe a chipmunk or something scurrying by. He really does listen to anything and anybody, but right now? An absolute Hellion. It doesn't matter that I pulled out my stern voice or yelled his name a dozen times; he just keeps running. A dog *that* well-fed shouldn't be able to run that fast. I pick up my pace a little bit more, not because I'm worried he'll get lost, but because I have no desire to pick a dead animal out from his teeth. It's then that I glimpse a familiar blonde, clad in tight black leggings and a gray top. Standing in the middle of the road with papers in her hand. Clueless to her surroundings. Her head snaps up when Benji lets out an excited bark. "Wesley?"

Benji uses her pause as an opportunity to come plop himself at her feet, tail wagging faster than I've ever seen. Patiently waiting for attention. She squeals. *Squeals* and crouches down to scratch his ears.

"Oh, my! You're so handsome! What's your name?" She talks in a baby voice, and my mood dampens just a bit at the much warmer greeting a dog got over me.

I scratch the back of my head and say, "Benji."

"You have a dog?"

"He's Wyatt's." She looks up from where she's kneeling on the ground, and every possible dirty thought my brain could manifest rushes to the surface. For a moment, we're no longer on the road but in a bedroom. Her knees digging into the carpet beneath her, her delicate hands reaching up to wrap around my – "Ah, that's whose farm is down the road. I came up a side road, so I didn't put two and two together."

I clear my throat, her voice washing away all my perverted thoughts. She blushes, hopping back up to her feet, and I wonder if she's recently taken on mind-reading. Or if she was visualizing the same damn thing. She shakes her head and asks, "Are you visiting him or something?"

"Yeah. Taking his dog for a walk." The idea of telling her I live on this road felt far too intimate for some reason. "You?"

"I was going for a run." She responds. A pregnant pause follows. I can tell by the way she's acting that she's distracted. Something's thrown her a bit off-kilter, and I can't help but wonder if it has something to do with her episode from the other day. We both just stand there, Benji looking between us like *he* can read the awkward air. "Well," She claps her hands. "I'll let you get back to it." She crouches again, giving Benji a pat on his head. When she returns to full height, she gives me a stoic look and dips her head. "Tell Wyatt I said hi."

She waves and then breaks into a run, and I'm not sure if it's because she's resuming her exercise or if she's trying to get as far from me as possible. "Come on, dude. I'm taking you home." I'm positive he sighs in return, but reluctantly forges ahead, wistfully glancing at Blake as she moves away.

Chapter 15

BLAKE

Passing my phone between my hands, I debate on what I should tell Vivienne when I call to break the news. I'm sitting on the porch steps of my mom's house, waiting for her to come home so I can share the news with her too. She'll probably keel over from happiness, and I can't wait to see her reaction. Jane and I spent hours going over the logistics of the home, and since she's letting me keep all the furniture and everything else that was in the house, I can start to move in this weekend. She's no doubt quick and efficient, and I can't help but appreciate it. If she made me take a few days, I probably would have talked myself out of it. Thankfully, Vivienne's job pays well, and I had already paid-up front for a couple of months in rent, so she could afford me pulling out. But the last thing I wanted to do was hurt her or make her angry for making such a huge decision without talking to her first. Vivienne has never actually visited Clover-Hills, even though Whitney lives here. She grew up in the city, thanks to the fact that they have different dads. The few times she's even met Whitney have always been in the city.

What do I even say to her? *"Surprise, I've decided to stay indefinitely, even though I've spent half my life hating this damn town."*

Do I even plan to stay indefinitely? It's not like I can't sell the house if I truly want to go back to New York. I sigh and drop my head into my hands, hating how much I overthink shit like this. "Fuck it." I say aloud and press her name. I wait as it rings once, then twice, and then her voice filters through the phone with a chipper, "Hello, Darling!"

"I bought a house." Cutthroat. Straight to the point. No point in tiptoeing.

She laughs loudly. "You're funny. So, what's up?"

"Viv, I'm serious." I start to bite one of my nails and then whip it back down to my lap, irritated at how nervous I am.

"Um...okay." Silence greets me from the other side of the phone, and I feel my nerves getting worse as each second passes. My knee starts bouncing, and then she giggles again and says, "Did you at least make sure it's a two-bedroom? Because I'm going to be pissed when I visit, and I have to listen to you snore all night long."

I can't help the laugh that escapes my lips as I protest. "I don't snore!" She hums, knowing damn well I do. "You're not mad?" I ask, needing the reassurance.

"Babe. Why would I be mad? A little shocked, yes, but not mad. Never mad. If this is something you want, I want it for you, too."

I sigh in relief and then wince when I say, "Will you be mad if I tell you it's a one-bedroom?"

She pushes out a long breath like it's the most devastating news she's ever received. "I suppose it will be fine if you have one killer couch."

"I love you. You're too good to me."

"I know. Now, tell me all about it. Do you have a hot neighbor?" I avoid the last part, because I have no idea who my neighbors even are, and tell her all about the house I stumbled upon during my run. There's a tone to her voice as we talk back and forth that tells me she's dying to ask a few questions solely unrelated to me finding a house. I debate on telling her just how well Whitney's doing, but I decide it's best if I don't. Even I can see it's time that the two figure their situation out on their own. They don't need a mediator. We're just finishing up the conversation as my mom's familiar white jeep pulls into the driveway. "Mom's home. I'll call you later, yeah?"

"Sounds good. Tell her I said hi. Love you!"

"Love you too," I say and put my phone down by my side as my mom steps out of her car, purse and keys in hand. She sees me, and her face lights up with a smile that makes my heart warm.

"Hey, kiddo."

"Hey." She sets down her stuff and sits next to me on the porch. I return her smile and say, "I have some pretty crazy news."

"Bet it's not any crazier than mine." A flash of worry appears in her eyes, and I don't stop the frown from working its way onto my face.

"What's wrong?" I ask, but she nudges my shoulder. "You go first."

"I bought a house. Just a few miles down the road."

Tears fill her eyes as she looks at me. She nods and turns her head forward before meeting my eyes again and taking my hand.

"Your dad got out early."

I spent the rest of the day hanging over the toilet, puking and puking until nothing was left.

Your dad got out early.

The sentence has been on a constant loop in my head for the past couple of hours. And while my mom tried to explain the situation to me, it ended abruptly when I started *this*. She now rubs my back as I dry heave into the toilet for what must be the 20th time. I lean back against the tub and bask in how nice the cool porcelain feels against my skin.

My father wasn't arrested for beating me, no. Nobody knew about that except for my mother, Whitney, and Vivienne. He was arrested because after he woke up and found me gone, he showed up at my mother's rehab center and trashed the entire place in a fit of rage. Drunk driving, aggravated assault, and criminal mischief. But no child abuse.

I suppose that's on me, as I made my mother promise not to say anything and to let me leave town with little protests. Not that she had much say when I turned eighteen. Even if she had tried, the police would have little to go on with said victim no longer even being in the same state.

Still rubbing my back, my mom murmurs, "Sheriff Eaton is still a good friend. Since he was released on probation, he won't even be able to leave the rehab center he's in, let alone come to Clover-Hills. You won't see him, Blake."

While it does ease some of the tension lining my shoulders, it does little to comfort me. *Especially* after my run-in with Jason. I haven't told my mom about it, and I sure as hell won't after hearing this news. She doesn't need another thing to stress about.

A part of me misses my father and wants to forgive him. He's just a man who needed help and was never offered it. He may have been violent and brutal in the end, but there was a time when he loved me more than anything else in his life. That's something I've come to terms with over the years. But another part of me wishes he was six feet in the ground and never allowed to see the light of day again. It's morbid and a little dark, but it's the truth.

I tip my head back and close my eyes. I have no idea what to say to her. The woman should be as freaked out as I am, but she is unnaturally calm. Just as she goes to open her mouth again, a knock sounds from the living room. She looks from me to the door, indecision written all over her features. "I'm fine. Go see who it is."

I hear a shuffle, and then what I assume is the front door swinging open. "Now's not a good time." I hear my mother's voice say, followed by a gruff, "I just need to talk to her for a minute."

At the sound of Wesley's voice, I groan as a burning sensation crawls it way back up my throat and scramble my body back to the toilet, lifting the lid and emptying what little is left in my stomach *again.* My mom protests, but he must have made it past her because his feet come into view a few short seconds later. I groan again and bang my head against the toilet seat.

"Go. Away." I growl.

"Oh, please." Wesley says as he falls into a crouch at my side. "I was there when you got drunk for the first time. This is nothing."

"What happened?" he asks, breaking the growing silence. I swear I can see a glimmer of worry in those blue eyes, but it's gone in a second. And before my mom can open her huge, gossiping mouth, I snap, "Food poisoning."

She gives me a weird look, but I shoot her a glare, and she holds up her hands, backing away from the doorway and thankfully leaving the topic alone. "I'll grab you some ginger ale."

Wesley has no idea what happened with my father, and it will stay that way. I made sure of that even *after* I had left town. I turn my attention back on him, his stupidly-handsome face putting me in an even worse mood than before. "What are you doing here?"

He holds out his hand with a smirk. "Hi. I'm Wesley. Your new neighbor."

"What?" I smack his hand away. "Shut up."

He just stares at me, still crouched with his forearms resting on his knees. If I wasn't so dizzy and delirious from the amount of vomit that's just left my system, I would probably be drooling from the way his arms look in his navy blue t-shirt. I close my eyes. "*Please* tell me you're joking."

"I would never joke about something like this, sweetheart."

"Don't call me that!"

"You can't be my neighbor." He says matter of fact. I pop one of my eyes open at that.

"We literally lived next to each other for 18 years of our lives. And I can do whatever the hell I please, Conway."

"This is different."

"I already put a deposit down."

"Un-deposit it, then."

"You *know* that's not how it works." I can't believe he's sitting here and arguing with me after just witnessing me puke my brains out. Only Wesley would be the type to not even bat an eye at something like that. I look and feel disgusting right now, and he's here in front of me looking like *that*. The thought alone makes me see red, and I'm scowling at him. Does he truly not know how to read a situation like this? Or does he genuinely not care?

"Leave."

"Not until you tell me you'll back out of the deal." *What the hell is his issue?*

"It's not going to happen. Now, leave before I castrate you."

He only looks amused at my idle threat. "Or worse. Call your mother." I add. That's got him narrowing his eyes at me. He knows I'll do it. It wouldn't be the first time. He stands and stuffs his hands in his pockets. An anxious tick of his.

"This isn't over," he concedes.

I flip him the bird and then shoot him a wink once I see that scowl on his face. "See you Sunday, *neighbor*."

Once he leaves, my mom appears back in the doorway with a mischievous grin on her face and a glass of bubbly liquid in one hand. "Don't even start." I moan.

She shrugs and hands me the glass. "At least you stopped puking." She wrinkles her nose and then adds, "Speaking of, I'll go grab a candle to light. "

I don't say anything else as she leaves or even when she comes back because she's right. As angry as I can, and will be at Wesley tomorrow, I am grateful for the small distraction he provided me. I sip the ginger ale my mother brought me and think of all the ways I can make Wesley Conway's life a living hell while living next door.

Chapter 16

WESLEY

I hate it. The sounds, the amount of people, the smell. New York City is the last place on earth I'd ever want to be. But here I am.

I didn't tell anyone I was coming, only let it slip to Harper that I'd be gone maybe a day or two so that she could hold down the bar. She didn't question me, only gave me a weird, long stare that had me fumbling to explain it was a 'business adventure.' It couldn't have been more of a lie.

I'm here because I just had to see her. Just once. I had asked Elise for her address, with the front of wanting to send her a letter. The truth is, I only ever planned on this. I now walk down the street her apartment is supposedly on, squeezing past the large crowds and ignoring the occasional man or woman trying to get me to stop and buy some useless knick knack. I abruptly halt when I see a mop of blonde curls walk into the open doors of a lavish restaurant. My heart skips, and my pause causes someone to barrel into me from behind, spitting out a string of curses that would turn even my mother beet-red. I mumble an apology but don't let my eyes leave her. I know it's her. I could spot her a mile away, an ocean away. I start moving again, now much more eager to catch up to her before she disappears. I reach the end of the building, where the windows to the restaurant begin.

I lose her as she moves through the building but catch her again through the shiny, tall glass as a man, both tall and lanky, dressed in a fitted suit that no doubt costs more than my house, stands to greet her. She smiles as he leans in to kiss her.

The excitement I felt, the adrenaline of getting to see her, just speaking to her at least once, is easily replaced with a sharp sting as she embraces another man.

She looks...happy. Not just happy, but euphoric. The city around me slows, reality slipping into a blur. I take one more look at her, allowing myself to selfishly soak her in from just a few hundred feet away while she's oblivious. Her long, blonde hair frames her soft, heart-shaped face. Her radiant honey-brown eyes and infectious smile. She's as beautiful as I remember. Yet somehow, nothing like the girl I knew.

At that moment, I turned back onto the busy street. I let her go. Let her fingers that have so delicately wrapped around my heart disappear. I let go of the idea that she's *ever coming back. I don't even peer over my shoulder as I get right back on the very bus that brought me here.*

***

I blink as I take another sip of my beer, irritated at the never-ending reminder of how my visit to New York City went just a little over a year ago. I knew the old woman who lived next door well enough and was devastated to hear of her passing. She was a nice lady, kept to herself, and had one hell of a sense of humor. We sometimes had coffee on my front porch, or I'd help her with something around the house when she asked. And I always did, even if I had to show up late to the bar to do so. I think I saw myself in her. My future self, that is. Old and alone. Nobody to share a home with. No one to call home. Content with the life she lived.

And now, Blake is living there.

Blake.

The one person I want to keep as far away from as possible. Having her back in town was hard enough to grasp. But having her a few hundred feet away *every* single day?

If I had known what she was doing when I ran into her the other day, I would have done everything in my power to talk her out of it. I mean, the woman said she didn't know if she was staying, yet she still went off and bought a house? It's too much. Too complicated. I want to be pissed but I'm also so curious. The idea of being so close to her when I can't even decide how to feel about her being here makes my skin crawl.

Does she not remember what it was like when she left? I had lost my father the year prior, and yes, I pulled myself away and struggled just as any teenage boy would. When she first left, I blamed myself. I thought maybe I had been a bad friend, and given her the impression I no longer wanted anything to do with her. But over the years, I've learned there is no one else to blame but *her*. Did she hurt the way I hurt when I woke up and heard she was gone? No explanation. No idea where she had taken off too. Nobody in our lives seemed to bat an eye after a few days. Everyone just moved on. She couldn't have been hurting, not really, if she could leave so easily. Does she truly not understand what it means? Where that plot of land is? What it meant to *us*?

Or is it all some sick ploy to get under my skin?

The questions have been never-ending since I've heard the news. I want nothing more than to stomp back to her mother's and demand answers, but I know I won't get them. She doesn't owe me anything, and I don't owe her anything. Seeing her at Elise's, emptying her guts over a toilet only made it worse. Because the entire time, all I wanted to do was fall to my knees and make it stop.

I shouldn't care if she's sick. Shouldn't care what the hell is happening to her, yet a part of me does. A part of me may always care. I hate it. I hate it because she *doesn't* care.

Like I said. *Fucking complicated.*

Chapter 17

BLAKE

Warm sunlight streams through the small break in my curtains, and I groan as I roll onto my stomach and stuff my face farther into my pillow. The sound of birds chirping and sheer silence outside of my bedroom is what causes me to lift my head high enough to peek at the old alarm clock centered on my nightstand.

5:55 AM.

As tempting as it is to rest my eyes just a few moments longer, I know I won't leave this bed if I don't get up now, and the last thing I need to do is piss off a pregnant woman by being late to work on my first day. I stumble as I catch sight of myself in my floor-length mirror. Something bright and orange stuck to...my *forehead*? I reach up and snag the piece of paper off my skin, flipping it around to see my mother's familiar scrawl.

When you decide to join the living, there's coffee

I scoff but can't deny the small tug that lifts the corner of my lips. I don't bother getting dressed yet, seeing as I have a little over an hour before I need to head to work.

The cold wooden steps bite and my bare feet make me wish I had grabbed a pair of slippers or fuzzy socks before making the trek downstairs. The noise of pans clanking, my mother's hum, and the smell of biscuits fills my chest with warm nostalgia. Nostalgia that feels just as painful as comfortable if I let myself dwell on just how long ago something like this was so ordinary in my life. The last step creaks, as it always has in this house once I hit the bottom of the stairs. "Morning, Mama."

"Mornin' Baby. How'd you sleep?" She cranes her neck to peer over her shoulder just as she finishes setting aside a wet, black pan onto the drying rack. I was lucky to favor my mother's features over my father's. Even with her messy curls thrown carelessly into a bun, bare face, and her ridiculously fluffy robe, my mom is beyond beautiful. It still stuns me that she never remarried. I know from her old high school war stories that there was more than one man envious of the attention my father won from her.

"Fine." I raise an eyebrow as I flip the note in her direction. She barely glances at her handiwork as she lets a small smile grace the corners of her lips. For as long as I can remember, my mom would leave notes like these for me to find first thing in the morning. Mainly on days when she knows I could use a little pick me up, or after nights I spent out late wandering the woods with Wesley. Something I know she's always pretended to be oblivious to. After a day like yesterday, I'm less than surprised to wake up to one smack-dab on my forehead.

My eyes roam over the dining room and kitchen, snagging on the heaping plate of biscuits and gravy. It's been so long since I've sat at this table, and possibly even longer since I've had any of my mom's cooking. My mouth waters at the sheer idea of a home-cooked meal. Neither Viv nor I could cook very well, so take-out was always our safest option. And any meals I spent with Marshall consisted of plates only large enough to feed a bird; more often than not, I'd have to stuff my face with junk food when I got back to my apartment. Alas, while burgers, pizza, or Chinese food are top-tier food groups for Vivienne and me, something about my mother's cooking will always take the cake.

With reluctant movements, I pass the food on the dining table and head to grab a mug from one of the cabinets. My fingers graze a familiar green handle, shocked to see it front and center. It's nothing special. A bulky, unsightly thing, truly. But it's a mug I made when I was little, and the little chip that still adorns the edge of it is what makes it my favorite. Even the most fragile and cracked things hold beauty. I spare a side glance to my mom, frowning when I go to reach for the black handle of the coffee pot, only to find it completely and utterly *dry*. "I thought you said there was coffee?"

She shoots me a look before leaning over and jabbing a button on top of the machine, brewing more rich, black liquid into the old coffee pot. "I thought you worked at a coffee shop?"

"Not my fault you're a java junkie." I outright cringe when I realize the word *junkie* probably was the last thing my mother should hear. I go to murmur an apology at the bad joke, but she silences me with a wave of her hand. "If we can't joke about it, then it wouldn't be in the past."

Fair point. A comfortable silence falls over the kitchen as I wait for my coffee, and it stays that way as she finishes up the last few dishes in the sink and I settle into my spot at the table. The scrape of my fork against the plate is the only sound until my mom's voice cuts through the air. "Sit on the porch with me when you're done?"

The fork freezes halfway to my mouth as her question takes me by surprise. Not at the idea of sitting outside on a morning like this, let alone with my mom. We have some of our best memories on the deck. Reading, coloring, gossiping. But I'm quick to realize what this is. My favorite breakfast. Coffee. A chipper but steady mood wafting off my mom at six in the morning.

My heart clenches, and it takes everything in me to meet her gaze. I know she wants to talk. To have a conversation about *everything*. But I'm not sure I'm ready for everything. So, I do what I do best. "I...um, I have to get ready for work. But tomorrow? Maybe?"

A part of my chest cracks wide open at the hurt that flashes across her face, but I busy myself with stuffing the last few bits of breakfast in my mouth and pushing away from the small, round wooden table. I hear her intake of breath, but I don't stick around long enough to see what comes of it.

***

After I change for work, opting for a plain pair of light-wash jeans with my Bell's shirt, I barrel down the stairs. I intend to escape before my mom can convince me to dally any longer than I want to. "Where are the keys?" I call out into the house, eyes scanning around the foyer.

I'm praying the old beetle even starts. It's been rotting in the garage since the dawn of time.

"Dish by the front." My mom hollers back, and I'm already ripping open the front door, shouting my good-byes. But my feet come to a screeching halt at the flowers I've nearly knocked over in my hurry. A *gorgeous* array of flowers. I cock my head and drop into a crouch, gathering the vase into my hands and turning back into the house. I hear my mom's footsteps rounding the corner of the kitchen and make quick work of glancing at the note stuffed in the center.

Something almost as beautiful as you.

My brows shoot sky-high. "Find them, honey?" Her light steps slow as her brown eyes land on the gift, and I fail miserably to hide my smirk at her shocked expression.

"Looks like you have a secret admirer?"

She blushes. My mom actually *blushes*. "It's probably just a friend from the center."

Still, she rushes forward to snag them from my hands, tucking them against her chest. I hum in a way that tells her I'm not convinced and skim a skeptical eye over her frame. But instead of teasing her any further, I shrug and lean forward to plant a kiss on her cheek.

"Thanks for breakfast. See you later!"

Chapter 18

BLAKE

I tell myself I'm absentmindedly walking, not heading in any general direction. Whitney gave me an hour for lunch, so my curiosity got the best of me. I was thankful the car started with ease this morning, otherwise, I probably would've settled on hitch-hiking the entire way to work.

I did work as a barista in New York when I first got there, so it wasn't hard to pick up on what Whitney needed from me in the shop, which I'm grateful for. It's an easy job, and one that will provide me with both a distraction and a good income. After yesterday, I want nothing more than to bury myself in work and any other silly tasks I can come up with. Moving, on top of my father's release, on top of Marshall's betrayal, has accumulated into a dark cloud hanging above my head, just waiting to let its core wreak havoc below. I'm going to do everything in my power to forget it all. If I managed to do it with my childhood trauma for six years, surely I can hold on a little longer.

I see the young girl from the other day locking up the door of the antique shop, and there's a slight pause in my steps. Unsure if pretending she doesn't exist will come off as rude. But Elain, if I remember correctly, takes it upon herself to strike up a conversation, not even turning her head when she blurts, "Sorry. We don't sell pot here. Just the turtles."

I outright laugh at her comment, and I see just a small smile tugging at the corner of her lips, her eyes lighting up at the fact that she had made me react so loudly. "Don't worry. I was just passing by. Looking to grab lunch somewhere, I guess."

"Me too."

She's fully facing me now, keys dangling from her hand. She looks tired, with light bags under her eyes that also look a little red. And for some reason, I have this odd desire to make her smile again. Brighten up her mood. She's just a kid, and it's summer. She should be hanging out with friends instead of working, so it makes me wonder if she even has any.

"Elain, right? I'm Blake." I peek around her shoulder, seeing Clover-Hills diner just a few shops away. "Do you want to go to the diner with me? My treat." I'm not hungry, but something tells me she'd appreciate the company. I think I would, too.

She contemplates it for a bit, but then she's shrugging her shoulders nonchalantly and saying, "Sure."

We settle into an awkward silence as we walk. "Do they still serve breakfast all day?" I ask. "They have the best pancakes in town."

"They do."

More silence that I can't stand. It truly makes me want to pull my hair out. I blame that on the reason I continue our conversation and not on the fact that I'm a nosy bitch. "So, do you enjoy working at the shop?"

"I just do it to help out my parents. I don't get paid." My brows shoot up at that. Maybe it's just me, but who doesn't pay their kid to work, even if it's a family-owned shop? And then a lightbulb goes off in my head, and I'm spewing the words before I even give it much thought.

"Do you want a job? A paying one, I mean." It would give me an opportunity to scope out her situation a bit more and the motivation to get the house fixed up faster.

"I don't want your pity help." She snaps, but it comes out weak rather than intimidating.

I shrug, feigning indifference. "You won't find a pity party here. I need help cleaning up a house. And you seem young and able."

Just to lighten the mood, I waggle my eyebrows and say, "Or maybe I just need someone to scare off all the ghosts living in my house." I lower my voice and do my best Beetlejuice imitation, "You get a free demon possession with every exorcism. Can't beat that, now can ya?"

Then, she shocks me when she laughs, tipping her head back and *bellowing*. My chest squeezes at the sight.

"Oh, you're weird." She adds, still laughing.

I laugh with her because I know my Beetlejuice voice is always spot on. One of my many talents. "I just bought the house. So, maybe some yard and interior work. I'll pay you, of course. And it'll be whenever you're free, really."

She's not full-on smiling anymore, but I see her mood is much improved from when I first saw her. "I'm free like all the time. I'll just have to ask my parents...but I don't see why they'd mind."

"Cool. I can always talk to them, too. Now, do you think they'll still use whip cream to make a smiley face on my pancakes? " She shakes her head, clearly done with my antics, but she's much more talkative and excited when we sit down for lunch. For the first time in a while, I feel at ease and happy about forming a new friendship, even if it's with a broody teenager. Elain even gets a smiley face on her pancakes, too.

Chapter 19

WESLEY

"**W**hat do you need?" I suppress a sigh as my brother walks right in, like he owns the place. The door shuts behind him with a click as he waves a couple of envelopes around in his hand.

"Some of your mail got delivered to the ranch."

"How do they keep messing that up?" I grumble as I set down my mug and newspaper, standing from my chair at the dining table. He throws the mail onto the wooden table and shrugs. Then he points at the paper I left next to my coffee.

"Who still reads the newspaper? Old ass."

"Whatever." I huff, picking up the mail and sorting through the few pieces. "You probably still hide Playboy magazines underneath your bed."

"I heard you terrorized Blake about moving in next door." I stop shuffling through the envelopes to look at him. *This* again? The way he so quickly redirects the conversation almost makes me laugh, but the mention of Blake is enough to sober me up. He probably does hide magazines under his mattress, but that's none of my business. "I didn't *terrorize* her."

He crosses his arms and leans against my table. "Why does it matter if she's there, Wesley?"

"This isn't a problem for you to fix, Wyatt." I bite back, hoping he'll drop it. He doesn't.

"I'm just saying, man, you guys aren't kids anymore. You're adults. Do something nice, welcome her to the neighborhood, but don't scare her off because you're holding some grudge against something she did as a teenager."

It's more complicated than that, but I'm not going to explain that to him. He is right in the sense that it's not fair for me to scare her off just because I'm not ecstatic about her being here. I know how much Elise has wanted her back home. Hell, how much *everyone* has wanted her home. My mom and Wyatt included. I can't take that from them. So, I just say, "I'm not going to scare her off."

"If that's the case, come up with a way to apologize for bombarding her the other day."

Apologize? Apologize for *what*? I don't have anything to apologize for. I suppose I can '*welcome her to the neighborhood*' as Wyatt suggested. If that's what it takes to smooth the waters and get the latter off my back about it.

"Just think about it, alright?" I wave him off and don't say bye as he leaves. I don't know much about this new Blake, but I do know she has a weakness for my mom's cookie recipe. Maybe I'll start there.

Chapter 20

BLAKE

"This place is a dump."

Elain and I stand in the middle of the living room of the new house, a couple of boxes behind us. Today, we're cleaning and throwing away anything that's not staying. Her parents gave her the go-ahead, seemingly happy to have her take on a job that doesn't take money out of *their* pocket. So, we got started on the house right away. Scratching the back of my neck, I mutter, "I didn't think it was *that* bad."

She looks at me, disbelief on her face. "It looks like it was built in the 18th century." Then, she wrinkled her nose. "Smells like it, too."

"She's right. It's a dump." Wesley's tall, broad frame comes into view, and Elain and I both jump at the deep voice. I try my best to not ogle him like some love-sick teenager. But I fail miserably. He's wearing dark blue jeans that hug his thick thighs and cowboy boots that are all worn and dirty. Nothing like the pretty and polished ones I've seen on the men in New York. His black t-shirt makes his tattoos pop against his sun-kissed skin, and I have the sudden urge to trail my fingertips across every single one of them.

But mainly my attention is caught on the fucking *backwards ball cap* that has no business looking *that* good on him. I cleared my throat, praying that my wandering eyes went unnoticed. "What are you doing here?"

I don't think they do because he smirks. *Smirks.*

"Welcoming my new neighbor to the neighborhood, of course." He sets a basket of what looks like various cookies on the dusty countertop, and as he passes me, the scent of something woodsy and green fills my nostrils.

Did he bake these? The thought of Wesley doing something as domestic as baking makes my stomach flutter. Then the idea of him in nothing *but* an apron has my thighs squeezing together. I internally sigh. I *seriously* need to get laid. Elain's looking at me like she can read my every thought, and my face flushes before I turn to look at the basket.

"Why? Did you poison these?" I snide and pick through them.

He smirks. "Don't know. Guess you'll have to find out." Looking at Elain, his head dips and his voice drops into a whisper as he says, "Just don't eat the chocolate chip ones." He winks. She laughs in return.

"Let me know if you need help with anything."

"We won't." I respond quickly.

He just keeps that insufferable smile on his lips. "Ladies." He tips his head and turns around, heading back out the open front door.

"That's your neighbor?" Elain whispers, even though he's pretty much out of earshot now.

"Mhm." I don't even try to hide my gaze as I pop a piece of cookie into my mouth and watch the way those jeans hug his ass as he walks.

"He's hot." That has me choking on the cookie in my mouth. This girl truly has no filter. I cough and slam my fist against my chest. He *is* hot. I'm not stupid, even I can see that. But I would never give Wesley the satisfaction of saying those words aloud. "Gross." I manage to get the word out in between coughs.

"Right." Then she grabs one of the cookies and bites into it before saying. "Damn, those are good." I sigh. Also, true. I'd recognize Ana's recipe anywhere. Then she's returning my sigh with her own as she finishes her cookie and wipes the crumbs from her hands. "Where do we start?"

Chapter 21

BLAKE

We spent hours dusting, sweeping, and wiping down every surface in the house on Sunday. Over the course of a few days, we've also bagged and boxed up items to donate and take to the dump. We haven't even started on the outside of the house, but we're feeling accomplished at how much we've done and how much better it already looks. I thought it was charming from the start, but I do suppose it did need a few touches to make it even more appealing. Elain even tagged along with me to pick up some necessities. The few times I've tried to ask about her parents or if she has any friends, she's shut down almost completely every time. I know there's more to Elain. A reason she works at the anti-weed shop for free. A reason why she took a job cleaning up an old house with a stranger. It's been abundantly clearer the longer we've spent together.

"Why did you move to New York?" Elain asks from where she leans against the island, flipping through an old, worn cookbook.

I pause, fingers stilling on a broken lamp as I mull over her words. It was a far more personal question than I was expecting, but I quickly shake it off and answer, "Dreamed of doing it since I was a little girl. I always wanted to write."

"Then why come back? I don't think I ever would."

The look in her eye is the same one I've seen in my own, and it makes my chest burn. Elain and I have gotten to know each other on a friendly basis while we've worked on the house, but we've never broached deeper topics in hopes of keeping the atmosphere light and playful. I think we've both been using this time as an escape and have been content with just that. But how do I tell her that even at my age, life is still just as hard? I have enough trauma to last me a lifetime, and it'd be a lie if I said I was completely healed, even after leaving the very town that was the root of it all. There's nothing like watching your family fall apart, and it's one of the many reasons I had always planned on leaving town the second I got the chance.

I decided right then and there that I'd try a new approach. Maybe sharing a piece of myself will make her feel more comfortable. Make her open up and talk about why her eyes look so sad all of the time. I didn't even consider it before because I didn't think I could handle someone like Elain looking at me differently, but something tells me she won't. I finish tossing out the lamp and taping up a few more boxes to donate when I ask a question instead of answering hers, "Do you want to know how I got this scar?"

I've seen her eyeing it a few times. Torn on whether it's inappropriate or not to ask such a question. It's faded, not nearly as horrible as when it was fresh, but it's still gnarly enough that it always catches glances when I do leave it exposed.

"My father was a drunk," I speak before she can utter a word. "After my parents got divorced and my mother went to rehab, it got worse. He was never violent before, but...but I think," I pause, looking down at the scar. "I think a part of him, the good part, died the day my mother left him for good."

I cast a glance at her as I finish, and she stiffens. Her hands halted on the book. "I'm sorry that happened to you."

"It got me to where I am today," I shrug. "So, I guess some good always comes out of the bad, right?"

"Yeah," She lets her shoulders drop a smidge. "I guess it does."

I can tell she wants to say something more, but I don't push it. I want to be someone she can run to, not from. Baby steps first.

Chapter 22

BLAKE

My phone buzzes with a text just as I finish dropping Elain off.

I laugh as I stare down at the texts from Whitney.

> Do they deliver?

> You're so funny!! I need to run some errands and get some stuff for the festival but can you pick it up and I'll meet you at your house? In about an hour?

I stare at the screen, now considering how I can get out of this. I do miss Whitney. We haven't hung out at all. And I can't avoid the bar forever. I know that. And *he* won't be there since he's home tonight. I know because I saw his truck in the driveway on the way to Elain's. I guess what better time is there to get it over with? Plus, I'm pretty hungry, too. My stomach growls as I type back.

> Me: Sounds good!

***

I step into the bar, some old country music softly playing overhead. I placed the food order quite some time ago, so I'm hoping I'm not too early to pick it up. While I was technically in here before, I didn't see much of anything. Too consumed with getting back to the house and under the covers that I didn't even stop to take it all in. Whereas the outside didn't change much, the inside of the bar is almost entirely remodeled. The memories made here are concealed by a bar I've never even seen before.

It almost looks like a cabin on the inside. Wooden floors, walls, tables, and chairs. The list goes on. It's all a matching mahogany, making the lighting and feel of the space cozy. The back bar is a decent size, with the bar top being just as long. Behind it lies bottles of liqueurs, spirits, and glasses placed neatly on stepped shelves. The same pool table from years ago is still here, a large antler-wrapped chandelier swinging above. An old jukebox in the corner. A brick fireplace. Various picture frames, newspaper articles, neon signs, and game heads take up the walls. Pictures of local people, Ben and the boys, and our moms.

I had been to more bars than I could count, but they were always ones that Marshall liked. Pristine and over the top. Hard to get into unless you know the right people and have the right connections. But this? This just screams small-town bar. My eyes snag on the booth in the back, and I want so desperately to go to it. To see why it's the same as I remember, and not anything like the new tables or booths that have been put in. But I don't let curiosity win me over this time. Instead, I spot the white bags sitting on the bar top and walk over to check the name on the receipt. Just as I go to pick them up, a woman comes out from the back of the bar. Brown hair pulled back into a low bun, and dark, rich brown eyes. Freckles splatter her nose. She looks young but not much younger than me. I recognize her from the time I came flying in here on a mission. She sees me, and her eyes light up. "Blake, isn't it? I recognize you from the other day."

I scratch the back of my neck and fight a blush from marring my face. "Sorry about that. I've been a bit off-kilter since being home."

She laughs; it's so pretty and light that it's hard not to be drawn in by her personality. Then she pushes out her hand. "No hard feelings. My name's Harper." I take it and shake hers, plastering a genuine smile on my face.

"Nice to properly meet you," I say while looking around, noticing it's rather empty. "Slow night?"

She nods, cringing. "It's been like that recently."

I crinkle my nose, and as I look around the space, a memory dawns on me that has me spitting out an idea. "Have you guys ever thought about doing karaoke?"

"What?"

"You know, karaoke. I think it'd be a real hit. In New York City, my friend frequented this bar that always did it on Friday nights. Brought in a big crowd. She always came home a little too drunk, but she always had fun."

Her eyes light up, and a smirk falls onto her red-painted lips. "That's one hell of an idea. I'll pitch it to boss man." I nod and smile. I turn to leave, hand already on the door, when I decide to spin back around.

"Do you have plans after this? Whitney is coming over." I ask, making a show of pulling the bags of food up. "And clearly, we ordered way too much food. Maybe you could join us?"

For a second, I expect her to decline, but then she says, "You know what? I'd love that. I get off in half an hour." She throws me a wink adding, "I'll even bring the booze."

I giggle. "Give me your number, I'll text you the address."

Chapter 23

WESLEY

It was exactly two in the morning when I woke to my mom screaming. The kind of scream that would haunt anyone for the rest of their life. So blood-curdling and bone-chilling that I thought she was dying.

She may as well have been.

It was 2:15am by the time the Sheriff and EMTs got to our door.

2:17am, when they pronounced my father dead.

It's not something you think is possible when you're young. Your parents are invincible, especially your father. I didn't cry at first; I couldn't feel anything other than blinding, unbearable pain as my brain tried to catch up with what I was hearing and seeing. I could only watch as Wyatt held my mom as she sobbed and shook while my father's body was wheeled away.

Our house was lit with flashes of blue and red. Sirens rang and orders were barked, but nothing except the sight of my dad's pale, blue face mattered. What were our last words? I couldn't remember, and I hated myself for the fact that I couldn't remember. So many moments I took for granted because I was naïve enough to believe he'd live forever. That I'd die before him. That he'd go peacefully. I didn't know what to do, and didn't know how to console my mother or my brother, so I raced through the front doors and ran. My brother yelled for me, maybe the sheriff too, but I ran, and ran, and ran until my lungs burned, my vision blurred, and I had no choice but to drop into a heap of exhaustion on the grassy ground.

It didn't take long for her to find me. I felt her before she spoke and wasn't surprised when Blake fell to her knees beside me. Her presence was like a tether to this world. A pull I could always rely on and could always find. Not saying a word, she wrapped her arms around me. She didn't say 'I'm sorry' or whisper any comforting, useless words into my ear. Just held me as I finally broke. What could one say in a moment like this, anyways? What kind of words could comfort a loss so huge?

Nothing could, I realized. Because this was the cold, harsh reality of life. Full of pain and sorrow and unforgiving changes you never see coming. I didn't have my dad or any feelings other than grief. But I had Blake. And she sat with me before our favorite pond, with our knees digging into the cold, wet ground as we cried until there was not a single tear left to shed –

”You alright?” My brother clasps a hand on my shoulder, his tense and tired voice bringing me back to the present day. I look at him, his face a mirror of my own pain as he watches our mother place roses on our father's headstone.

“Just reminiscing. Hard not to think about how different life would be if he were still here.” He nods in understanding, and we don't say anymore, not needing to. We both feel it, this mutual emptiness but desire to be strong for our mom every time a reason to visit our dad rolls around.

I stare as tears slip from my mom's chin and splash on the deep red of the rose petal. “He is so proud of you boys,” she tells us.

I know she's right. Our dad was always supportive. Proud of us, even when we both deserved a good walloping. But it's hard not to doubt it some days. Even from the grave, the aspiration to be everything our father hoped we would be is a weight so suffocating it's a miracle I haven't drowned.

***

My keys swing from my hands as I walk from where I parked my truck a few shops down from Buddies'. Harper had texted me that it was dead tonight, so I cut her shift early and told her I'd come in to take over. I could just have her close the bar entirely but coming in and doing something sounds a hell of a lot better than sitting on my couch at home, mourning another one of my father's missed birthdays.

When I see Blake swinging open the entrance to the bar, I pause and duck behind the side of the building. I nearly started banging my head into the brick wall for letting her ward me off from *my* space. Regardless, I'm still pathetic enough that I don't move from my hiding place, choosing to whip out my phone and pull up the bar's cameras instead. There's no audio, so I can't hear anything, but I can see the way she pauses when she walks in and takes in the inside. How she pauses when she sees her untouched booth. I curse at the sight.

Harper comes into view shortly after, and they chat for some time. Blake says something that has Harper tipping her head back and laughing. I decide then to tuck my phone away and lean against the hard wall. She must be picking up food, not stopping in for a drink. So, I wait until I hear the door open again and only peek around to make sure she's walking away before I come out from my spot and head inside. When our bell chimes, Harper whips back around, likely thinking it's Blake again or a new customer, but it's just me. She throws her hands on her hips and cocks her head. "Were you hiding outside?"

"What?" I feign confusion and scoff. "No."

She hums, clearly not believing me. She takes off her apron and hangs it on the hook behind her. "Well, I'm off then. Call me if you need me to come back in."

"Thanks, Harper." Only when she gathers her stuff and leaves do I see Mr. Sanders sitting at the end of the bar, again, with a shit-eating grin on his face.

"Keep looking at me like that, and I'm going to start feeding you rat poison, old man," I threaten.

He only laughs into his mug and goes back to playing his crossword puzzle.

Chapter 24

BLAKE

"I've officially declared it girls' night," Harper announces, grinning as she steps into my doorway with her arms packed full of goodies. "We've got alcohol and good food. Time to talk about *everyone* who's wronged us."

Whitney and I laugh, and I just know Vivienne would adore a moment like this.

We spent the night talking about everything under the sun. We laugh until we're near tears, and we eat both junk food and takeout until we're so full we can't possibly eat another bite. Harper and I have a few drinks while Whitney sips down mocktails. They question me on everything about New York City, and Harper, despite only knowing her for a mere five minutes, even gets me to open up about Marshall. The way she responded has me thinking she can relate to that sort of situation better than anyone else.

Somehow, hours into our night, the conversation takes a turn. What started as a mention of Ben's birthday slowly drifts into talk about my "hot" neighbor—Harper and Whitney's words, not mine. Before I know it, he's the center of the conversation. I'm not as irritated as I usually would be; if anything, I'm grateful. The distraction dulls the guilt of not visiting Ana or going to Ben's grave on a day like this.

"You two have history, don't you?" Harper is the first to prod.

"More than I'd like to admit." I sip my cocktail. The sweet mix of cherry and pineapple makes it almost too easy to forget just how much rum I had watched Harper pour into it. Dangerous, but delicious.

"Then what's the deal? You two always seem so tense around each other."

"Oh, come on." I protest, "That's not true –"

"Yes, it is." They say at exactly the same time.

I sigh. "It's...complicated," I look at Whitney. "You *know* it's complicated."

"Maybe it doesn't have to be?" Whitney asks. "I'm just saying...maybe you guys should try to be friends? I mean, it's been, what? Years? I'm sure things have changed. You guys aren't kids anymore."

Harper nods along, adding, "And unfortunately, in a town this small, we're all linked in some way. It can get a bit awkward if you two can't even stand to be in the same room."

"Or when you look at each other like you want to rip your clothes off." Whitney mutters, and I gasp, launching one of the marshmallows I was prepared to shove into my mouth at her.

I smirk, opting to give her a taste of her own medicine. "Oh, and what is it you call it when you ogle the *other* Conway boy-"

She cut me off by launching the marshmallow right back. We all break out into a fit of giggles, which soon turns into laughter so loud it has us doubling over and fighting off tears. This night has been fun, the most fun I've had in a long time. Once things dwindled down and we all started yawning, we even promised to make plans for next weekend to do it again, and I find myself rather excited at the idea. That night though, once I'm tucked in bed and trying to drift off, all I can think about is our earlier conversation.

Maybe you guys should try to be friends.

Maybe they're right. Regardless of the small town and friends we share, we're linked through our moms until the end of time. And we are neighbors, after all.

Chapter 25

WESLEY

"Alright. Last one, okay?"

I throw a piece of leftover bacon from this morning into the air and watch as the black lab at my feet jumps to catch it in his mouth. For a dog that gets exercise every day and walks at least a mile down to my house day and night, he's seriously a chunk. Wyatt thinks it's because I feed him, but he's always been like this. Plus, they only live for so long, so why not let them enjoy the finer things in life? With that thought, I pat his head and toss him another piece. "Don't tell your father." I point a finger in his face in warning and turn around to throw a lob of butter into the heated pan on the stove. The lacrosse game I have on blasts from the small TV I have hanging in my kitchen. Just as I go to throw some vegetables into the pan, a knock sounds from the front door, and Benji barks before bolting to it and sniffing the bottom of the door like he can somehow figure out who it is that way.

I wipe my hands on the apron and join him at the door. What I don't expect to see is Blake standing there in tight pink biker shorts and a cropped black tee. A ballcap adorning her head, hair pulled into a messy bun in the back. She looks fucking *delectable*.

She tucks a loose strand of hair behind her ear, offering a soft, almost timid, "Hi," like she's not sure she's supposed to be here.

"Everything okay?" I ask, looking over her shoulder, not seeing anything. Can't think of any other reason why she'd show up to my house unless she was being chased with a chainsaw.

"Can I come in?" Her tone piques my interest enough that I don't say anything, and against better judgment, I step aside and motion with my head for her to step in. She gives Benji a quick greeting, and once he's satisfied with her attention, he waddles over to the dog bed I bought for him. Her eyes light up as she takes in my space. It's an open concept. Cathedral ceilings with wooden beams. A spacious kitchen with an island and a living room with a real fireplace. Tall windows all around. No curtains, so the light is always streaming in. I'm an early bird anyway, so it never bothers me much. Plus, when you live in the middle of nowhere, there's not much need for that extra wall of privacy. It's not much, but I built it myself, and it's home. My mom always chastises me about how it could use a 'woman's touch.'

"Wow. Who knew you had such taste?"

"Says the girl who likes the Yankees." I huff, making a show of glancing at her hat. "So, what's up?"

"I...well, I was just going for a walk and wanted to see if you wanted to come. I saw the truck in the driveway."

I'm stumped. Stuck standing there with my mouth gaping like a fish. I half expected her to ask me to kill a mouse for her or something, but not hang out. We don't even like each other half the time, and she's acting like this is something normal. Like it's something we'd do every day. I warded her off after finding out she was moving in. Granted, I did bake her favorite cookies, so she must be feeling some sort of guilt for the way we've been acting around each other.

"...You want to hang out?"

Her face reddens, and she scrunches her face. "Forget it. It was a dumb idea." She whirls around and bolts for the door, already having thrown it open. Somehow, I wasn't pleased when I saw her on my porch, but knowing she *wants* to be here has made me feel differently. Turns out I'll still take whatever she'll give me.

"Blake, close the door and get your ass back here." The blush on her face deepens, if that's even possible, but she closes the door. "You hungry?"

"Starving," she admits.

I nod and say, "Good, it'll be just a little while, but you can hang out on the couch. Want a beer?"

"God, yes - holy shit. Is that Aaron?" I turn as I see that she's gaping at the TV where the lacrosse game was playing. Now there's an interview going on of Aaron Moore. He used to go to high school with us and left town once he got a full-ride scholarship to play. I almost laugh at her expression. He's a big deal, so I'm a bit shocked Blake hasn't heard about him while living in the city. Right then, her phone begins to ring, and I watch as she fishes it out from the pocket on the side of her shorts. Her eyes light up a bit at the name, and red-hot jealousy courses through me because I want nothing more than to know *who* she's smiling about. I busy myself with opening the fridge so as to not look like I'm snooping.

"Vivienne." She says it as a way of greeting. That immediately eases the tension in my shoulders. I've heard about Vivienne through her mom. Not much aside from the fact that they're close friends who met in the city.

"What? How did you even know that? Creep. No, No. It's Wesley." She lowers her voice when she gets to my name, seemingly thinking I can't hear her. But I can. And when I turn back around with a beer in my hand, I can also see the blush creeping up her neck when she says it. That has me feeling smugger than I should. She continues talking in a hushed voice. "Yes, yes. Okay, I'll call you later. Bye."

She looks at me with a soft smile on her face and tucks a piece of hair that fell back under her cap. "Sorry. She gets a bit cranky if I don't answer."

I huff a laugh at that. "Makes sense. I'm sure she misses you," I take a deep breath before continuing, "Did you enjoy it? The city?" I, of all people, know she did, but small talk was better than standing here all awkwardly.

"Yes. And no. Vivienne was probably the best thing about it. She is, I mean." Her wording doesn't invade me. And I'm dying to know if that means she's torn up on whether or not she wants to go back. She did buy a house, though, so I can't imagine she's that torn.

"Why'd you leave then?"

"It's...complicated." The way her tone falters just a bit at the end and the way she pauses when she speaks those words confirms that it runs deeper than even I could have anticipated. "Let me guess," I drawl, leaning against the island and cocking my head. "Crazy ex or something?"

"Or something." She stills, tracking my movements with those brown eyes. "I quit my job." She shifts in her seat, thoughts wrinkling the space between her brows. I want nothing more than to pluck each and every one of them from her mind, just to ease whatever weight she's carrying. "Or lost it? I don't know, I guess."

With that, I nod and slide her the beer can I popped open. Out of everything that's happened since she's been back, that's probably the most shocking. If Blake was one thing, it sure as hell wasn't a quitter. I look at her, hoping she'll elaborate, but she just says, "It's a long story."

I raise a brow in answer. "I've got time."

"He cheated." Now I'm the one who stills as she pulls in a breath. The small sound is the only thing reminding me to move. I straighten from where I lean against the counter but keep my eyes trained on her as she adds, "With my boss."

I clear my throat, choosing to place my hands back on either side of the counter. I think if I leave them anywhere else, I'd start breaking every damn thing in this house, and I can't imagine that'll help the situation in even the slightest. "I'm sorry."

She replies with a curt nod, feigning indifference. But the way she fiddles with the rim of her beer can tells me she's anything but indifferent about the situation. "Like I said," She shrugs, "Complicated."

"What could possibly be complicated about that?" I tease, hoping to brighten both of our now sour moods, but I only get a twitch of a smile in return. While I may not know this new Blake, I do know that cheating on anyone is unimaginable. If you're not interested, just say so. Don't lead someone on, and don't waste their time. And cheating on Blake? *Blake*? The idea of that is downright unfathomable. All I know is that I pray I never set my sights on the guy.

"Yeah," a breathy little laugh catches in her throat, "At least walking in on them mid-sex proved it wasn't just *me* he sucked at getting off." My brows shoot up as a red-hot color slowly creeps up her neck. She slaps a hand over her full lips and blinks like she can't believe she voiced those words out loud. "That...was widely inappropriate of me."

"No," I shake my head. "More like a damn shame."

That blush somehow deepens, and she coughs, slicing that growing tension in half like a hot knife slicing through butter. "So, you have a girlfriend yet? Or still trying to find someone who will take your virginity?"

"Why? You interested in deflowering me, sweetheart?" I tease.

A sputtering comes from her mouth as she tries not to spit out the beer she just took a sip of. Smirking, I turn around to throw some chopped vegetables into the pan I had heating.

"No. No girlfriend. Just me," I respond, looking at her over my shoulder and finding her staring at me. Or rather, my arms. I'm wearing a cutoff since I've just been at the house, so my tattoos are on full display. Suddenly, I'm regretting not throwing something else on when she got here. My entire right arm is covered in black ink, a sleeve of memories and moments that trail down to my knuckles. There are a couple of random lyrics and other miscellaneous shit I got back when I was young and didn't give a damn about the world. A bull I got with Wyatt—his prissy ass needed a lot of convincing for that one. A carnation for my mom. A rose for my dad. And up on my bicep, there's a pond, still and quiet, with tall pine trees rising behind it, their reflections rippling across the water like a memory you're not sure is real.

Her eyes flutter shut. "Is-Is that...?"

"The pond? Yes."

She stands up so fast that she nearly knocks over the stool she was sitting on at the island. "I'm sorry. You know what? I just realized I may have left the stove on. I should get going." Then she wiggles the beer can and tucks it in her chest. "Thanks for the beer."

She practically runs for the door, not even saying bye to the dog. I look to him, now sitting by the door, looking over his back like I disappointed him. "Don't look at me like that," I grumble and fix my attention back on the vegetables that now lay burnt in the cast-iron pan.

Chapter 26

BLAKE

The pond. The pond. *The pond.*

How the hell didn't I recognize it? The very one that lays in my yard is our pond. *Was* our pond. Is that why he built his house on this road? Because of the nights we spent wandering those exact woods? When I saw it, it dawned on me. What other reason would he have for permanently putting something like that on his body?

I could look at that pond in any format and know exactly what it is. Yet I didn't realize that it was the one now on the property I *own*. Granted, it looks different than it did six years ago. But still. God, I feel so stupid. I want so badly to know what it means to him. Why he'd get something like that. The questions will follow me around until they get answers. And I so desperately wish I hadn't listened to the girls. Going over there was stupid, and telling him about Marshall was even more stupid. Embarrassment trails me like an old friend, and I want nothing more than to go back home and hide myself so deeply beneath my covers that no one can find me.

I park my car a few shops down from Bell's, confused as to why the street is so packed this morning. It's usually so easy to find parking. This is now my fourth week at the coffee shop, and I truly enjoy it more than I could have ever hoped. As I step out into the crisp morning air, I blink as I take in the huge orange banner hanging overhead.

Now *that* makes sense.

Clover-Hills Harvest Festival
September 12-14
Est. 1877

Next week. The infamous Harvest Festival, of course. How could I forget? Everyday, it feels like I'm remembering more. Uncovering aspects of this life that I buried so deeply in hopes of just healing. I hadn't even realized it was already approaching September. It's always a huge event for the people of Clover-Hills. Every storefront, streetlamp, and shrubbery possible will be decorated by the end of the week. That's exactly why people are milling around now, some shouting orders about what decorations go where and some just walking around to watch it all take place.

The town holds a scarecrow contest that each business owner participates in. The shops do a trick-or-treat for any littles who dress up. Games, food, raffles, a costume contest, a chili contest, pony rides, the list goes on. It's a big deal, and people come from all over to participate. Surprisingly, it's not nearly as extravagant as the Christmas Festival, though. I find myself excited for the changing seasons. Christmas in New York City is nothing compared to Christmas in a small town.

Thankfully, the coffee house doesn't open for about another half hour, so there will be a small reprieve from the crowd. I have a feeling that once the open sign flicks on, we'll have a full house. I go to push my key into the lock of the front door of the shop, only to see that it's unlocked. Whitney beat me here. She beams at me as I step in. I beam right back, shooting a teasing grin her way. "Looks like it'll be a busy morning, huh?"

She sighs and gives me a look that says *tell me about it.* "I swear it feels like these damn festivals happen every week."

"That's because they do," I respond in a sing-song voice.

"I bet you're excited, though?"

"Actually, I am." A knowing smile lights up her face.

We busy ourselves with getting the shop ready and making small talk. Menu ideas for the festival, what she plans on doing with her scarecrow, how she and the baby are, along with all sorts of random day-to-day things. I've always loved how easy the conversations flow with Whitney. That's exactly what made us such fast friends. After our morning rush, Whitney's rear-ranging some books that were left out and I'm wiping down tables on the coffee side when the bell dings, signaling we have a customer. I slap a charming smile on my face and turn to greet them, "Good morning!"

"Ma'am." He tips his head in greeting, and the towel I've got slips through my fingers at the small distraction before me.

Well, small wouldn't be how I describe him. I can't imagine there's anything *small* about him. A tall man, at least six-feet or so, with cropped black hair, a devastatingly gorgeous grin, and deep, rich brown eyes consumes my vision. Tattoos cover both of his massive arms, and there's a tiny scar on his bottom lip. Black shirt, jeans, combat boots. A look that shouldn't work, but that's so fitting to this man's hard features. It just screams tall, dark, and handsome. I don't even try to stop my roaming eyes when he's distracted by my small hiccup. He squats down to pick it up before withdrawing back to full height and holding out his hand to offer the rag.

I softly take it back and quirk an eyebrow at him, "Ma'am? Can't say I've ever been called that."

He smirks at me in a panty-melting kind of way. One that tells me he has zero trouble with getting laid whenever he wishes. He shrugs one of his shoulders, "I can call you whatever you'd like."

I feel no romantic spark, of course. I don't know this guy, but I am just a girl. I'm not immune to good looks and getting flustered at a handsome man's attention. And the horndog in me who reads all-smut, no-plot books would be crazy for not wanting to climb this man like a tree.

I huff a laugh. "You are a shameless flirt. What can I get you?" I tuck a piece of hair behind my ear and steer the conversation in a different direction before meeting his gaze again.

He leans against the counter and rubs his strong jaw-line like he's thinking *really* hard about what he wants, "Your number?"

I can't stop the teasing grin from slipping onto my lips, "Straightforward. I'll give you that."

"Maybe. I'll take a black coffee, please." I turn around to grab one of the to-go cups, and he rattles on behind me. "You new to town? Can't imagine I'd forget you."

I roll my eyes. *This guy.* "Something like that," I respond.

"You know how to keep a man curious. I like it."

His eyes roam over my frame as I turn back around with his cup. It doesn't make me feel self-conscious at all. Living in the city forced me to get used to crappy lines and all sorts of roaming eyes. Yes, the guy is hot, but he's not really my type. Everything, and I mean *everything* about this man is the opposite of someone like Marshall, or any of the guys I met in the city. He screams trouble. He screams something a woman *wants* but sure as hell does not need. Not what I need or look for in a man. Not like the one

I *want*, but that is completely off-limits for more than one reason. But...I could use a little fun. So, what's the harm in dishing it right back?

"So, your number?" He asks again, and I let out a dramatic sigh. "Maybe try again tomorrow, and we'll see if you happen to get lucky."

He nods his head and tilts it to the side, staring directly into my soul, like he can read every thought and see every gear turning. It's a bit odd, but this entire town has a way of making me feel that way. He takes the warm paper cup from my hands, raises it, and says, "See you tomorrow, then." As he walks out, I notice while he has a nice ass, it doesn't nearly fill out his jeans the way Wesley's does. It also dawns on me that even at six-foot, Wesley no doubt towers over him. I nearly smack myself in the face for that thought. Thinking about *fun* things should not include thinking about my neighbor.

Whitney's high-pitched squeal flows to my ears, thankfully pulling me away from my internal sabotage. "Did you just *flirt* with that man?"

"Yes...yes, I think I did," I laugh. "You know him?"

"I know of him. And trust me, from what I've heard, you do not want to go down that road. Dude has got a great personality, but he needs some serious therapy." That has the woman in me wanting to fix all his problems. Or at least find him someone who will. At my silence, she goes on. "He's great eye candy, but not great boyfriend material."

It's a good thing that's exactly *not* what I'm looking for, but I don't say that.

"Now, back to work and stop ogling all the hot customers," She laughs loudly and ducks as I throw the wet rag at her head.

Chapter 27

WESLEY

"What's got you in a chipper, sober mood?" I poke fun at Haden, who came sauntering into my bar with a shit-eating grin just a few moments ago.

"Hot blonde who made my coffee this morning," He winks, shooting me a grin behind his cup. My brows shoot up. There's only one blonde working at the coffee shop, and it makes my blood run cold at the idea that Haden is setting his sights anywhere near her. He's talking about Blake. My Blake. An "Uh-oh" rings out from where Mr. Sanders sits at his usual spot at the end of the bar. I shoot him a look that would send most men running, but it only gains me a shit-eating grin in return. I decide to focus it on Haden instead, knowing it'll be more effective.

"Don't even think about it."

He looks taken aback, "What?"

"She's off limits." The old man sing-songs.

Yes. And no. She's off limits to nobody, *but* Haden. He's a playboy. She doesn't need a playboy. Especially not after what she went through with her piece of shit ex.

"Shut it." I point at Sanders without even looking. He raises his hands in surrender before picking his mug back up and busying himself with the newspaper.

"Doesn't seem like she is. So why does it matter?" Haden butts in.

"Because she'd probably make you cry before you could even score a first date." I busy myself with sorting out cash in the drawer. That part is true. She's a bully. Haden wouldn't know what to do with her. Hell, half the time, I don't know what to do with her.

"Alright. Alright. I'll back off. Unless she comes to me first." His laughter grates against my ears, and I roll my eyes, knowing he was only trying to get a rise out of me. And succeeded.

"What do you want?" I bark.

"Our darling Harper said you wanted to see me." Shit. That's right. *Harper. Job. Haden.* I've been so busy and distracted that it completely left my mind. Leave it to that woman to give me no choice but to deal with it.

"Of course, she did," I mumble. He scrunches his brows at that, so I cut to the chase. "I need some extra help around the bar. You want a job?"

He laughs like it's outrageous. "No."

I didn't expect him to take the job, but his tone only riles me up more, "Why not?"

"Because I have better things to do. "

I place my hands on my hips and fully face him. "Like?"

"Like taking your hot blonde on a date."

"That's it -" I growl and lunge forward, but he's already bouncing back. I go to follow when Harper's stern voice cuts through our soon-to-be brawl.

"Alright, boys. It's barely ten in the morning. No fighting in the damn bar."

We both stop dead. I'm confident Harper could kick both our asses. She's maybe 5'3, not very tall, but she packs some muscle, and I've seen her break up more than one bar fight. We both know it. We just won't say it out loud. That's why we both mutter "Yes, Harper" and step away from each other. Then the asshole flips me off when she turns her head. But somehow? She still sees it.

"You're a child, Haden," she scolds.

He smirks at her backside. "You love it."

She doesn't deign him a response, only rolls her eyes and turns a look at me once she's done setting her stuff down. "I want to start doing Karaoke Nights every Saturday," she says matter of fact.

"Karaoke?" I don't hide the disgust in my tone. Or face.

She crosses her arms like she's ready for a stand-off. "Yes. Karaoke."

"I hate karaoke."

"We need the business." I sigh. She's right. I hate it when she's right.

"And what gave you this brilliant idea?"

She smiles like she knows something I don't. "A friend."

I ponder it for a few minutes while she stares at me, waiting for a response. "Friday nights. And if it doesn't take the first time, we don't do it again."

She squints her eyes at me. "If it doesn't take the *second* time."

I close my eyes in feigned annoyance and shake my head. "Deal. But all the planning and running around to get shit is on you."

Her returning grin is evil. She knew I wouldn't say no.

Chapter 28

BLAKE

Viv:

O.M.G.

YOU SENT ME THE TURTLE!?

This is why you're my best friend

So glad you love it. Keep it as a reminder that I am the first and last friend you've ever gotten high with.

It's going at the very center of the shrine I've created for you.

Closing out my texts, I look up at the big Victorian-style home before me. I haven't seen Ana yet, and I've been dying too, so it was easy to accept the invite. Clearly, I'm late to the party, though. A familiar blue truck is parked next to a newer truck I don't recognize. One I can assume is Wyatt's. I guess I should have known it'd be a full-blown family dinner. I have a feeling she omitted that detail on purpose.

My foot barely hits the first step when Ana's swinging open the door and barreling towards me. I glimpse her black hair and blue eyes right before she envelopes me. "Oh! My girl! Look at you! You're as gorgeous as you were the day you were born." She squeezes my face and plants kisses on either side before bringing me in for a hug.

"Hi, Ana." Relief fills my body from her embrace, like it always has. I relax in her arms. "I missed you." She squeezes me tighter at my words, and I *swear* I hear a rib crack. I didn't realize having her and my mom in one setting would make me want to crawl into bed between them like I used to and cry until no tears remained. Thankfully, my savior sneaks up behind her.

"I don't think she can breathe, Ma." Wyatt says from behind her in the doorway. He joins us on the front porch and slings an arm over my shoulder once his mom lets me go. "What's up, little lake? Heard you're my new neighbor."

"You heard right."

We make our way inside, where my mom and Wesley are chatting in the dining room. "*There* you are." My mom says, moving in to give me a hug and a kiss. "I'm starting to feel like you're avoiding your mother."

I try my best not to roll my eyes, but I'm not sure I succeed. "You know I've been busy."

"I'm just teasing," She pats my cheek and motions with her head. "Come on, have a seat. Food's almost ready." Then she pats the chair that's *right next to Wesley.*

Reluctantly, I sit. Asking to sit somewhere else is far too petty and would just look weird. "Hi," I greet quietly.

"Hey," His response is just as quiet. And so close. Our arms are nearly brushing, and I can *smell* him. Heat flares in my face, and I do my best to avoid the mountain of the man sitting next to me. He smells like pine and woods, like *home*, and he looks like a Greek god in a button-down shirt rolled halfway up his arms. Wyatt and my mom sit across from Wesley and I, and Ana sits at the head of the table. The other end of the table is empty, but it's still set for one. The same spot their dad would sit if he was here. They've always saved a seat for him. It's been that way since his passing.

"How's the new house coming along?" Ana rips me away from memories of Ben with her question.

"Good!" I clear my throat. "Still a long way to go, but it's coming along."

"I was so happy to hear that you decided to stay."

I just give her a little smile in return. I don't say anything. Because yes, while I bought a house, I'm not quite sure what the hell I'm even doing. It gets quiet, and the atmosphere turns awkward at my lack of chatter. Wyatt nods in my direction, cutting through the growing tension. "That reminds me. I'm free tomorrow if you want to come see the place," the older Conway boy says, tossing me a lifeline.

"I have to work in the morning, but how about noon? I have an hour break."

"Works for me." He smiles, showing that same dimple he and Wesley share. He goes back to stabbing his green beans as my mom then turns to Wesley.

Ana shimmies in her chair. "So, tell me *all* about the city. You had a roommate, right? Vivienne? I'd love to meet her sometime. How did college go? I'm so sad I missed your graduation."

The rapid-fire questions spewing from Ana's lips are enough to make me dizzy. I settle on answering the simplest question out of the bunch. "I'm sure she'll want to plan a trip down here soon."

She hums. "Oh, and that job! Your mom told me you were working for this big newspaper. Do they have you working remotely while here or something?"

I falter at that, not truly healed and ready to discuss it with the entire table. Thankfully, just as I start to clam up, Wesley's deep voice cuts through the dining room. "The first night of Karaoke at the bar is Friday."

The way he changes the subject comes off like he's merely uninterested in my life, maybe even downright rude, but I know that tone. I understand what he just did for me. His voice causes goosebumps to rise on my exposed flesh. I shuffle in my seat and place my arm closest to his in my lap. *That* shocks me. More than the fact that he just swooped in to save me. I did not think Harper had it in her to convince him, but I guess I was wrong.

"Mr. Sanders told me," Ana exclaims. "How exciting, honey!"

"Wow." I cut in, clearing my throat. "What a fun idea."

He narrows his eyes at me and leans back in his chair. "It was your idea, wasn't it?"

"I don't know what you're talking about." I shrug and busy myself with taking a sip of my water. I can feel his eyes on me, but I don't meet his stare. I'm a shit liar. And he knows it. When it comes to the little stuff, at least.

"So, Blake," Ana leans forward from her spot at the table. "Are you dating anyone in town yet?"

I choke on the piece of chicken I just put in my mouth, and Wesley pats me on the back dramatically. I shoo away his hands with a scowl, clearing my throat. "No. Nope. Single pringle over here."

Single pringle? I cringe at my own words. *What am I? Five?* Wesley snorts beside me, and I shoot him a glare. Ana hums and widens her eyes. Taps her chin like she's deep in thought. "You know...there's this *very* handsome boy who works at the convenience..."

Both Wyatt and Wesley cut her off with a groan and a chorus of "*Mom*"s, but it's Wyatt who throws his head back and says, "Come on, Mom. Seriously?"

"What?" She asks incredulously. "If you two won't give me a grandbaby, Blake might as well!"

"Oh my god." I bury my hands in my face. "Please make it stop." I mutter to Wesley. My face feels like it's on *fire*. And their reaction tells me that this is *not* the first time she's played matchmaker with the people in this room. I pray to the man above to make the rest of this a normal family dinner, but even I know there's no such thing when the Conways and Warners come together.

Chapter 29

WESLEY

After dinner, Blake and I are alone in the kitchen. Our moms are on the porch drinking wine, and Wyatt rushed out of here to help with a problem on the ranch. So, that left us two to deal with the clean up.

"I wash. You dry."

I nod and take up position beside her. A comfortable silence fills the space between us. I go to break it, but she beats me to it. "Thanks for that. With your mom." She doesn't need to elaborate. I know exactly what she's talking about. I adore my mother, but she tends to pry more than she should. I could see how quickly Blake became uncomfortable and changed the topic for not just her sake but for us all.

"Does your mom not know about your ex?" I ask.

"His name is Marshall. And no," she shakes her head, "She doesn't."

The way she says it tells me she wants to keep it that way too, so I don't prod any further. Instead, I let out a scoff and raise my eyebrows. "Marshall? What a shit name."

A laugh bubbles from her chest in return, and damn me if that smile doesn't make my pulse skip a beat. I feel like I'm sixteen again, begging for her attention when I know it's not fair to do so with so much already on her plate. She gasps, letting her laugh turn into a giggle, "It really is, isn't it?"

I nod, and we're quiet again for a few minutes, nothing but the sounds of glass clanking and running water floating in the air. Thinking about my mother's earlier questioning again has me opening my loudmouth and shoving it into a completely different direction. "I heard you met Haden."

"Haden?" she asks, confusion wrinkling her pretty features.

"Tall, dark hair, tattoos." I elaborate.

"Oh!" Surprise coats her tone. "You know him?"

I shrug. "He's a buddy of mine."

"Huh," She shakes her head. "That's so weird. Never would have guessed. He was so nice."

The way she says it grates against my nerves. I roll my eyes as I pass back one of the plates she gave me. "You missed a spot." She didn't. But it'll drive her crazy that she can't see it.

She squints her eyes at the plate but shrugs and pushes it back under the water. It hits at just the right angle and causes water to shoot straight onto my clothes. She gasps and covers her mouth to hide the amusement lighting up her eyes. "That was an accident. I swear."

"Hey, it's okay. It happens," I wave my hand in a *for-get-about-it* motion. But when she turns around to grab some paper towels, I reach forward, cranking it all the way to cold, pull out the sink hose, and spray her from head to toe.

"Wesley!" She squeals, turning as the cold water hits her. She throws her hands up like she can stop it.

I gasp dramatically and bring my hand up to cover my mouth. "It was an accident," I say innocently.

"You little shit!" She lunges forward and snatches the hose from my hand in an attempt to turn it on me. We both wrestle for control until I gain the upper hand and back her against the counter. I let go of the hose, letting it find its way back to the sink. I don't care where it goes, don't watch the mess it makes as our bodies press together. Her hips, now trapped beneath mine. I can see and feel her every breath. We both stop dead as we realize just how close we are. Her eyes bounce between my eyes and my lips, and her chest rises faster and faster.

"Missed a spot." She whispers as she brings the tow-el she's been holding up to wipe at the corner of my mouth. She pauses, towel in the air between us. She licks her lips, and I *groan* at the sight.

"Don't do that." I whisper.

"Why not?" Her hot breath fans against my lips, and I instinctively lean closer –

"Hey, kids! Bring us more wine!" My mom's voice is like a bucket of ice pulling me back to reality, both of us back to reality. We jump apart, her cheeks vibrant and red. She avoids meeting my eyes as she scrambles away from me. I sigh as I watch her leave the room, soaking wet. I lean against the cool marble and try not to think about the fact that I almost just fucking *kissed* Blake Warner.

Chapter 30

BLAKE

"Harper knows how to plan a party." I say to Whitney as I staple the bright orange paper to one of the bulletin boards on the street. She stopped by this morning to give us some fliers to help promote the karaoke bar this Friday. I turn to Whitney. "It's been like, what? A day? And I'm pretty sure she bought out the convenience store's party supplies."

Whitney chuckles. "Sounds about right."

"Hey, I'm headed to the Ranch to see Wyatt during break. You want to come along? We can grab something on the way back."

We both grabbed a rather large breakfast together this morning, so I'm sure she won't mind putting off lunch. Her nausea has been kicking her ass lately too, so I doubt much sounds good right now. "I'm down. I could use some fresh air." She wrinkles her nose. "My car, or yours?"

"We can take mine."

***

Whitney and I finally hit the entrance to the ranch shortly after she agreed to join me. The drive here was fairly quick, considering how small the town is. Whitney and I spent the trip placing bets on who will be the most shit-faced by the end of the Harvest festival. My money's on Ana, but she's betting on Haden. I don't know much about Haden's drinking habits, but I know Ana could rival a frat boy on spring break.

I notice on the drive down just how quickly the weather is changing. Green leaves transform into various shades of reds, oranges, and yellows. The breeze feels just a little bit harsher with the windows rolled down. I'll have to check out the boutique for some cold-friendly outfits here soon.

A "Buddies' Ranch" sign swings overhead as we approach, and what I assume is one of the ranch hands swings open the entrance gate. I've seen it before, but I don't really remember it. We didn't spend much time here as kids. Most of our days consisted of hanging out at the bar or one of our mom's houses. Wyatt was here more often than not, though.

"Holy, shit. This is huge." I speak.

"Yeah." Whitney replies as she looks out the window. "He holds a few rodeos here and there. But not as often anymore."

I hum. "Wonder why?"

"Beats me." She sighs.

We pull to a stop when we see Wyatt standing near one of the gates where some horses are being worked on. As we step out, Wyatt comes around to greet me. I give him a quick hug, and his smile falters a tad when he sees whom I brought.

"Whitney." He says, a bit shocked, it sounds like. Some tension that I remember from the first day in the coffee shop makes an appearance again.

"I asked her to tag along. Hope that's okay." I cut in.

"No problem at all." He gives us a tight smile before motioning with his head for us to follow. I turn to ask Whitney a question but find that she's no longer at my side. She's stopped at a gate where a man is whipping a large, black horse.

"He's being a bit rough with her, don't you think?" Whitney asks Wyatt, but he just shrugs.

"She's stubborn. Gives us all a real hard time. I've had my fair share of difficult ones, but she hasn't budged. This guy was on the list of people to call if all else fails."

She cocks her head at him, and I just wish I could understand what's going on inside that head of hers. Then she hops over the gate.

"Whitney!" I shout and lounge forward. At the same time, Wyatt grits out, "Don't you dare!"

She rode quite a bit when we were younger, competed in competitions, and whatnot. So, it's not that I don't think she can handle it. But she's pregnant, for God's sake.

"Oh, stop it!" She snaps over her shoulder. "I'm pregnant, not helpless."

That stops Wyatt dead. He turns to me. "She's pregnant?"

I peek at him shyly. "You didn't know?"

He shakes his head as he watches her. Something like wonder on his handsome face. Then he mutters, "The damn horse is scared of men."

"What?" I ask confused, but then I turn my head and see Whitney petting the horse's nose as it nuzzles its head into her side. From the way the man with the whip tucks his tail and runs, it seems like she scared him off fairly quickly, and I'm a bit down at the fact that I missed it. I take another glance at Wyatt. "Careful. You're drooling, Conway."

He rolls his eyes. "I am not."

I give him a look that says *you're not fooling anyone.*

"Who's the dad?" He asks, quiet enough so that she can't overhear us.

"Your guess is as good as mine. She won't talk about it much." He doesn't respond. His face is scrunched in confusion. So, I decided to change the topic instead. "I'll have to bring Elain down sometime. She'd love this."

"Yeah. Yeah, tell her to come down whenever she wants. Y'all are always welcome." But his response is half-hearted. He's so focused on the woman before us, I'm not sure he's seeing or hearing anything else.

Chapter 31

WESLEY

I regret every decision that has ever led me to where I am today.

I need to get *her* out of my head. Out of my system. She's the one who left. She's the one who wanted nothing to do with me. And fresh out of a relationship, she sure as hell is still the one who wants nothing to do with me. So, after whatever happened in the kitchen, I picked through the hideously large list of numbers my mother gave me a few months ago.

Brittany McIntyre. We knew each other in school, and she's been trying to get me to take her out for years. I've never been interested, and it's not anything against Brittany herself. I'm sure there's someone out there for her, but she's not for me. I could tell that from the moment I picked her up. She's wearing too much perfume, her makeup looks like she let a kid run crayons all over her face, and she no doubt got a boob job. Not a very good one from the looks of it. If her top was any smaller, I'm certain one would pop.

And now we're going to Bell's. The one place that won't help me forget about the very thing I'm avoiding. Blake *hates* Brittany. They've had some weird vendetta since high school. I can only pray that she's not working today, but the odds of that are slim to none.

"We could always go to the Diner." I try my best to sound casual, but I'm not sure it comes out as anything other than desperate.

Her high-pitched laugh grates against my ears like nails on a chalkboard. "No way, Wes. Bell's has the best coffee and pastries on the street."

Once we make it to the door, she pauses. And I realize she's waiting for me to open the door. I jump into action, reaching forward to pull it open. I've always been one for manners, but clearly, I left those, along with any brain cells I have left, at home. "After you." I motion with a hand, and she runs her nails down my bicep. I refrain from shivering at the touch. The last thing I need her to do is take that as a sign that I like her touching me.

"Such a gentleman," she purrs. I give her a forced smile and follow in after her.

Chapter 32

BLAKE

"**A**s much as I admire your hard work, I'm a bit scared you're going to break that mug."

I'm furiously scrubbing at a spot on a white ceramic mug, glaring at the blonde bimbo sitting at a table with Wesley when Whitney comes up beside me. I mumble an apology, cheeks turning red, but only replace the mug with a new one. If I don't, I might launch it at the very booth they're sitting in. "You, okay?"

"Fine!" I answer in a perky tone. But my teeth are clenched, and I'm on the verge of blowing a pupil. She clocks the two sitting in front of us, shock etching into her tone.

"Is that –"

"Yup."

"Is he–"

"Mhm."

Whitney looks from me to Wesley, to me again. Her mouth is wide, and brows shot halfway up her forehead. She looks like she just saw a man with three heads walk by. I can't imagine my expression is much different.

We both know Brittany. She's one of the only mean girls we've ever encountered in this town. The girl went after every guy I talked to in high school and made it her personal mission to embarrass me at every chance possible. One time, she even went as far as to tell everyone I slept with the *whole* football team just to win votes for homecoming queen. My date dumped me the day before, and I lost homecoming queen to her. Not that I cared very much about winning to begin with, but we were sixteen at the time. It was the most exciting thing to happen at that age, and the most devastating to know I lost it to my *mortal* enemy.

And now she's on a date with Wesley? He's on a date with *her*? After he almost *kissed* me?

I know that I am acting like an emotional teenager, and I know I need to get a grip, but I want nothing more than to go over there and poke one of her fake boobs with a ball-pen. I, of all people, have no room to be this upset over what Wesley Conway does with his life, not when I'm the one who's meant to be recovering from a fresh heartbreak. I dated after leaving, it was stupid not to think about how he probably has, too.

"If it makes you feel any better, she didn't age very well," Whitney mutters next to me. She's turned around now, leaning against the counter, and trying to stifle a smirk.

"Clearly, he doesn't think so."

"Are you...*jealous*?" Whitney whispers, but she may as well have shouted into a megaphone. I slam the mug on the counter, and it hits with a large thud. Unfortunately, drawing the attention of Brittany, herself. Whitney and I both cringe when her gasp floats through the shop.

"Oh, wow." Brittany laughs, jumps from the table, and makes her way toward the coffee bar. I don't miss the way she adds an extra sway to her hips for Wesley or how she bends over the counter like she's putting on a show. Her eyes rake down my frame with distaste written all over her face. "Blake? I haven't seen you since...what? High school?" She waves her hand around. "What a nice...*job* you have here."

"So great to see you, too, Brittany." I smile sweetly. "What can I get for you?" But she ignores me and chooses to hike a thumb towards her date, who now looks like he's currently trying to hide behind his menu. He briefly greeted me when he came in, but otherwise seems to be avoiding any further conversation like the plague.

"You know Wesley, right? You two used to be so close," She says, a knowing glint in her eye.

I frown. She knows just how close we were. Everyone in this damn town knows how close we were. "Our moms are friends," I mutter, my voice tight.

I don't look at Wesley, but I know that comment strikes a chord when he lets out an awkward cough.

Stoic silence fills the air, and she hums. Then she leans in a little more, whispering so quietly that only Whitney and I can hear her. "He got hot, didn't he? I'm so hoping he takes me home after this." She winks at us like we're all best friends, and she just let us in on one juicy secret.

"Wesley has always been hot." I fire back. Heat blooms in my cheeks before I can shut it down.

Whitney coughs next to me. *Fuck. Me.* Did I seriously just say that out loud? I grimace, peeking over at Wesley, thanking the god above that he remains blissfully unaware of my idiocy. Brittany straightens, her face screwing into a nasty look of disapproval. She spews out a stupidly complicated order, and I pretend to write it down on the notepad before me. But I'm really just playing Hangman. I may or may not add horns to the stick figure, too.

Whitney takes the notepad, gives her a warm smile, more forced than friendly, and lets her know we'll get it right out to her. Once Brittany returns to Wesley, I watch as Whitney glances down at the paper. An uncontrollable giggle bursts from her lips, and she slaps a hand over her mouth when Brittany shoots us a weird look.

"Who knew you were such an amazing artist?" She whispers. I glare at her, but she only chuckles again in return. "I won't fire you if you want to punch her in the face. Or spit in her coffee."

I want to laugh, but it comes out as a huff. A scowl so firm it feels like it will be permanent is the only thing I can manage. "Oh, please. I don't hold grudges."

Lie. Lie, lie, lie. Because this...I've never felt this before. I could dig her grave and etch "*Bitchy Brittany*" into her headstone with a jackhammer, dying happy knowing it'll still be there long after I'm gone. That revelation is like a slap to the face. Wesley isn't *mine*. Who cares that he's on a date with someone? I peek over at them, only to watch as she lays a hand on his, and he gives her a smile that pops one of those stupid dimples on his cheek. I need to go before my sanity finally crumbles.

"I'll put some of these away!" I snatch some of the books from Whitney's hand that she's just picked up and scurry toward an aisle of books I can hopefully get lost in. The silence doesn't last long when a towering, familiar shadow fills up the space behind me.

"Can I help you?" I ask Wesley as I shelve one of the thick books clutched in my hand. Ironically, the title reads *The Jealousy Cure*.

"Looking for the bathroom."

It sounds more like a question than a statement, and I can't help but laugh in his face. He knows where the bathroom is, and it's not between the bookshelves. I turn toward him with a sigh. "What do you want, Wesley?"

"I don't know." He stuffs his hands in his pockets. "You seem upset."

I narrow my eyes at him. Is he serious right now? Of course, I'm upset. Yes, I know whatever happened in the kitchen meant nothing. Physical attraction doesn't mean romantic attraction. It makes sense that he'd try to lay one on me if he's just trying to get laid. Clearly, he decided Brittany was the more rational alternative. And that's *fine*. But it doesn't mean I'm immune to feeling scorned over the revelation.

"I think you should get back to your date. Don't you?"

He watches me for a few beats, but doesn't say anything else as he turns to leave. I lean back against the bookcase. My shoulders slump, and I finally let loose a breath I didn't even realize I was holding.

Chapter 33

BLAKE

"**S**hould we have gotten fall decorations?"

Elain and I just got back from Jake's Convenience. We spent a good hour picking out some décor for the house so that it won't look as '*boring*' as Elain says it does.

She wrinkles her nose. "It's not even September yet."

"It's like the end of August. It's *practically* September." I argue, crossing my arms.

She gives me a '*really?*' look, and I pout. "You're no fun." Then, I stick my tongue out at her like a five-year-old. She rolls her eyes, opens her door, and reaches into the back to grab some of the bags. I go to follow her, but the minute I reach for the car door, I trip. The world spins, my arms flail, and then – faceplant.

Pain lances up my exposed thigh and face. I cry out as I make contact with the hard ground.

"Shit!" Elain screeches, scrambling over and dropping to her knees beside me. "Are you okay? Ew. Ew. Ew! You're bleeding!"

I groan as Elain continues to shout, rolling over onto my back. I lift my head to look down, seeing a bloody tree branch broken in half right next to my leg. I'm covered in dirt, and I can feel tiny rocks digging into my skin.

A *fucking tree branch*? Who cuts themselves on a *fucking tree branch*? I'm screaming at myself in my head. Or maybe out loud. I don't know. I throw my head back against the dirt road. "Thank you so much for pointing out the obvious."

I go to shift into a sitting position, but wince. A few tears breach the corner of my eyes. It hurts like hell, but I think most of it's from the fall. The cut's bleeding, sure, but it doesn't look *too* deep.

"Maybe you shouldn't get up." She squeaks.

I wave her off from where I lay. "I'll be fine. Just give me a minute."

"Just – just wait here for a second, okay?"

I mumble a few curses, relinquishing any efforts to pull myself up. Elain quickly disappears. I stare at the blue sky above me, praying it would turn cloudy and thunderous and a lightning bolt would just strike me right where I lay pathetically against the ground. I'm not sure how much time passes while I wallow in the pitiful unfortunate events of my life, but footsteps drawing closer cause me to pop my eyes open.

"You've always been a little too clumsy for your own good." A rough voice grates against my ears as Wesley falls to a crouch beside me.

"Really?" I lift my neck to shoot a glare at Elain. "Him?" She doesn't even try to hide her evil little smirk. She's holding what looks like a bunch of medical supplies.

"Come on, up you go." He wraps one arm behind my back and the other under my knees. He hefts me up, effortlessly, and cradles me to his chest. I flush when I feel his muscles shift beneath mine. We make our way inside, and he sets me on the bathroom sink. I don't miss the way he seems to know the layout of the house better than I do. Elain drops the stuff off on the counter and shuts the door behind her as she leaves. Wesley taps my knee, and I blush when I realize he's telling me to open my legs so he can get closer. Once he does move in, he reaches over and grabs some of the alcohol pads he brought with him.

"Might have to amputate it." He quips.

"That's no good." I breathe out. Trying not to focus on how his hand nearly takes up my entire thigh. They're so warm, so big, I can't help but imagine how they would feel everywhere else.

"Is that blush because you enjoy the sight of me between your legs, Blake?" He doesn't even look up as he says it, focusing on cleaning up the blood and dirt. But that so-called *blush* on my face disappears in a second, and that same feeling from the coffee shop comes back with a vengeance.

"Careful." I say, "Not sure your girlfriend would appreciate you talking to someone else like that."

His head snaps up at my tone. "She's not my girlfriend."

I scoff. "Right. So, you're just fucking, then?" Venom drips from my tongue, and I hate how annoyed I sound. It shouldn't matter who he's seeing. And it sure as hell shouldn't matter that it's Brittany. He pauses, then drops both palms on either side of me, effectively caging me in. The bathroom is small, and with the layout of it, we had to close the door for this position to even work. It feels more suffocating. Like I'm stuck in a cage with a wild animal, and I'm the prey. He's so tall that even though I'm seated on the sink before him, he still needs to dip his head down to look at me. It's too similar to the situation in Ana's kitchen. The lack of space. How *easy* it would be just to lunge forward and run my fingers through his hair.

"Does it matter to you who I'm fucking, Blake?" The way the word *fuck* rolls off his lips sends a thrill shooting through me, and I almost forget what this conversation is even about.

I'm going to *kill* him. *And* Elain. "Why–" I ask through gritted teeth, "Would it matter to *me*?"

He chuckles and then bends down, blue eyes never leaving mine. He blows on the wound he's finished wiping down. Goosebumps cover my flesh. I try to keep my breathing under control, praying he can't hear my heart beating against my ribcage.

"Can you hurry up?" I snap. "I don't want to catch anything with you being this close."

He breaks our staring contest when he straightens back to his full height, slapping a huge bandage on my thigh. He only meets my gaze again when he says, "All done."

"Thank you." I say, but it comes out as a whisper.

He's so close, and I find myself locked on his eyes. How bright they are, and how they just get a little bit darker around the edges. He's still standing between my legs, and I swear I see his eyes drop to my mouth for just a split second. But then he's stepping back, and a cold draft that wasn't there before floods my system. Clearing his throat, he nods and extends a hand to me, helping me hop down from the sink. "Anytime, *neighbor*. See you at the bar this weekend?" He asks.

I nod, not able to form any words. Not sure I trust myself with speaking. Because I'm sure I'd ask him to kiss me until I die from the lack of oxygen if he sticks around any longer.

Chapter 34

BLAKE

I stand in front of my old wooden mirror and do a little spin to make sure I'm comfortable. There's nothing I hate more than going out in something that makes me feel like I'm not even wearing my own skin. More than not, I'd wear only specific dresses Marshall had picked out. One he deemed acceptable for whatever lavish occasion we had planned that night. At first, it was sweet. Cute, even. But over time, it was a bit exhausting being told I couldn't wear the new skirt I had bought myself or the chunky boots I was obsessed with the minute I spotted them at the thrift store. Now, I see that behavior for what it truly was. Marshall didn't want people to sample what he had, even though he could gorge on others himself.

Literally.

I'm more than comfortable tonight, though, and a little smile lights up my face because I'm positively glowing. I haven't felt or looked this good in a long time. I'm thankful that my thigh is better, and it didn't end up ruining going out. I typically wear little makeup, but tonight was clearly an exception. I spent extra time doing my face. A bronzy eyeshadow that makes my eyes pop and a soft peach lip color that makes them look full and glossy. My blonde curls are blown out to frame my face. A little cropped, black vest top that makes the girls look perfect, a jean mini skirt, and black booties to match. I don't dress up often, not anymore, but *god*, do I love it when I do.

Look good, feel good, and all.

Before I can stare too long and possibly convince myself to change, a knock rings out from the front door. I yell, "Coming!" and after a few seconds, I whip open the door, shocked to find Elain standing there, nervously twisting her fingers and peering up at me from beneath her hoodie. I crane my neck to check the clock on the wall behind me. "Did you walk here?"

"Rode a bike." She hikes a finger over her shoulder where a bright green bike leans against a tree trunk.

"Your bike?"

"Do you really want to know?"

Jesus. I look to the ceiling and draw in a long breath before looking back down at her. "No. I can't bail you out if I'm privy to the crime."

She smirks, but it falters just a smidge when she looks over my outfit. "I'm sorry, I didn't realize you were going somewhere."

"Karaoke is tonight." I open the door wider and motion for her to step in. "Come in." As I close the door with a click, I turn around and find her sitting on the couch with her hands tucked beneath her legs. "Everything okay?"

"Can I stay the night?"

I nod. No hesitation. "You're always welcome here, Elain."

"Did you want to talk about it?"

"Not tonight." She avoids any eye contact, but I shrug.

"Okay. Well, I'm going to the bar. You want to tag along?"

Her eyes light up. "Can I really?"

I almost laugh. Not much will bring a smile to her face, but the little things always tend to. "Yes, just don't even think about trying to talk me into getting you drunk. It's not happening."

She giggles but jumps up from her seat on the couch. "Let's go."

✳✳✳

When we get there, the night is already vibrating with life. Music blasts, and people are talking, laughing, and drinking. It's the busiest I've seen it since I've moved back.

"I'm gonna grab a soda." Elain shouts over the music. I nod my head. It's not like the bar is very big, so I'm not worried about her getting lost.

"I'll join you in just a sec. Gonna look for Whitney and Harper." She shoots me a thumbs up before spinning around and weaving through the crowd. Just as she disappears, a deep voice sneaks up behind me.

"You followin' me?" I turn to find the man from the coffee shop behind me, two beers in his hands and a teasing grin on his face. Haden, I guess his name is.

I cock my head. "Kinda feels like you might be following me."

He pushes one of the beers towards me and whistles as he takes in my look. "Lookin' mighty fine tonight, Ms. Warner."

My brows raise as I take the bottle. "Funny. I don't remember giving you my name."

God, please tell me I do not have a stalker on my hands.

He laughs like he can read my thoughts. "Turns out we have a lot of the same friends."

I nod along, just watching him. This flirting, I've done this flirting before. The kind that turns into a one-night stand or fling. When it's clear that it'll be nothing more than a physical connection. Before I can finish my thought, a large presence pushes against me. So close, too close, that I can feel his chest brushing against my loose curls. Goosebumps and a thrill I can't place rushes through my blood. Something earthy floods my nostrils, and I know immediately who it is. Haden's eyes catch on the man behind me, and a teasing grin pulls at his cheeks. "Wesley," He greets. "I was just asking Blake here if she wanted to dance with me."

I don't turn around to greet him. I see that glint in Haden's eyes as he looks back down at me. The teasing. As handsome as he is and as fun as the banter may be, I won't be someone he uses to get a rile out of another man. We aren't twelve. So, I reach over and pat Haden on the shoulder.

"As flattering as that is, I'm not sure you could keep up," I say with a grin. "But thanks for the drink."

I give the beer a little wiggle in front of his face before turning away, effectively dismissing him – only to be met with a smug look stretched across Wesley's face.

He looks down to take me in. For just a moment, I swear his eyes darken, and he's merciless in the way he lets his eyes roam over my body. When they snag on my cleavage and linger there, I can't fight the way my thighs squeeze together.

"At least he was right about one thing. You do look pretty damn good tonight, sweetheart." Wesley says gently, a hint of a smile tugging at his lips as his eyes slowly make their way back up to mine.

Even in the dim lighting, his eyes are so blue they send a shock of warmth throughout my body, and my face heats at the fact that those eyes are locked solely on *me*. Not on anyone else in this room. "Just tonight?" I ask, breathless.

He licks his lips. "You always look good, Blake."

That movement has me remembering exactly how our last encounter with each other went. How he almost kissed me. I won't lie and say I didn't want it to happen, but it was a moment of weakness for us both, one I know we can, and will never act on. It's just too damn complicated if we do. I don't respond, so breathless and brainless in his presence, it's nearly impossible. So, he just chooses to look around the room before saying, "I suppose I should thank you for this idea. Haven't been this packed in a while."

I watch the crowd. The door that's propped open. The loud noise spilling in and out. Some people coming and going. The entire bar is alive tonight. The entire street. I shake my head. "This is all you, Wesley. Your father would be proud."

I know I'm right. As I watch the bar and the crowd with him, it's easy to know how happy Ben would be at the sight. He always wanted the bar to be a space where people could come together. Where this town could come together. I turn back to find him watching me. A glint in his eye that's sad? Happy? I can't tell. Never can with him.

"Do you regret leaving?" He asks me. It may sound like a random question, but I know what he's asking. The atmosphere, the people, the simple life. Still, it hits something in my chest.

"Every day." I whisper back. Despite all the noise, I know he can hear me. Only me in this crowded bar.

I pull in a long breath as I fully turn my body back towards his and stand a little taller, looking up at him below lowered lashes. I haven't even sipped my beer yet, but something about this moment makes me feel a little braver than I usually do. "I know...I know things aren't the same. Maybe they never will be. You want answers that I don't know how to give you. And you have every right to hate me for it. But I think it's safe to say there's no way to avoid each other in this town. I - let's start over. I'm willing to if you are. We can be...friends."

Friends. The word makes me want to throw something, but I don't let him see that. Wesley and I could never just be *friends.* I'm not stupid enough to truly think so. But we can damn well try. He runs his tongue along his teeth and nods. "Friends?"

I hum in agreement. "As long as you promise not to do that caveman shit again." I hike a finger over my shoulder, so he understands who I'm talking about him being a caveman with.

That evokes a laugh from him. "Caveman shit?"

I dip my head in agreement, a smile tugging at my lips, and stick out my hand like we're striking a deal. "What do you say?" He takes it and steps in a little closer. He speaks just loud enough so that only we can hear.

"Friends it is then."

Chapter 35

WESLEY

Friends.

That word makes me want to punch something. To throw her over my shoulder and show her just how much I don't want to be *friends* with her. But I don't do that. I sit at the bar like a loser as I watch her dance with the other girls. How she breaks away to check on Elain or pulls her into the crowd to dance with them. She's had a few drinks here and there, but not enough to be wasted.

She looks gorgeous. Carefree. Relaxed. Happy.

Everything that makes her who she is. That's the Blake I knew growing up. It makes me happy to know she's made new friends and rekindled old friendships. That she's moving on and healing from the prick who left her so broken in the first place. She may think she doesn't belong here anymore, but she was quick to make this town as much hers as it was the day she was born. The way she takes change in stride has never failed to impress me. I can't understand how Marshall, or any man, could fumble a woman like that.

And that skirt? That fucking *skirt*.

It's a miracle I *didn't* throw her over my shoulder and haul her out of this damn bar.

I was so angry when she came home. Confused. But the longer she's here, the more she pops up in my everyday life, it's easier and easier to forget why I was so upset to begin with. Easier to get excited when I get an excuse to see her next door or when she pops up at *my* door and *asks* to hang out. Just as I take a swig of my beer, Harper drags Blake over to the Karaoke station. I can tell she's a bit nervous by the way her eyes dart around and her cheeks turn pink, but she must have just enough liquid courage because she doesn't bolt away. Just as they start to sing some old country song I don't recognize right away, an older guy I've never seen before takes up the seat beside me. "This was my wife's favorite song."

"How did you meet her?"

Was. The look on his face is sorrowful but so full of love that it cracks my heart just a little. No one should go through life without the one person they want to spend it with. It's the same way my mom looks when she talks about my dad. "Childhood sweethearts. I let her go once, and never made that mistake again once I got her back."

I nod. But my eyes drift back toward Blake at his words. I don't know why. The old man clocks it because he leans in and lays a hand on my shoulder before pointing in her direction, "Don't let that one go."

"Oh, we're not –" I go to protest, but he smiles like he knows something I don't, and the look has me slamming my mouth shut. He just tips his cowboy hat at me and saunters out of view without another word. I just look back towards the blonde singing her heart out, back-to-back with Harper, and that sentence echoes in my head. *Don't let that one go.*

But I already did. Didn't I?

Chapter 36

BLAKE

I feel good. And I'm having fun. It's been so long since I let loose like this, and I just know Viv would be so proud to see me right now. Wesley and I had a mature conversation. Harper, Whitney, Elain, and I spent the entire night dancing and laughing. I make my way to the bar to grab Harper and I some more drinks. My moment of bliss comes to a screeching halt when I see Brittany leaned over the bar, talking to Wesley. He's leaned back, sipping a beer, and he's *laughing*.

It strikes me right there, seeing him happy and flirting with another woman. I suddenly feel so stupid and can't understand for the life of me *why* I blew off Haden earlier. I whip around without a second thought, my eyes landing on the tall, dark man leaning against the pool table. I'm not drunk by any means, but I'm buzzed enough that I stalk up to him. Maybe even putting a little extra sway into my hips as I do so. He grins once he spots me. "Back for more? Thought you said I wouldn't be able to keep up."

"Figured I'd give you a chance to prove me wrong." I know I said I wouldn't let him use me to get a rile out of Wesley, but after seeing him with Brittany? I'm not sure I give a shit anymore. I steal a loose napkin from a nearby table and dig around in my purse to pull out a pen. I lean over the pool table and write my number down on the paper before pushing it toward Haden. "If you don't text me tonight, no date."

He stares at the napkin, looking smug. "If that's the case –" He leans forward, and for just a second, I think he might make a move on me. But he doesn't, his arm just snakes around to reach into the back pocket of my jean skirt. "What are you doing?" I blurt.

He shrugs like it's obvious. "Putting my number in your phone."

Once he's pulled it from my pocket, he flashes it toward my face, using the face recognition to unlock it. Then he types away and hands it back to me. I look down to read the screen and fight off the laugh bubbling in my chest. "Wesley's *hot* friend? Really?"

He only smirks in response, then leans it and brushes his lips against my ear, "I'll be seeing you for that date, Blake."

Chapter 37

BLAKE

"I swear to god, if there's a ghost down there, I'm burning this house down."

I stand at the top of the basement steps, talking to nobody but myself. I've been trying to find the courage to go down there for the past half hour. It's creepy as hell, and it has a weird, damp smell to it that makes me want to gag. Cobwebs cover the wooden steps.

I'm suddenly regretting not having Elain here with me to help. I gave her the morning off since she's been helping me like crazy, and she wanted to go see the animals down at the ranch before we go meet my mom. She seemed a bit tense, and she'd been staying the night with me here and there, so I had no qualms about letting her go out and get some fresh air. I slowly creep down the steps and nearly fall the rest of the way when the door slams shut behind me. "Seriously!" I shout. I swear the light at the very top of the staircase flickers in response.

Once I finally make it to the bottom, it's not nearly as bad as I expected it to be. It's empty save for a few large grey totes, a worktable, and some tools scattered around the space. Light shines in from the small grimy windows, and a clunky hot water tank sits in the corner. I go to flip the only other light switch down here and nearly groan from not thinking of grabbing a flashlight first when it doesn't respond. In my pursuit to find just that, I bump my shin against one of the boxes, and that's the exact moment something scurries across the ground and crawls right over my foot. I let out an ear-piercing scream that echoes all around me as I bolt back up the basement steps.

Tripping only once.

I go to rip open the door only to realize there's no fucking doorknob on the cement slab. I try pulling from the bottom, pushing, kicking, whatever else comes to mind, but nothing works. It won't budge an inch.

What. The. Fuck. Fuck. *Fuck, fuck, fuck!*

I pull out my phone from my back jean pocket and text one short *help* to the only person that comes to mind. I have one bar until my phone dies. And it does just that right as I click the *send* button. That's what I get for not charging it.

This is my worst nightmare come to life.

I take a few deep breaths. I can only pray that it sent in time. If not, someone will probably find my corpse down here after a few days.

"Blake?" I hear a shout from upstairs.

"Yes! Yes, I'm down in the basement!" I shout back, hoping he'll hear me.

"What's wrong?" He steps down on the first step, letting go of the door behind him, and just as I shout "No!" the door clicks shut behind him.

"What?" Then he turns and tries the door himself, to no avail of course.

"Oh, my god." I press the heels of my palms into my eyes. "We're gonna die down here."

"Why didn't you say something before I came down?"

"I think the one-worded *help* was enough information! What if there was a serial killer down here? Would you just come barging down?"

He looks at me like I've grown three heads. "Yes."

***

A couple of hours have passed now. Or maybe it's a few minutes. I don't know, but Wesley keeps messing with the door, and it's driving me crazy.

"Will you give it a rest? We aren't getting out of here until someone comes looking," I snap.

Eventually, he gives in and listens. He comes to sit across from me, letting his hands rest on his knees. We just sit there, not saying anything. I'm not sure how much more time passes, but it's so quiet that I can't stand it.

"I'm pretty sure this basement is haunted."

He scoffs. "I'm pretty sure you've said that about every old building in town before."

"Whatever," I mutter.

More silence.

"We're friends, right?" I ask, bringing up our previous conversation from the bar.

"We are."

"Tell me something you haven't told anyone else."

He's silent for a few minutes, thinking of what kind of information to give me, then a slow mischievous grin spreads across his face, causing a dimple to pop up. "I'm the one who stole Mr. Finnigan's mailbox."

"Oh my god, I knew it was you! He called the cops on every kid that walked past his house after you did that."

Our laughter fills the air, so loudly that it echoes against the stone walls in the basement, and tears spring to my eyes.

When our laughter slows, I ask him, "Is my mom seeing the Sheriff?" The pace at which his brows rise is almost comical.

"Why do you ask?"

I shrug, not deigning with a response. He sighs, rubbing the back of his neck. "A lot of us have noticed the way they interact. Wouldn't hurt for you to ask her yourself."

I swallow, looking up at the ceiling. "I just…I thought she'd tell me if she was."

"Did you tell her about Marshall?"

Fair point. Wesley doesn't prod me any further, letting me think about the question in whatever way I need to. I can't expect her to lay everything out on the table when I get home when I haven't even given her the time of day since I've been back. It's not like she hasn't attempted to get me to stick around for a chat. I know I owe it to her – to let her explain, and to explain myself too.

I consider asking about his relationship with Brittany, too, but creating a tense atmosphere that we could be stuck in for a couple more hours is less than appealing. We continue to play this game of questions for quite some time until I prod deeper, which surprises us both.

"Tell me about the pond tattoo."

He sits there, contemplating what he wants to say. He's quiet for so long I'm not sure he's going to answer the question at all.

"I got it for you," he says looking directly at me as he says it, so sure and confident in his answer. Like it's not a big deal that he's tattooed a piece of me on his body forever.

"Why?" I ask softly.

"You already got your question. It's my turn." He nods his head toward my arm. "How'd you get the scar? I don't remember it happening when you were here."

"It did." I answer truthfully. When silence greets me, I push on. My nerves rising, and my palms sweating.

I look into his comforting blue eyes. "Look, Wesley. There's something I want to tell you –"

Right then, Elain's voice sounds from the top of the basement steps, and we both jump to our feet. "Downstairs!" Wesley shouts. We both head to the steps where Elain waits with the door swung open. He turns around, pausing halfway on the stairs, and looks down at me. "What did you want to tell me?"

"Um, nothing important." I shrug.

"You sure?"

"Yup. See you." I say with a forced smile.

"Right." He says, stuffing his hands in his pocket. "I'll come by at some point to fix that." He nods over his shoulder to the basement door. "Holler if you need anything."

I dip my head in acknowledgment before busying myself with brushing off invisible dust on my clothing. I only look back up when his voice takes on a teasing tone as he says, "And uh, maybe charge your phone before doing anymore ghost hunting, yeah?"

I roll my eyes and stick my middle finger up at his now turned back. "I saw that." He calls back. I let my laughter flow freely after he's gone.

Chapter 38

WESLEY

I find Blake standing on the porch and digging through her purse. She pulls out her keys at the same time I slam shut the door of my truck. When she sees the toolbox in my hand, she nods toward the door. "I was just headed to grab Elain, but feel free to let yourself in."

"Will do," I reply. It's nice to see how close Elain and Blake have become, and it's such an unlikely pair that it makes me want to laugh. I don't know Elain well, but I have seen her around town. She's quiet and tends to keep to herself. No doubt much more reserved than most kids her age.

I notice Blake doesn't meet my gaze for very long and hauls her ass down the steps before I can say anything more. Our conversation in the basement unlocked something between us, and now I know there are questions we both want answers to. I make my way inside as her car starts. The smell of her, something sweet like lavender, fills my senses far quicker than I'd like.

I've seen the inside of the house before. A couple of times now. I take a moment to look around. It's impressive how far it's come. Blake's touch and good eye make it look like a completely different house. Inside and out. My eyes catch her calendar hanging from the fridge, and I can't help but notice a date circled on it. Today's date.

Date with Haden, it says.

You have got to be fucking kidding me. I thought she blew the bastard off, and now she has a date? With *him*?

I don't even turn to see if she's fully pulled out of the driveway before I stalk towards it and wipe it off her calendar with my hand. It's childish, I know it's childish. But right now, I don't give a fuck. I told him once before, and I'll have no problem telling him to back off again. I pull out my phone and click the call button right underneath the contact.

Chapter 39

BLAKE

One morning after Elain stayed, she mentioned how she hadn't met my mom yet, and she's been dying to. We decided this morning we'd stop by to have breakfast with her. It didn't take much convincing on her part, as I've been planning on working to see my mom more often. Elain's busy asking my mom to show her old pictures of me when my phone pings with a notification.

> Sorry, I have to cancel on tonight, something came up

I don't answer right away, just staring at the screen. Something came up? That's the oldest excuse in the book. The guy practically begged for a date, and now he's blowing me off? Over text?

"What's wrong?" My mom sing songs from her rocker.

"Haden canceled our date for tonight." I mutter back. My mom hums like she's in deep thought, but it's Elain that pipes up first. Face scrunched in curiosity. "Sure it's got nothing to do with him being Wesley's friend?"

I narrow my eyes at her. "What are you talking about?"

"I'm just saying that he probably had something to do with it."

"You don't think...—" They give each other a look, like they know something I don't. It only makes my nerves worse. If that's true...no. There's simply no way he'd interfere like that. What I do with Haden is none of his business, in the same way that what he does with Brittany is none of my business. I turn my attention away from the two before me and furiously type back.

Is this because of Wesley?

It's best if I don't get in the middle of it

"What a douche!" I shout. And then wince once I see Elain and my mom giving me a weird look. I don't pay them anymore mind and go back to fuming at the texts on my screen. Wesley is so dead.

And the fact that Haden let someone push him around about taking me on a date caused any sort of attraction I had toward the guy to fly out the window.

"Do you mind if I run an errand?" I ask the two sweetly. They share a nervous glance, but my mom just shrugs, and Elain only shoots me a thumbs up in return.

Chapter 40

BLAKE

"Did you seriously tell Haden to back off?" I'm fuming at the sight of Wesley. His go-to black shirt, jeans, and boots adorn his hulking body. Swinging my basement door back and forth to make sure it's working. I wasn't entirely sure he'd still be here. Either way, he wasn't getting off scot-free.

"What are you barking about?" He has the audacity to sound amused, and it only makes my temper skyrocket. I cross my arms over my chest.

"Haden blew off our date."

He shrugs a shoulder as he shuts the basement door. "Maybe he just changed his mind."

"Bullshit." I jab my finger at his chest. "That's bullshit and you know it."

He smirks. "If he's the type of guy who scares off so easily, maybe it's for the best."

"Stop smirking! We're in the middle of an argument!"

"I'm not arguing. You are."

"That was not your decision to make!" I'm yelling at him, but despite my anger and his own seething off him, he doesn't raise his voice at me. Not once. But my tone does sober up his own.

"He isn't good for you, Blake." He pivots away from me, walking to clean up his things.

"Don't turn your back on me!"

His steps falter for just a beat, but he keeps on walking. "Right, like you've never turned your back on me."

I don't miss the double meaning in that. But how *dare* he? He reaches over to pick up his flannel, hanging over one of the island stools. "That is different." I say firmly, voice rising with each word as frustration bubbles to the surface. "*This* is different. It's not your responsibility to decide what's good for me."

That causes him to straighten, leaving the piece of clothing discarded on the chair beside him. He whirls around to face me. "The girl I knew would have never let someone like Haden take her out."

"I'm not the girl you knew anymore, Wesley. Stop pretending that you know anything about me." I snap. He flinches. Flinches like I just slapped him in the face.

"Noted." He picks up his toolbox and flannel up from where they lay and turns his back to me once again. "Doors fixed. Let me know if you have any more problems with it."

I just watch as he walks out my door, not even slamming it. A part of me hates how calm he is, how composed. I want him to turn back around and yell at me the same way I did to him. And I realize that's a walking contradiction, but it doesn't change the facts. I turn to grab a water from the fridge, maybe more so to give my hands something to do, but it freezes on the handles when I realize my calendar was haphazardly wiped clear.

***

Today has been one clusterfuck of a day. Watching Gilmore Girls and drinking nearly an entire bottle of red wine by myself has done *almost* enough to distract me from Wesley and I's fight. My mom texted me, telling me that she and Elain were going shopping and that she'd take her home herself. So, I've been sitting here stewing, debating on whether I should just walk right over there and slap him or pull him in for a hug and apologize. I know the bigger picture is there, I know he was simply watching out for me. But he and I have way too much history for the words we exchanged not to sting.

Was it fair for me to hurl those words at his face? No, probably not.

Have I even given him a chance to know this 'new' me? Am I truly *so* different from the girl I used to be? Or am I just praying that I *am* different?

Sometimes, I think the idea of being that small, breakable girl I was for so many years is terrifying, but she is entirely what's made me the woman I am today. Maybe trying too hard to shove her as far away from who I want to be, is the problem.

Who knew your twenties would be so fucking confusing.

A knock vibrates from the front door, and I sigh as I must relinquish my wine and pause the TV to go answer it. I swing my legs off the couch and hurtle the blanket off my thighs. "Coming!"

A strong wave of nausea coats my throat at the sight before me. Marshall stands at my door, suitcase in hand.

"You can't be here." I swing the door shut in his face, only for it to stop when his hand hits the door.

"Blake. Please." The way his voice cracks is enough for me to crack the door open just enough to peek at him. Disheveled hair, like he's spent hours pulling at it. Bags under his eyes that make it seem like he's been getting little to no sleep. I let my eyes scour his face, looking for a hint of that spark I felt the first time I met him. Now...now he seems so plain. Nothing like the rugged, hard lines of most of the men in this town. His green eyes that I once believed to be so charming don't hold a candle to the blue ones—

No. No. I internally chastise myself for even going there when my goddamned ex is standing in my doorway. This isn't about Wesley.

Wesley…while Wesley may have tried to protect me from Haden, he doesn't have any room for me in his heart. Not truly. And this is…this is Marshall. While he has his faults, I gave him over a year of my life, and he gave me the same. There were moments so good that it's hard to remember the bad. Hard to understand why someone I poured so much love into would want to hurt me. Hard to understand if it was ever intentional or just a mistake that could be corrected. But isn't that the same grace I gave my father? The very thing I spent years running away from?

Why is it that we always chase and crave the things we *know* are bad for us?

There was a time when he wasn't just my boyfriend, but my friend too. There's a battle waging in my heart, and he obviously notices my hesitation. "I'm sorry."

I cross my arms, letting go of the door. "You're sorry?"

"Please…just let me in. I just want to talk." I sigh and look behind his shoulders, noting the lowering sun, and not seeing a car in sight. Meaning, that he got a taxi here. The idea was laughable because Marshall Donovan wouldn't be caught dead riding around in something as cheap as a taxi. If anything, it was a power play. Intentional, so that I'd have to ask him to stay.

It works. Or maybe it's just the wine making me act like a complete idiot. Because I don't say anything, I just reach out to widen the door some more and leave him to follow while I go to my bedroom. Suddenly, I'm overly self-conscious about the tiny top and oversized shorts I wear. I know he's following me by the heavy thuds of footsteps, but I don't say a word as I rifle through my top drawer in search of a t-shirt. I'm throwing it on as he walks into my room, which suddenly feels far too small with the two of us in here. "I got you your job back."

"My job back?" I ask. "My *job* back? The one you fucked out of my life?" My words may have been harsh, but they came out less aggressive. More... tired.

"And I left her."

"Is that supposed to make it better?"

"Of course not."

An uncomfortable silence fills the air. I go to sit on the bed, facing away from him. I don't look at him, finding it impossible to do so. Because I have a feeling the second I do, I'll give into whatever he asks of me. Because forgiving is far easier than hurting. "You of all people should have known how much that job meant to me."

He doesn't waste a second coming around to kneel before me, taking my hands in his. It isn't lost on me how soft they feel. How different they are from the rough hands that have seen and done so much more than sit behind a polished desk. "I did. I do. That's why I'm here."

I shake my head, still avoiding his gaze, but he pushes on. He dips his head so that he's below me so that I have no choice but to look into his green eyes. "It meant nothing to me, baby. Nothing. If I could take it back, I would. But I can't. So, I'm here. Promising you that I can do better. That I *will* do better. If only you give me the chance. I want to be with you. Just *you*. Forever."

Forever. I almost laugh at the idea. Do we even want the same things? A quiet and cozy life? I'm not sure it's even what I want anymore. But I'm twenty-four. My life wasn't perfect in the city, but it was good. As good as it would get for someone who came running from a sleepy, dead town and had nothing but a shit background to her name. I built that life for myself. I earned it. After everything I've been through, I deserved it. Didn't I? Now, I wasn't so sure. Part of me wanted to cling to the idea that I did so damn bad, it felt like I was finally saying goodbye to everything I worked so hard for if I finally cut ties with Marshall. "I...I need to think about this."

He looks like he wants to argue but thinks better of it at my expression. "I...I can work with that."

I nod, and the air becomes thick with silence. He abruptly stands, straightening his shirt. "How about I make you some tea? And we watch a movie?"

"That sounds nice." I give him a smile, one that feels too forced.

Chapter 41

BLAKE

My phone dings from the kitchen island, and I reach forward to set my mug on the coffee table, excusing myself to go check it. "Need anything while I'm up?"

I'm dumbstruck when his eyes roam over me in a hungry and fervent way. Although Marshall hasn't made any moves on me since we've cuddled up on the couch to watch a show, I can't tell if I'm surprised or relieved that it doesn't heat me the way it would have just months ago. Now, it just feels more overbearing. Oppressive, even. Carrying a weight that feels intrusive, as though expecting submission rather than my reciprocation.

Currently, I'm in an overly large T-shirt and basketball shorts. Something I wouldn't be caught dead wearing in front of Marshall when we were dating. He often was only impressed by the silky little things he'd buy me.

But this is my home, and he's the one who showed up unannounced. He's embarrassed me enough; the last thing he deserves is to see any more skin than this outfit allows. He shakes his head, "All good."

I nod and walk toward the kitchen, ignoring the way I feel his gaze burning a hole into my backside.

Viv:

Did you see this?

Attachment: 1 Photo

What a douchebag!

You have no idea.

My phone continues to blow up, Viv hounding me with questions, but I ignore them. Letting my eyes jump from the photo Vivienne sent to the man on the couch, who's now watching the TV with rapt fascination. The rage seeping into my vision is blinding. How dare he come here and beg for my forgiveness after what he put me through? Only to turn around and throw it right back in my face?

I do the only thing any woman would do. I take a deep breath, close my eyes, and count.

One.

Two.

Three.

When my eyes flutter, I pull up the local taxi app on my phone and order him a ride to the airport. Then

I turn onto my heels and into the bedroom. The very room where I let him whisper sweet nothings into my ear. Where I let him apologize. Where I let him kneel before me and promise me something he could *never* give me. I grab his suitcase, swing it over my shoulder, and make a show of stomping to rip open the front door. I waste no time in throwing my entire body weight into flinging the over-packed luggage over my shoulder and off my porch. I revel in the way it smacks against the dirt road, coating the white suitcase in dust.

I hear the distinct sound of tires rolling up the road the same instant I turn around to find Marshall gaping at me. Perfect. Fucking. Timing.

"What are you doing?" He has the audacity to look confused.

"Get out." I snap.

"Blake, darling. You can't be serious." The endearment grates against my ears, sending my temper into the clouds.

"Get the fuck off my porch, Marshall." I brush past where he stands in the doorway. Evading his hand when it reaches for my arm.

"Where is this-"

"Don't!" I whirl, lightly shoving him. Just enough to get him closer to my porch steps and far away from me. "Don't act like an idiot when you damn well know what this is about!"

"Blake –"

"When were you going to tell me? When were you going to tell me that you proposed to *her*?" If the picture wasn't confirmation enough, the way he blanches tells me everything I need to know. "After you try to worm into my bed? After you told me you *loved* me?"

I startle, my walls cracking for a fraction of a second as a heavy foot slams onto the first porch step. The realization hits me – the car I thought was Marshall's ride wasn't his after all. "Not now." I bite out at the same time Marshall looks the newcomer over with pure disdain. "Who are you?"

"Could ask you the same thing." Wesley's eyes narrow, and his voice is sharp enough to cut through steel.

Marshall stands a little taller as if sizing Wesley up. Clearly not liking the former's tone. I don't let my eyes wander to my childhood best friend, too hell bent on getting this sorry excuse for a man out of my town. The reminder of why I left the city is a smack in the face, but the realization that this town is *still* my safe harbor bites harder than I could ever imagine. I scoff at the incredulous look on Marshall's face and turn to head back inside. "It's time for you to go."

"I'm not leaving. I never would have given the ring to her if you hadn't run off-" He rushes forward mid-sentence, reaching to grab for my arm, but I sense his motive before he gets the chance to touch me, and doge from his grip. His lips peel back in a snarl as his eyes bounce between Wesley and me. "Is this what you've been doing? Dressing like *that* and fucking the first low life who gets you to spread your legs?"

A growl rips from Wesley's throat, his rage a reflection of my own. But I'm faster. I whip around, fist already drawn back, and strike. Marshall crumples to the ground in a pathetic heap, blood spattering across his shirt and the dirt beneath him. "Bitch! I think you broke my nose!"

Wesley's shock lasts for all of a second before he turns to face me. "Is this Marshall?" I don't look at him, don't respond, but I suppose my discomfort is answer enough, because he's barreling down the steps and lifting him effortlessly by the back of his shirt.

"You're lucky she got her hands on you first. Now get your shit and go back to your fancy fucking city before I let her call you an ambulance instead." Then he leans down and whispers something into Marshall's ear. Too quiet for me to hear, but by the scarlet shade his face turns, I know damn well I wouldn't want to be on the receiving end of Wesley's wrath.

I don't spare them another glance, not even as Marshall finally gets loaded into his cab and peels out of my driveway. I plop into the rocking chair on my front porch and drop my head into my hands. Only then, when I finally inhale a breath that feels a little less angry and a lot sadder, do I feel the pain shooting through my knuckles. I reel back to peek at them, cursing when I see I've split them open.

"Are you hurt?" Wesley drops into a crouch before me, the smell of mint and pine overriding my senses.

I shake my head, "I'm fine."

"Let me see." He rolls his eyes, peeling my hand from where I cradle it against my chest, inspecting the damage. His touch is so gentle, so at odds with so many of the men in my life who have done nothing but take, take, and *take.*

"Come on." He mutters, reaching forward to scoop me up into his arms.

"Where are we going?" My words have little bite, and I don't fight the urge to cuddle further into where I already press against his hard chest. The beating of his heart is like a harmony to my own. It's easier to breathe, and the fact that we fought just earlier today means nothing in this moment. The only thing that matters is that *he's here.*

"My place." And while I know that's a bad idea, I don't have the energy to argue with him.

"That was one hell of a punch." Wesley's tone takes on a teasing edge as he slips my shoes from my feet. I grunt in reply. Safe to say, I'm my father's daughter. After cleaning my knuckles, he insisted that I take a bath and lay in bed. When my second shoe falls to the floor, his hands fall to wrap around the back of my knees. "Look at me, Blake."

I shake my head, but a gentle tug on my chin has me relenting. I had avoided his gaze for as long as possible, scared of what I might find in them. Rage, sorrow, even a glimpse of pain in those blue eyes. But no pity. That alone causes me to crack under his stare. A shattered sob rips through my lips, and I let it consume me. Letting sob after sob rack my already shaking body. It was so easy to be consumed with rage before, but now? With Wesley's gentle hands and soft heart, it was far easier to break under the weight of everything. I feel the bed dip beside me, and broad arms pull me into his lap, letting his hand fall to the back of my head as he tucks me into him.

I don't know how much time passes, but only when my sobs slow does he stand to set me back on the bed. I scrub my hands over my face as I hear the faint sound of footsteps and then water running. He returns, setting a fresh towel down next to me, dropping a kiss to the top of my forehead. We both still. My eyes flicker to his, and they widen as if he didn't mean to do it. As if it was so natural, it wasn't even a thought. He clears his throat, straightening to his full height. "I'll come back to check on you in a few."

He doesn't wait for my response; only the sound of the door clicking signals his departure. I realize now that I'm in his room. His bedroom. Alone.

It feels wrong to be given free access to something that has the power to tell one's entire personality. The king-size bed is adorned with a dark grey duvet. The grey walls were only a few shades lighter. Everything is so neat with a quick sweep of my eyes, but the clutter on his nightstand is undeniably Wesley's. A small smile breaks through my dried tears at the picture of him and his dad after a baseball game. Ben looks so proud standing next to his son, and Wesley looks so happy. Beaming from ear to ear, one of his front teeth missing. Nothing like the hardened man I've come back home to.

I make my way to the bathroom, and nearly collapse from the warmth wafting from the full tub. The ache in my shoulders and hand from earlier comes to a full crescendo at the idea of sinking into the warm, bubbly liquid and easing my sore muscles. It's a huge claw tub. Big enough to fit two people, maybe even three.

I try, and fail, not to imagine why Wesley, who lives alone and is single, would need such a big tub.

When he returns, I see he's changed into shorts, and a mug of warm, hot liquid is in his large hands. I'm already undressed and fully submerged in the water. Nothing is visible beneath the white bubbles, only my collarbone peeks out over the soap. Something flares in his eyes at the sight of me, but it's gone in an instant. When he sees I haven't made a move to grab the soap lining the side of the tub, he sets the mug down and reaches behind him to pull off his shirt. Then, he shocks me to my core when he gets behind me.

I'm too dumbstruck by the sight of him shirtless to do anything but scoot farther down the tub, giving him more room to settle in behind me. He nudges me, telling me to dip my head back just enough to wet it. Then he's reaching around me for the shampoo. "Do you want to talk about it?"

I suck in a breath as he begins working soap into my hair. A moan nearly slips from my lips at the sensation of his hands massaging my scalp. His touch is in no way sexual, but it's intimate in a way I've never experienced. For a few moments, I'm utterly silent. Debating on if I do want to talk about it. If talking about it makes me weak, or if it'll help this ever-growing hole in my chest. I decide he, of all people, deserves a piece of me, no matter how small the piece is that I can offer.

My lip trembles as I close my eyes. "I'm sick and tired of men just taking and *taking*."

His fingers still in my hair for a heartbeat before he's back to it. "Do you love him?

I bite my lip, but the answer isn't a hard one. "I-I think I loved the idea of him more."

He doesn't respond, but I feel the movement of him nodding his head. He cups some of the water, bringing it over my head to rinse the soapy residue from my strands. Once he deems his work worthy, his fingers glide over the back of my neck, sending goosebumps over my exposed flesh. He stiffens but only wrings out my hair and sets it over my shoulder. He clears his throat and stands from where he's nestled behind me.

Despite the warmth of the tub, I feel much colder with his body no longer pressed against mine. "I'll let you finish up, get you some clothes, and you can take the bed for tonight."

I reach out, snagging his hand. A bolt of electricity runs up my wrist at the same time he settles his gaze onto our intertwined fingers. "Thank you."

He dips his head, shutting the bathroom door on his way out. I sink further beneath the water, trying to sort out how the hell I got here.

***

Once I'm dried off, my hair is brushed, and I'm dressed in the clothes Wesley gave me, I finally make my way out of the bathroom. I find him tossing back the large comforter and rearranging the pillows. He nods towards the living room. "I'll be just out there if you need anything."

He turns toward the door without another word, and I don't know if it's the adrenaline of today or from the way he took care of me in the tub, but I call out for him. "Will you stay?"

He looks from me to the door, hesitation written on his features, but nods. I scooch over as he comes to crawl into the bed with me. Once he's settled, I lay my head on his chest, focusing on his deep breaths. I know we should talk about today's fight. And he deserves the full story on Marshall's appearance after everything that's happened today. But I am so, so tired, and the idea of even using my last bit of energy to apologize to him sounds excruciating. Wesley's hand rubs soothing circles on my back, and I swear I hear him whisper "Always" as I drift off to sleep.

Chapter 42

WESLEY

When I woke up this morning to Blake snoring on my chest and her legs wrapped around my own, I was fully content with ignoring any work I needed to get done for the day and making her a breakfast so big I'd have to wheel her back home.

But now? Now, I sit across from a spitfire brunette who talks and talks and talks, and I wish I would have thrown my work boots on before the sun even rose.

"He just kept sending gifts and flowers to the apartment. Eventually, he found out she was gone and went ballistic. I knew when she texted me something was wrong. So naturally, I bought the first plane ticket out here."

She was so giddy when she got here that I almost let her go wake Blake up, but we both agreed she deserved the extra few hours of sleep. I made her coffee, but she declined any breakfast until Blake awoke. Now she sits across from me on the couch, filling me in on 'Princess Marshall', as Vivienne likes to call him. I couldn't help the laugh that came barreling out of me at that name.

"So, how long have you known Blake?" I ask, setting my mug on the side table.

"We met when she moved to the city, so-"

"Six years." I nod my head in confirmation.

"Right." Vivienne draws out the word, raking a skeptical eye over me, like she just *knows* something I don't. Usually, I wouldn't be so intimidated by a woman so small, but I'd do just about anything to get the hell out of this conversation as soon as possible. "We've been roommates for forever," she adds.

"Well-"

"Vivienne?" Blake's soft voice interrupts from the hallway, making me nearly groan in relief.

Thank god.

Before I even have time to process, the two are a jumping, screeching mess. "Oh, my god!"

"I missed you so bad!"

"When did you get here?"

"Are those his *clothes*?"

Vivienne practically whisper-shouts that last one, her eyes bouncing between the two of us. Blake looks ready to throttle her best friend, not as oblivious to the fact that I can hear them. She *is* in my clothes. Where she slept in *my* house. In *my* bed. And goddamn if I don't want to take her right back to the bedroom and rip that top right off her body until she's a screaming, weeping mess beneath me. The shirt is three sizes too big, falling right above her knees. The thought of Marshall sneering at Blake's attire yesterday has me seeing red. I knew from the stories that he didn't deserve her, but I didn't realize just how bad it was. This woman could walk around in a garbage bag and still steal the very breath from my lungs.

I went over there last night with the intention to apologize for being an overbearing dick. The last thing she needs is me dictating her love life, even if I loathe the idea of Haden getting anywhere near her. The things we said... I couldn't stop pacing when I got home. Couldn't concentrate on work or even a stupid TV show until I went over there and made things right. I still need to apologize, but I'm glad I got there when I did. Seeing Blake pop her ex in the mouth may just be the highlight of my week. Life is more like it.

At the reminder that I'm here, she turns her honey-brown eyes on me. A little smile graces her pink lips, and I hate the way my heart skips a beat. "Hi."

Her eyes are still puffy from the night before, but she seems much more at ease. Whether that's from Vivienne's presence or from sleeping like a rock on my chest, I couldn't tell. I'm just glad she's better than when I found her. "Sleep, okay?" I ask.

She nods, scrunching her eyebrows and turning back to Vivienne. "Does Whitney know you're here?"

I pull my eyes from Blake to look at Vivienne. "You know Whitney?"

"No, she doesn't." Vivienne replies before turning her attention on me. "She's my sister."

Now, *that* I wasn't expecting. It's easy to see now, the dark hair and big, round eyes. The two aren't identical by any means, but it's obvious to anyone passing by that they're sisters.

"Well, shit. Congratulations on-"

"Making it here!" Blake interrupts me with a high-pitched enthusiasm that has me raising my eyebrows. "Was the flight horrible? I know you hate planes." Blake pulls her in for another bone-crushing hug and gives me a look over her shoulder that just screams *'Don't you dare mention that her sister is pregnant you gigantic fucking idiot.'*

I give a subtle nod. Noted. Vivienne doesn't know that she's going to be an aunt soon. I clap my hands, deciding to help Blake out with our little hiccup. "Everyone want breakfast?"

✳✳✳

I'm flipping a pancake when Blake creeps up beside me. I peek at her, seeing her set a near-empty coffee mug on my counter. "Did you get enough coffee? I can make you another cup."

"I just want to say thank you for last night. And I wanted to apologize for yesterday."

I turn off the stove, registering that this isn't going to be a conversation about coffee. I set everything aside to give her my full attention and in hopes of not burning anyone's breakfast. "Blake. You don't need to-"

"I do." She cuts me off with a shake of her head. "You...you were right. I don't need another douchebag. You were protecting me. Even..." She sucks in a breath. "Even after all this time. After *everything*. You still are. So, thank you."

As if I need any other reason to be pining after this woman, my heart fucking melts when she gets on her toes to kiss my cheek. She goes to move away, but I'm quicker. My hand shoots out to grab the back of her head, holding her just mere inches away from my face. I tilt her head just a little bit to meet my eyes. Her warm breath grazes my own when she gasps, and when she licks her lips, I have to refrain from running my thumb over her plump bottom lip. Seeing tears stain these cheeks just 24 hours ago...it makes me want to rip this fucking town apart.

"I'm sorry too, sweetheart." Not just for my words or my actions, but for everything that's been burdening her. She straightens, releasing herself from my grip and lifting her chin at me. Seemingly trying to shake off the tension that's crackling in the air between us.

"All is forgiven." She glances toward the pan and raises an eyebrow. "So long as you don't burn my pancakes."

I don't miss the extra swish in her hips as she leaves me in the kitchen.

Chapter 43

BLAKE

"What if she tells me to get the fuck out?"

I roll my eyes at Vivienne. She has been panicking the entire way to the coffee shop. Nervously twisting her fingers, playing with her earrings, and pulling at the threads on her pants. "For the hundredth time, Viv. She's going to be ecstatic. Trust me."

I couldn't be happier that she was here. I needed her more than I realized after this shitshow of a week. I'm glad that she'll finally get to find out about her soon-to-be niece or nephew. What I was nervous about was how Vivienne would react to me knowing Whitney was pregnant, and not telling her. I nearly pissed my pants when Wesley almost let it slip.

This morning...I thought he'd try to kiss me. And I'm not foolish enough to pretend I wasn't disappointed when he didn't. The way he was with me last night...that's the Wesley I fell in love with as a little girl. That thought alone scares the shit out of me. If it weren't for Vivienne showing up, I would have been content staying in his bed for the entirety of the day.

We pull into a parking spot just a few doors before the coffee shop, and when I look over to ask Vivienne if she's ready, the girl is already bolting out of her seat.

"Guess that means you're fine?" I grumble, but quickly unbuckle and catch up to her. For being on the shorter end, she sure is eating up the distance faster than I can keep up. I suppose she's probably doing her best not to chicken out on herself right now.

The coffee shop doors do that familiar chime I've grown so fond of, and Whitney looks up from where she's writing on a notepad. Whitney's face goes from bright red to ghostly white when she sees her sister. She drops her pen and walks around the counter, never taking her eyes off Vivienne.

"Vivi?"

"Hey, sis." Vivienne cracks a small, sweet smile. One I know feels a little broken to her. The two meet each other in the middle, enveloping themselves in a hug. Whitney's eyes clash over her sister's shoulders to meet mine, and when she draws her back to scan her from head to toe, her mouth hangs open as if she can't truly believe what she's seeing.

Her hand falls to her stomach, and I can see that it was such a natural gesture that she freezes when Vivienne catches it. The latter takes a step back, throwing a hand over her mouth. "You're fucking *pregnant*?"

Whitney cringes. "Is it that noticeable?"

"When were you going to tell me?" The way Vivienne's voice cracks has me instinctively reaching for her, but I take a step back. Knowing these two *need* this moment. I know she's refraining from looking at me, poised to strike the question at me next. But it's not my business to share, and as much as I value and love Vivienne, it's Whitney's decision when and where to tell her little sister.

Whitney's eyes begin to water. "I...I've been meaning to. I just didn't know when a good time would be. I was hoping I'd get to come see you but-"

Vivienne cuts her off with a hug, a sob slipping from her lips as she holds her as tight as humanly possible. Soon, Whitney's sobs mesh with Vivienne's. My own heart tugs in my chest at the sight.

"I'll give you guys a few minutes, yeah?" They both shoot me grateful, watery smiles.

***

"How was it?" I ask. Whitney and Vivienne got to talk for quite a while before the former had a plethora of customers come in. We're walking the town now, so Vivienne can get the full experience of Clover-Hills.

"Good, I think." Vivienne replies, looking at me. "She wants to meet at the bar later. Guess she's got a pretty hard-core obsession with the fries."

I laugh, linking my arm through hers. "That she does."

We continue to walk in silence. Grateful for the decent weather and the chatter of those milling about. I don't miss the few men who outright gawk at the sight of Vivienne. She's stunning, and newcomers are easily spotted in a town this quiet. We're passing Clover-Hills Veterinary Services when she asks me, "You guys have a vet here?"

"Of course, we do."

"Huh."

"What are you thinking right now?"

"What if...what if I moved here?"

I abruptly stop, jolting her with me. She winces, but I force her body to look directly at me. "You can't be serious, Viv."

She shrugs. "I don't have anything in New York aside from work. And I can do that here. I...I want to be here for Whitney."

Tears shine in her already swollen eyes, and any argument I may have had about her dream job in the city flies out the window. I give her a small, understanding smile. "You know, anything that you want to do, I will support. And you're more than welcome to stay with me."

She nods, casting one more glance at the old vet shop. "Now." She slings her arm over my shoulder, blinking away any lingering emotion. "Where is that little shop with the turtles?"

Chapter 44

BLAKE

I sit on my bed flipping through a book as Vivienne curls Elain's hair. When we stopped at the shop, Elain was working. I was so happy that she was – glad that she'd finally get to meet one of my dearest friends. Her mom was there too, so I asked her if I could steal Elain for the night. She looked rather relieved at the idea of Elain getting out of the house.

Both of us had to practically drag Vivienne away from the glass turtles before she bought out Elain's family's shop. "Soooo...got a boyfriend?"

Elain blushes. "No."

Vivienne and I raise an eyebrow at each other, looking in the mirror at the same time to give Elain a *really?'* look. "Okay. Fine. There's this one guy." Elain rushes out. "Maybe. I don't know."

"Has he asked you out?" I ask her, feigning indifference, but realistically, I'm overly giddy at the idea of Elain making friends.

"No."

"So why don't you ask him out?" Vivienne probes, letting a curl fall from the iron.

Her eyes widen, and I almost laugh at how shocked she looks. "I can do that?"

"Of course, you can. This isn't the dark ages, honey. Boys *love it* when a girl makes the first move." I smile as I watch them. Vivienne goes on to explain how she made the move on her first boyfriend, and I can't help but imagine if this is how Vivienne and Whitney would be if they were given the chance.

I look down at myself as they prattle on, glad Vivienne convinced me to pair this outfit with heels. I chose a simple pair of jeans with a low, long black sleeve top and matching pumps. My boobs look rather fantastic in this top, and I find myself excited to go out tonight. Even more excited at the prospect that a certain blue-eyed neighbor might be there.

"Hello?" Vivienne's voice drawls. "Are you there? Or too busy thinking about Wesley's sexy-"

I jump from the bed, bolting after Vivienne, who squeals and runs from the room. Elain's laughter trails after us.

***

"Any weird cravings aside from these?" Vivienne leans forward to steal one of Whitney's fries.

We finally made it to the bar after everyone was ready, and I was deemed the winner in our very short-lived pillow fight. Elain immediately got bored of the adults and is currently practicing playing pool across the bar. "Uhh...not really. No."

"Liar!" Harper points an accusing finger at Whitney. "I caught you trying to eat a spoonful of minced garlic last night! After telling me you already had, and to *not* let you do it again."

"Harper!" Whitney groans dramatically, throwing a hand over her chest. "I told you that in *confidence!*"

We all break into a fit of giggles. Harper slides another drink to Vivienne once she sees it's empty. "Oh, fine. One more. But that's it. I have to head to the airport tonight."

"You're leaving?" Whitney turns to face her sister, eyes softening when they look at her.

"I just have to sort a few things out at work. I'll be back soon, okay?"

They seem to have a silent conversation with their eyes, and Vivienne nudges her with an elbow. "Plus, no way in hell am I missing out on my niece's birth. It's a girl, right? Please tell me it's a girl."

Whitney bites her lip, looking around at all of us girls. "I get the results back in a few weeks but...I have this hunch that it is, you know?"

We all squeal in tandem as Whitney talks about her symptoms and whatnot, her face lighting up at the idea of having a little girl. We order another round of green tea shots to celebrate (with the exception of another Shirley Temple and fries for Whitney). The door to the bar swings open, and heads swivel in the direction of the noise. Vivienne leans over to whisper in my ear, never letting her eyes leave the tall, broody man now taking up the space. "Who is *that*?"

I snort. I should have *known* this was coming. But gods, yes. It's the most brilliant idea I've ever conjured. "Haden." I shove her shoulder lightly and nod my head in his direction. "You should go talk to him."

"Don't have to tell me twice." She shoots me a wink before hopping out of her barstool and sauntering to where Haden settles in at a table. Everyone slowly drifts off into their own conversations as the bar crowd picks up. I smile as I watch those all around me laugh and smile as if every problem in the world is gone for just this one night.

"Having fun?" The hairs at the back of my neck prickle as Wesley's deep, baritone voice flows over my shoulder. I turn to look back at him, noting the way his white long-sleeve shirt hugs his broad arms. The very arms I spent the night wrapped up in.

"I didn't realize you were working tonight." I spin my chair, fully facing him.

"I'm always working, sweetheart."

I blush, quickly covering it up with a smirk as I turn back around to look at Vivienne and Haden over the rim of my glass. "You and me both."

His eyes follow my line of sight, and an insufferable sigh leaves his lips. "God, those two? They would wreak havoc."

"20 bucks says they'll get married one day."

He scoffs. "You're on."

Wesley goes to get a refill as I sit back and watch my friends once again. Whitney and Harper are teasing Wyatt (who surprisingly showed up shortly after Haden with Benji in tow), Elain is playing pool with old man Sanders, and Vivienne and Haden are bickering about something that has her rolling her eyes.

Home. I realize. This is what *home* feels like.

Chapter 45

BLAKE

I'm cuddled up on the couch, flipping through the TV when a scream pierces the air, filling me with fear that has me throwing back the blankets and following the sound before my brain fully registers what's happening.

"No! No. No, no, no!"

Elain.

I rush into the bedroom where Elain's thrashing in the bed. Screaming at the top of her lungs and fighting off invisible hands I can't see. A nightmare.

I run to her side, dropping to my knees and shaking her as hard as I can. "Elain," I yell. I need to yell it a few more times before it stops, and her eyes pop open. She launches up, chest heaving and tears flowing down her cheeks. She continues to gasp for air as she looks around wildly.

Immediately, I pull her in, rubbing a hand down her sweat-drenched back. "It's okay. It's okay. It was just a dream."

"No." She sobs. "No, it wasn't."

I hold her for a few more minutes until her chest begins to slow. I loosen my grip and whisper, "scooch over." Once she does, I tuck myself under the covers with her, laying on my side and facing her. She still sits up, staring ahead. She often asks me to stay the night, and I never tell her no. Some days, we'd crash out in the bedroom gossiping, but this time, I had trouble sleeping and went out to the couch to avoid waking her up. As far I know, she's never had a bad dream while here. Vivienne took off to the airport a few hours ago, so it's just us in the house.

"You want to talk about it?" I ask.

She looks at me, tears still pooling in her eyes. "You...you promise you won't tell a soul?"

I shake my head. "I can't promise something like that. Not when I don't know what it is. But I do promise I can help if you tell me what's going on."

"My dad...he hits my mom." Her lip wobbles.

I close my eyes for just a brief second. Letting the confirmation wash over me in waves. I knew something was going on. But this? This is not what I thought it was. And I *hate* it. I hate that anyone is forced to go through life with a story even slightly similar to mine. I *hate* that I didn't dig deeper in the beginning, that I didn't see the signs of a little girl living in a broken home. Once I open my eyes again, I brace myself for the rest. Because I will be strong for her. For both of us.

"He's never...come after me specifically. But there's been times where I've got caught in the middle." She hiccups but continues, "He always apologizes. To us both. And says it will stop, but it doesn't. It only gets worse. It's all getting worse. His drinking is getting worse. I don't think he even realizes who is who anymore."

Another sob racks her body, and my heart squeezes painfully at the sight. "I'm scared, Blake. I'm so scared."

"In the morning, we can go to the Sheriff –"

"No!" She yells, jumping up and ripping the blankets off herself. "No, you can't. I can't. They'll put me in the system. My parents will *hate* me."

I cup her face in my hands so that she's looking directly at me. So that she can see what my words may not convey. "Look at me, Elain. I *know* this is scary. I *know* you're scared. I know it's your father. But that doesn't mean he gets the right to lay a hand on either you *or* your mother, okay?"

More tears pool in her eyes and slide down her cheeks, but she doesn't say anything. Just stares at me. A mirror of my younger self.

"When someone has an addiction, they need someone to take it out on instead of blaming themselves. If you don't go to someone, it won't get any better. It can only get worse. It can only get more dangerous. Do you understand?"

She sniffs in response, nodding her head, so I pull her in close. "Come here, kid. I got you."

I hug her for as long as she'll let me. And once her sobs turn into silent snores, I don't leave either. I stay there, lying awake and making sure those dreams don't come back to wake her. Tomorrow, I will take her to the police myself. I'll stand by her side while she gives her statement that will forever alter the course of her life. But tonight, I'll be that shoulder she can lean on. I'll let her process what this will all mean for her and her family.

I'm not sure of this process because I ran instead of facing my monster. But I am sure that I can't let this happen to her. If I had someone who spoke up for me, maybe I would have never left. Maybe my father would have gotten the help he needed. Maybe I wouldn't chase after men who treat me like garbage. Maybe my mother and I would be as close as we used to be.

The idea of Elain feeling or going through everything I did...the feeling is indescribable. I may not have known this girl for long, but she's become a vital part of my life. One that will make me lay down *everything* to make sure she never gets hurt again. She deserves to be a normal kid. To go to school, to have friends, to have two parents who love her more than life itself.

Elain and I met for a reason, that, I was sure of, but now knowing exactly *why* only solidifies the fact that I will stop at nothing to make sure she lives the life she deserves.

I wasn't sure why Elain came into my life when she did, or why we grew so close so quickly, but after tonight? It's never been clearer to me why she was planted into my life. After tonight, I'll make sure that the threads that bound us in the first place aren't misplaced.

Chapter 46

BLAKE

"Will your mother back you up?" I ask Elain as we pull into a parking space near the shop. We're stopping here first to grab some clothes for her since her parents should still be out of town getting stuff for the festival this upcoming week.

"I don't know." She answers honestly as she looks out the window towards Maurice's.

"They might ask us for some kind of evidence. Just in case she doesn't, okay?" She nods, and I place a hand on hers. "You've got this kid. Let's go."

We both unbuckle and step out onto the street. As Elain works on unlocking the door, I realize I don't have my phone on me. "Hey, I forgot my phone. Be right back."

I run to the car, just a few shops down, and look for it. It's taking longer than usual, and I'm starting to wonder if I left it at home. "Where the hell did I put it?" I curse under my breath. Right as I see it wedged between the two seats, I hear someone cry out. My head whips to the side, so fast that I swear it cracks a little.

"Elain?" I call out. I don't hear anything for a few beats, but then she calls back. My heart starts beating fast. Too fast. Panic and worry and dread fill every inch of me at her hurried tone. I rush towards her cries, nothing else matters except that I get to her as quickly as possible. The endless possibilities of what could be happening make my stomach curdle. Just as I round a corner past Maurice's, I hear a man's angry voice hiss, "I thought I told you to stay away from her!"

I shout as I see what I can assume is Elain's father, gripping her arm hard enough to bruise and pulling her down an alleyway. "Hey!" I rush towards them, hating the fear etched all over Elain's face and the fact that his grip only tightens as she tries to pull away. "Hey! Hey, enough!"

I shove myself between them, putting my hands up, but before I get the chance, the floor is swaying beneath my feet, and a sharp pain lances up the side of my fore-head. "Mind your business, skank." Elain's father spits at me as he throws me to the ground.

It's fuzzy for just a moment, but I sit and touch my head. Red coats the fingers I pull back into view. I look up, seeing him drag Elain by her arm. I stumble onto my knees as I keep my eyes locked on them. What was once an unfamiliar face is now replaced with my father's features. Elain's small frame morphs into my own. The memories of defenseless nights and broken glass blur my vision.

The entire world around me blurs as anger so hot it feels like it's burning me alive *consumes me.*

On steady feet, I stand. A few strides, and then I'm grabbing his meaty shoulder and whirling him back around to face me before letting my first fly. It lands with a sickening *crunch.*

If my father taught me anything, it was how to take a punch. And dish it right back out.

He falls back from the sheer shock of it, and I use it as an opportunity to crawl on top of him and bring my fist down again. Over and over. His hands flail as he tries to fight me off, but red is flooding my vision, and there's nothing but pure adrenaline and anger flowing through my veins now. I've become unstoppable, my hands merciless and unforgiving. "If I see you lay your hands on your wife again, I will kill you." *Punch.* "If I see you lay your hands on that little girl again, I will kill you." *Slap.* "Do you understand?" *Punch.*

I've never hit anyone in my life before Marshall. And now *this?* I hear shouts, someone calling my name, but I ignore it. I'm so full of bloodlust that I don't even notice when the fight has left his body, and he just takes every punch and slap I deliver. I don't feel remorse. Not at this moment. And I'm sure I would have killed him if it weren't for rough hands lifting me off the man below me. I'm still swinging blindly, pushing and clawing at the arms wrapped around my middle.

"Blake." I only stop my struggle when Wesley's face comes into view. "Blake, sweetheart, you need to calm down."

Everything comes back into focus at his voice. Reality seeps in as I take in the scene before me. A woman at the end of the Alley on the phone, Elain behind Wesley and I, tears streaming down her red cheeks. The man on the ground lets out a string of curses as he holds his bloody nose and kicks out at me. Wesley kicks it back with his own. "Stay down." He growls. "You're lucky I pulled her off you."

I don't heed them anymore attention. I'm pushing behind Wesley and crouching before Elain. My eyes fly over her wildly. "Are you okay?" She just stares at me, sobs racking her small frame. "Elain! Are you okay?"

"Yes." She cries. "Yes, I'm okay." She then flings herself at me, and I embrace her.

"Okay." My lip wobbles. "Okay. You're okay." I rub circles on her back, doing my best to control my breathing. I don't know if my words are for her, or if they're for me. But I repeat them until I'm breathless. Adrenaline is the only thing keeping me moving. We only pull away as sirens fill the air and a few cops fill up the street. One of them approaches us, one I recognize as Sheriff Eaton.

"Thank god." Elain's father growls as the officer approaches, throwing a hand in my direction. "Cuff this bitch! Do you see what she did to my face?"

"You ladies, okay?" Eaton asks. We nod, and he dips his hat in acknowledgment. He turns to the bloody and seething man before him and pulls out his cuffs. "Mr. Maurice, you are under arrest for domestic violence and child endangerment."

"What?" He shouts and flings an arm towards me. "What about her?"

Wesley bares his teeth at the guy and steps in front of us. But it's Sheriff Eaton who speaks first. "As far as what I've heard from our callers, it was self-defense. And you put your hands on your kid."

"Now stand up and turn around. Don't make this more difficult than it needs to be." Surprisingly, he doesn't struggle when he gets placed in cuffs and keeps his mouth shut as the Sheriff goes on to read him his rights and places him in the back of a cop car.

Chapter 47

BLAKE

We spend the next half hour giving statements. We'll have to come back into the station within a few days to work everything else out. Elain called her mother, so she's on her way back into town to meet us. Wesley drove both of us back to my house, and Elain took off to take a shower and clean herself up.

After we hear the shower turn on, Wesley doesn't miss a beat laying into me as I dab a wet cloth against the top of my head. It's a small cut; thankfully, I won't need stitches. Just some water and a good bandage. My knuckles are busted back open too, and much sorer now that the adrenaline wore off, but I'll survive.

"What the hell were you thinking? You're lucky you aren't in the back of a fucking cop car right now." He points an accusing finger in my face. I flinch at his tone, not worried that he'd ever lay a hand on me, but because I've never seen Wesley *so angry* before.

"What was *I* thinking?" I snap. I look at him and shake my head. I can feel the stinging creeping into my nose. Is it really this hard for others to see? Do people truly never know what's going on behind closed doors? Notice a little girl's behavior or see the bruises and not question it for one second? I shouldn't be the one being chastised. The entire goddamn town should be showing up at that asshole's door with pitchforks. In a quieter voice this time, one that sounds much more broken than before, I say, "You have no idea what you're even talking about."

I go to move past him, over this conversation, but his fingers wrap gently around my wrist. He holds me in place, like he knows that something else is at play, and he just *wants* me to break. "Stop! Stop running from me, Blake."

"What did I tell you about me not being your problem?" I bare my teeth at him but haven't moved away from his touch yet. "Back. off."

He moves us so that we're fully facing each other now, both of his hands wrapping around my biceps. "*Everything* when it comes to you is my problem, Blake. What about that don't you understand?" I shake my head, but he presses on. "Just tell me why it matters *so much* that you'd risk your own life for a girl you've only just met?" His voice comes out as a plea, and much more vulnerable than I expected. It only causes my temper to flare.

"Because someone should have helped me!" I yell as I rip my arms away. "Because I was that little girl, Wesley!" I'm full-on shouting now. Not even thinking about how someone may overhear us. I'm spilling everything I've kept a secret from him. I'm angry, so unbelievably angry that I can't stop this kind of outburst. "I mean seriously? Why do you think I left? You think I wanted to leave my home? To leave our moms. To leave *you*?" My voice breaks on the last sentence, and my entire world feels like it comes crashing down at the same time.

"What did you just say?"

My chin wobbles as I turn back to look at him. His voice is both calm and lethal, and his eyes so dark they could rival the midnight sky. His entire demeanor sends shivers down my spine, but I ignore them. I knew the day would come when I'd have to tell him, I just didn't expect it to come so soon. Too soon.

"My father. The night I left...I shouldn't even be alive, Wesley." For a few minutes, he doesn't speak. His eyes just jump between mine, trying to read whatever may lay within them. Then they land on the scar that's on full display. The one that he's only seen since I've come back to town, and one I definitely didn't gain from my reckless childhood. He runs his hands through his hair before stepping forward, and I don't move back, too scared I'll crumble with one step.

"Why?" He reaches for that arm with the scar and gently runs his thumb over the raised skin. His touch burns and something unreadable falls on his face. So many emotions, and I can't help but be in awe at how quickly he processes them. "Why didn't you tell me?"

The question makes me laugh. I laugh at how thick his voice is. But there's no humor in it. It comes out all wrong and broken. He's now piecing together that I've had this scar since I arrived home. It's not like it's hard to miss. But just the mere thought of where it came from...I can't stomach the idea of Elain having to carry a visual representation of her abuse for the rest of her life. One that people will always question, never allowing you to just *forget.*

"And what could you have done?" I ask him, "We were kids, Wesley. I was just a kid. And so is she."

I finally crack on that last word, a dam bursting open in my chest. A few tears leak down my face. And then I'm sobbing. It doesn't stop, only gets louder, and faster. Everything is suddenly *too loud.* I can't breathe. I hurt; it all hurts, and this time, not just for me, for Elain, for myself, and for any other child who can be so thoroughly shattered because of another's harsh hands. "So is she." I say again. Again, and again, and again.

My knees give out, and I fall to the floor and wrap my arms around myself. I don't stop saying it until I feel warm hands pulling me into a lap and placing a hand on the back of my head. "It's okay, baby, It's okay." He rocks me, running a gentle hand over the spot where his hand came to rest.

But that touch, *that gentle touch*, is what has me coming back to my senses. To the reality of my situation. I scramble out of his hold and get to my feet. "Don't. Don't! I don't want pity." Snot and tears mix, and I'm glad I'm too upset at the moment to care. "Not from you."

He just stares at me, and he looks so heartbroken that it physically hurts to look at him. I whisper so quietly that only we can hear. "This - this doesn't change anything. It *can't*."

So, I turned and walked out, leaving him there on his knees. Not sure where I'm going, but knowing I need to get out. I know it's my house, but Wesley won't leave. Not now. And I need space. But as I walk away, I'm left with a sinking feeling that I've shattered his heart for a second time.

And I'm not quite sure how I'll forgive myself.

Chapter 48

WESLEY

This doesn't change anything.

But it did. It changed everything.

Blake was wrong. I don't pity her—I admire her. A little girl who carried the weight of the world on her shoulders, and a woman who found the strength to rise after watching it all crumble beneath her feet.

The anger that I felt for her is gone in an instant. All six years of it. Replaced by anger at myself for being so blind, and anger at her piece of shit father. At my mother for not telling me, at Elise for not telling me.

That's exactly why I find myself pulling into my mother's driveway, knowing the two of them are spending the day together. I slam shut the door of my truck and take wide steps to the porch before pointing an accusing finger at them as they sip coffee in their porch chairs. "Did you know?"

My mom looks appalled by my sudden appearance and hostility, but I forge on anyway. Too angry to see anything other than two women who could have changed the way this went. If Elise knows, my mother knows too. "Honey, what are you-"

Elise places a hand on hers before shaking her head. "Ana." She stands not even close to meeting my height but somehow managing to look down her nose at me. "Is this about Blake?"

"You know exactly what it's about."

"It wasn't my story to tell, Wesley."

"The hell it wasn't. That fucking bastard should be in jail!" I yell, and if I wasn't so blinded by rage, I'd be horrified. I've never raised my voice at any woman in my life. "Where is he now?" I ask.

They share a wary glance. Elise is the one who pipes up first, though. "He was released from prison a few weeks ago. But he's not even in the same state. He's on house arrest, Wesley."

"Where?" I snap. I'll *kill* him. I don't care if it happened nearly a decade ago. And once I'm done, I'll make sure to visit Elain's father too.

"Wesley." My mom snapped. "Watch your tone."

Elise shakes her head. "It's fine, Ana. He has every right to be angry."

She looks at me. "Do you think I didn't want to get his ass locked up? Go after him myself? Blake is my daughter. But there was *nothing* I could do to stop her from leaving. *Nothing.* She was legally an adult, and without the victim present, it was a bit hard to even convince the police to show up at all. I called him after both she, and the cops left. I antagonized him, and he reacted exactly as I expected he would. He showed up at the center. He may not have been arrested for hurting my baby, but I damn well made sure he didn't get off scot-free."

Tears slip down her face, and she doesn't wipe them away as she continues, "I blame myself every day for what happened to her. For not being home. For leaving her with that monster. I've come to live with it. The only thing I can do now is be here for her. For however long she'll let me. In whatever way she'll let me. I can pick up the pieces and let the woman who's struggling to come back up for air breathe again."

I shake my head, avoiding her gaze. Elise continues, stepping in closer to me. "She doesn't need you to save her, Wesley. She did that all by herself. But maybe she just needs you to be her friend again."

When I meet her brown eyes, the ones that look so much like the woman I've spent years chasing, the feeling of tears prickle the back of my eyes. I should have tried harder to bring her back home. I should have paid more attention. I should have noticed what was going on.

How many of those scars on her body are from his hands? How many nights did I spend safe in my bed with my perfect parents just across the hall when she was cowering in hers? Elise, as if she can read my every thought, doesn't hesitate in wrapping her arms around me. I bury my head in her shoulder. After a minute, my mom's own gentle hands swallow us both.

And I let myself cry. I don't care if it makes me less of a man. Or if it makes me look weak. I don't cry for me. I cry for Blake. The two women hugging me do, too.

Blake and I sit at the edge of the pond, pants rolled up and socks off as we swing our feet back and forth in the cool water. It was one minute before midnight, and Blake and I would finally be turning eighteen this year. Celebrating our birthdays on the pond had become a tradition, one I made sure we never missed. We'd sneak out and stay out for a couple of hours until midnight hit, so we could always be the first to say happy birthday to one another.

"Happy Birthday." I nudge her shoulder. "Now, make a wish."

She turns to look at me and huffs out a breath. "I can't in front of you, or it doesn't count."

"Best friends are exempt from that rule."

"Are we? Just best friends?" She looks into my eyes, searching. She knows the answer, but I just smile at her, tucking a piece of blonde hair behind her ear. "We'll never be just best friends, Blake."

She looks up at the night sky. At all the stars twinkling above and closes her eyes as she speaks. "I wish...I wish I could call my older self. Just – just so I could ask how she's doing. If this life gets any easier."

"It's stupid. I know." Blake adds as she opens her eyes and sees me just watching her.

"It's not." I say softly.

"I want to leave, Wesley. If I don't, I might never make it out."

"Then I'll go with you." I lean my forehead against hers. "Where you go, I go."

Chapter 49

BLAKE

"Did you take MMA classes or something?" Elain asks me from behind her steaming cup of tea.

I almost laugh. No, I didn't. I can't explain where that rage came from. I've never even been in a fight, and I doubt I could make something like that happen a second time. I made my way back here after I went for a walk, remembering that Elain had been in the shower during Wesley and I's fight. Thankfully, the former had already left by the time I returned.

"Are you mad at me?" I ask.

"Why would I be mad?" She questions. "He got what he deserved."

I toy with the tea string hanging from my cup, and she reaches over to place her hand over mine. "Look, I'm not going to pretend like it doesn't hurt. He's my dad, of course it does. But...talking with you? Being around you...It's made things clearer. What he's doing...It's not okay. He needs help."

Tears spring to my eyes. This girl is so strong. Stronger than I was. She's not scared to fight, and she's not running from her demons. The front doorbell rings, and it makes me jump at the sudden interruption. Elain stands from her seat at the island. "That's probably my mom."

I nod and go with her, knowing she's not going to want to face this one alone. She opens the door, and her mom rushes in to hug her. "Oh, babe. I'm so glad you're okay." She sobs. "I would have gotten here sooner, but traffic was really heavy."

"It's okay," Elain says as she lets go. "I'll go grab my stuff." But her mom catches her shoulder as Elain turns and blurts, "No. Don't."

Both Elain and I pause, sharing confused glances. "I...I was thinking that I need to go away for a little while." She looks at me. "Your mother stopped by to see me before I came here. Gave me some information on the center she went to. She helped get it all arranged."

A knot forms in my throat. Of course, she did. A part of me wants to fall to my knees and never get up at the fact that women even have to go through this sort of pain; another part of me wants to squeeze my mom until she pops for being so brave and lending a hand to another who needs it.

"And...and if it was okay with you, I want Elain to stay with you. Just...just until I get myself together."

She looks between us two, nervously rubbing her hands against her jean-clad thighs. I look at Elain, and tears are pooling in her eyes, but she doesn't seem mad. She looks like she understands. Like, she's happy. Like, she may have even expected this. "She's always welcome in my home." I say. "I'll give you guys a minute."

They both nod, and I busy myself with cleaning up the kitchen. I don't attempt to listen in. They need their moment, and quite frankly, it's none of my business. But before her mother leaves, she comes to me in the kitchen, leaving Elain leaning by the door. "Thank you." She says to me, "Thank you for doing what I should have."

I smile at her but don't say anything. She hugs me too. So, I mutter in her ear, "She won't forget this. I know. I know it's hard. It will never be easy. But it's the right choice. And I'm proud of you for making it."

She pulls back, sniffling, and gives me a broken smile. She stops and crouches before Elain on her way out. "Remember. You can come and visit or call me whenever. I love you, and I am so proud of you, baby. Never forget that." She gives us both a watery smile and Elain and I watch as she hops into her car and drives away.

"So, did you take MMA classes? You never answered." Elain's wobbly voice cuts through the sorrow-filled air. I tip my head back and laugh. Slinging an arm over her shoulder, I pull her close and steer her toward the kitchen.

"Come on, kid, let's figure out what to make for dinner."

Chapter 50

WESLEY

I've heard of mothers being able to lift cars when their children are in danger. A spike of adrenaline so strong, they can defy the laws of physics. The same theory must have applied to Blake with Elain. I've known her my entire life, and I've never seen someone so small pummel a grown ass man like that. If I hadn't been so pissed at her for putting herself in harm's way, I think I would have kissed her until we were both breathless. I stand before her door now, having spent the past half hour pacing the inside of my house, thinking about things to say. I was going to wait until tomorrow, since it's late and she's had enough bullshit for one day, but I wouldn't have been able to sleep.

Thankfully, Blake's the type who loves going out and partying. But when it really comes down to it, she'd much rather curl up on the couch with a book or binge reruns of Gilmore Girls. After a day like today, she is definitely lounging on the couch and stuffing her face with popcorn.

I knock once on the door, as quietly as I can, so as to not wake anyone who may be sleeping. The door swings open before I even pull my hand away.

"What do you want?" Blake doesn't even glare at me as she looks up. She sounds tired and drained. Her hair is thrown up in a messy bun, and she's wearing a nightgown that I'm positive should belong to her grandmother. Yet, somehow, she still looks just as alluring.

"Please," I say, bringing my hand back down to my side. "I just want to talk."

She doesn't say anything, just opens the door wider. But she's the one who steps out. "Elain's asleep inside." She says as she closes the door softly. I watch as she brushes past me and walks along the porch. She leans against the railing, refusing to face me. I stop a few feet behind her.

"I am sorry that you felt like you couldn't come to me, Blake. I'm sorry that I was ever angry at you for leaving." I swallow. "I will live with that regret for the rest of my life."

"Don't." She whispers. "You have nothing to apologize for. We were just friends." She shrugs as she picks at the railing's wood chips. "I am just the girl you grew up with."

I take another step closer. "You aren't just the girl I grew up with. You never have been."

She turns toward me at my tone. "Wesley, I left..." She animatedly throws her hands in the air. "It's...It's been years. So, don't say that. Not if you don't mean it."

"I was a damn fool for letting you go six years ago, Blake."

Another step.

"I won't make the same mistake twice."

"Wesley." She whimpers as she closes her eyes. "I'm a mess. I don't know what the hell I'm doing half the time. You deserve someone who can give you everything that I'm not sure I can–"

"I came to New York for you." I cut her off, running a hand through my hair. "Three years ago. I came looking for you. I had to see you. Just once. And when I saw how content you were, how happy, I couldn't ask you to leave that behind. So, I turned back around and made myself forget everything when it came to you. I tried drowning myself in whiskey. I tried to date. I tried to throw myself into work. But none of it mattered because *you weren't here.* I'd have to be dead to forget about you, Blake, and even in death, you'd still haunt my thoughts; you'd still be the one I'd crawl through hell to get back to."

"Don't you understand?" I ask. "I don't want to start over. Not with you. I don't want to see other people. I don't want to see *you* with other people."

A few tears have slipped down her round cheeks, so I close the last two steps to her and press my brow to hers. "I want everything. The good, the bad. I want it all, Blake. I want *you.*"

All control snaps between us as that last word echoes in the air. She lunges, crashing her lips against mine.

Chapter 51

BLAKE

His hands tangle in my hair. My hands trail down his chest. This kiss…It's not sweet or romantic. It's bruising. It's hurried. It's as if we can't get enough of each other. Can't get close enough.

Running away has always been easier than facing the alternative, but being here? On this porch? I can't fathom why I ever ran from it in the first place. From him. We may have been kids, but maybe it would have been different if I had just stayed. So many what-ifs. I pull back, panting from the heat and lack of oxygen. "Elain's inside…I can't…We can't."

He pulls back, too, just far enough that he's still gently brushing his lips against mine.

"Let me take you on a date tomorrow."

"What…what about Brittany?

"What about her?" He looks at me like I just asked him to commit arson.

"I thought…"

"We went on *one* date." He interrupts me. "One. And I'll never make that mistake again." He looks so disgusted at the idea that I let a laugh burst from my chest.

"Thank god." I sigh and tilt my chin to look up at him. "I suppose I can squeeze you in after Haden, after all."

That earns me a little growl and nip on my bottom lip, and I giggle in response. Once we've put enough space between us, I motion a hand between us. "What does this mean, then?"

"It means we stop pretending like we don't feel whatever this is between us. We don't have to label it, not if you don't want to. But let's just see where it takes us."

I give him a small smile. "That…that I can do."

Chapter 52

WESLEY

"Blake?" I call out. She doesn't answer, but the doors propped open, so I assume it's safe to let myself in. But a man's voice I don't recognize stops me dead.

"You like having your mouth fucked, baby? Is this making you wet?"

The man's voice filters out from her speaker that I spot sitting on the kitchen island. Erotic and filthy words continue to spew from the speaker, and soon another voice, a woman's voice, joins the audio. My eyes bounce to where Blake stands slack-jawed, having dropped the small bag she was carrying. She screeches, "Oh god!" and runs toward the speaker.

"Please, please cover your ears." Embarrassment coats her tone. The pink flush all over her cheeks and chest makes me want to put her on her knees and reenact the whole scene just to keep it there. She manages to turn it off after a second and whirls around to look at me. "That *never* happened." She huffs and points a finger at me, brushing a piece of hair back that fell onto her face.

Once my shock has washed away, all I can focus on is the matching tiny little top and grey shorts that she's wearing. They do nothing to cover her ass or her perfect tits that are on full display. "I have a feeling you *won't* want me to forget that, sweetheart." I say as I let my eyes devour her.

She drops her finger. "I hate you." She mutters. "You didn't tell me you were coming over."

"I texted you."

"I didn't see it, then." She slaps her hand against her head, and the slight jump it creates causes her tits to bounce. Once she catches my gaze on them and realizes what she's wearing, she crosses her arms. "You could have knocked!"

"Door was open." I chirp back.

She squints her eyes at me, a little less embarrassed and more of a challenge swimming in those brown pools. "Give me a few minutes to get dressed." She bends down to pick up the bag she dropped.

I smirk. "Sure you don't want to wrap up your book? I don't mind waiting for you to finish."

She then hurls the bag at my head, and my laughter follows her into the bathroom. Such a violent little thing.

"Where are we going?" Blake hollers from the small room after a few minutes. I walk around her living room, looking at some of the pictures sitting on her fireplace mantel.

"Just wear something comfy." I call back.

"That's helpful." I can hear her roll her eyes from here. I pick up a picture of her and her friend, Vivienne. How happy and content they look holding up their diplomas together brings a smile to my face. Vivienne really does look a hell of a lot like Whitney.

"Goin' through my stuff, Conway?" I turn at Blake's entrance and whistle. She's wearing light-wash jeans with little rips in the knees, white sneakers, and a pink top. Her hair is thrown up in a half-up, half-down look. She looks gorgeous. She always does. I take her hand, pulling her to the doorway and out to the truck. Her hands are so soft and small in my rough ones. Her man-icured nails make me wonder how the color would look wrapped around my cock. I push the thought down, but it lingers – just like she always has.

"Can I drive?" Blake quips from my side, stealing me away from the lude thoughts.

"No."

"What?" She gapes. "Why?"

"Because your driving scares me." She looks offended as I rip open her door and help her hop in. It's true, though. When we were younger she used to take cor-ners like we were in a damn action movie. I'd be lying if I said I didn't pray a little every time she got behind the wheel. Warm vanilla and something lavender fill my nostrils as I reach over to buckle her in. "Plus, you just look too damn good in my passenger seat." I wink before slamming the door shut, savoring the pink flush that creeps up her pretty neck.

Chapter 53

BLAKE

"**B**odies? Seriously?" I ask as I slide a new CD into the truck's stereo.

"What?" Wesley asks incredulously. "It's a classic."

I sigh. "So, you gonna tell me where we're going yet?" I've been nagging him nonstop, dying to know what exactly we're doing. I *hate* surprises.

He rolls his eyes. "We're almost there."

And he's right. A couple more minutes and we're pulling into an open area surrounded by trees.

"What is this?" I scrunch my nose. Then, I look at him with wide eyes. "You're going to murder me, aren't you?"

I'm convinced he would be the type to play *Drowning Pool* before hauling someone off into the woods. A bunch of random junk is littering a white folding table, and a tree stump is right next to it holding what looks like…an old TV?

"Well, I was going to take you to dinner." Wesley sighs, completely ignoring the murder part. "But Elain said you'd hate that. So, I came up with something else."

My heart squeezes at the fact that he asked Elain for help planning a date with me. Something so small, but it still holds so much meaning. She was right. I've gone on plenty of over-the-top dates when in the city, and they were not impressive. It got old, fast. I miss the days when ordering pizza and throwing on a show was fun and not something that just gives the guy the idea that he's going to get laid.

"But don't worry. I'll make sure to feed you before taking you back home." He grins. He then reaches around me to dip his hand into the back of his truck and pulls out two baseball bats. "Oh!" I squeal and clap my hands together. Not even embarrassed at the fact that I sound and probably look like a child. "Did you *make us* our very own rage room?"

"After Marshall *and* the other day…I think it's safe to say you need to let off a little steam. And this is the safer way to do so." He says pointedly.

I just look at him, those blue eyes and the little dimple poking out from his cheek. I give my head a little shake. I can't place why a date like this makes me want to cry and hug him at the same time.

"Thank you," I whisper. "I can't remember the last time someone put this much effort into hanging out with me."

He stares back at me for a beat and shakes his head. "That's a damn shame."

"Now come on." He hands me a bat. "There's a microwave with your name written on it. I even glued a picture of Dean from Gilmore Girls onto it."

I tip my head back and laugh so loudly that it sounds foreign to my ears. It's different from any of the other ones I've given him. I feel it, in every inch of my body. It fills me with ease and makes me want to do it again. Just so that it keeps that smile he's got lighting up his face, too.

Chapter 54

BLAKE

We pull back into my driveway a couple of hours later. The house is quiet, with all the lights off. Elain is doing a supervised overnight visit with her mother tonight, so it's just me in the house. I turn my head to Wesley. "Do you want to go for a swim?"

He looks at me like I've grown another head. "It's 10 p.m."

I shrug. "So? You got better plans?" I open my door and jump out, not waiting to see if he'll follow. But when the engine turns off and a door slams, I know he does. We make it to the pond, standing on the old dock. He's just standing there like he's not sure what to do. So, I kick off my shoes and lock eyes with him as I unbuckle my jeans. Once that's done, I cross my arms and rip my top off – happy I decided to wear a matching pink set that makes my skin look tan. Pink's fun. Most people hate it, but not me. And I have a feeling Wesley doesn't either. Not with the way he's looking me over like a man starved.

There's a breeze, and I can feel my nipples harden beneath the lacy fabric. But I'm not sure if it's from the chilly air or the man standing before me. There's no one here except us for miles but being so out in the open...it's erotic. The moonlight feels like a spotlight, and his gaze feels like a cold caress.

"Your turn." I say softly. He doesn't hesitate to reach for his belt buckle, and he doesn't rip his eyes away from mine. Something about the movement makes me want to drop to my knees and ask him to just *fuck me* already. I choose to turn and dip a foot into the water, deciding it's best not to jump his bones and scare him off before the night's even through. I eventually fully submerge, and soon after, I hear a splash and feel Wesley swim up behind me. I turn when I feel him creep closer. The pond isn't very deep. Just reaching underneath my breasts. But with Wesley's height, it leaves most of his chest exposed.

My mouth waters at the sight. I saw him in the bathroom the night he took care of me, but I didn't allow myself to take it all in the way I am now. His chest is toned and narrows down to a taut waist. His broad shoulders and tattoos are on full display. Water and moonlight glistens on his tan skin.

"You imagining me naked, Blake?" He's smug as he catches my roaming eyes.

"Yes." I breathe.

No point in lying. I'd be an idiot for saying anything else. I'm practically drooling at the sight of him. I turn back around; his stare too much. It sends a pool of heat straight to my core. I can't focus. And it doesn't get any better when I feel him finally push against me. I nearly whimper from the feel of his hard length pressed against my back.

"Tell me I can touch you, Blake." I lose a shaky breath. My head feels like it's floating in the air above us. "You'd like that, wouldn't you?" He asks. "I can see it in that pretty pink color you light up with every time I come around, Blake. You want me just as bad as I *need* you."

I need you. God, those words. *That voice.*

"Please, Wesley." My moan escapes as a whimper.

"Fuck." He mutters as he bends his head down to plant a kiss on my neck. "You sound so pretty when you beg, baby."

His hand snakes around my waist and pulls me taut against his chest. He's agonizingly slow in his touch. Trailing over the material of my bra, down the middle of my stomach. I moan when he just skims the top of my lacey panties. And then he pushes it farther down to cup me. Only when I'm practically grinding against his hand does he finally move my panties aside and slip a finger in. "Oh, god." I cry. It's been so long since I've been touched, and I could fall apart with just this.

"So fucking wet for me." He groans. "So desperate." He pulls out just to pinch my clit, before adding another finger. As one hand continues pumping, his other comes up to grip my chin. He turns it so he's pressing his lips to mine in a bruising kiss. Slipping his tongue in and claiming my mouth as his.

"Tell me." *Pump.* "When you were listening to your book earlier, were you thinking about me?" *Pump.* "Wishing it was me whispering those filthy things into your ear?" *Pump.* "Doing those filthy things to you?" *Pump.* I only moan, unable to voice any words, but he yanks his fingers out, choosing to tease my folds instead. He grips my chin tighter. "Answer me, Blake."

"Y-yes." I cry out again. "I was thinking about you."

"That's what I thought."

"Now, squeeze that tight pussy around my fingers, and let me make you cum all over them, yeah?" I nod eagerly, pressing my body further into his. As if I can somehow make his fingers go deeper. Make his body melt into my own. Soon, waves of pleasure are racking my body from both his filthy words and fingers, and I'm doing exactly what he told me to.

Chapter 55

WESLEY

As soon as Blake comes down from her high, I'm picking her up, internally beating my chest at the way her legs immediately wrap around me. We're both soaking wet, but I don't stop to grab our clothes or find something to dry us off with. I stalk up to her front door. "Elain's not home, right?"

"No." She shakes her head, breathless and mindlessly grinding herself against me.

"Good," I growl, and just as the lock clicks behind us, I push her up against the door, one hand wrapping around the back of her head, and the other reaching down to squeeze her ass. Forcing her plump lips to meet mine again. I pull her away from the hard surface, both of us keeping our lips locked. "Light?" I mumble against her lips, She reaches over and flicks on a nearby switch. We stumble through the house, stopping here and there just to savor each other's kiss. Then we finally make it to her bedroom.

I'm much softer when I lay her down at the top of the mattress. I'm just as desperate for her as she is for me, but the idea of Blake underneath me, moaning my name and crying out for more, is something I *want* to savor – n*eed* to savor. Once I lay her down, I take a moment to step back and just soak her in. The ends of her hair are still wet, falling to frame her breasts that are concealed by the tiny pink set I know she purposely picked out. One that I've been dying to rip off her body. Her skin is flushed, nearly the same color as her lingerie, and her brown eyes are wild with arousal. Her nipples are hard and peaked underneath the flimsy material, and water drips down her skin. She's beautiful.

So heartbreakingly beautiful, and so *mine*.

"You are..." I shake my head, pure disbelief at the sight of this woman splayed out on the bed like my own personal feast. "A fucking *dream*, Blake."

"Then stop standing there gawking and do something about it." She snaps, all sass. Any trace of shyness she had before is gone.

I smile, but it's not warm. Not sweet. "Come here."

She doesn't move right away, a challenge sparking in her brown eyes. A test to see who *wants* it more. She won't find that I give so easy, not when *I'm* the one who's always doing the chasing. It makes her feel empowered, thinking she's the one in control. But she's not. After a minute of neither of us budging, she goes to stand from the bed, but I shake my head.

"No. Crawl to me, baby."

She's practically gaping at my demand. "Show me that you can listen, and maybe I'll let you wrap your pretty little lips around my cock."

That has her pivoting so that she's on all fours at the top of the bed. She's listening, and it sends a sick thrill through me at the fact she's so *willing*. So *desperate*. My dick throbs at the sight of her. She doesn't break eye contact with me as she slowly makes her way down the bed, and I just know she's as turned on as I am right now. Once she hits the bottom, she leans back to rest her ass on her heels.

"Atta girl." I grip her chin, trailing my thumb across her bottom lip, swollen from my own. I apply just a little bit more pressure, prompting her to open. She doesn't hesitate in capturing it in her mouth, sucking and moaning around it like it's a lollipop she's never had before.

Fuck. *This girl*. I reach down, pulling my boxers down until my cock springs free. Her eyes widen as she takes me in. I reach forward, wrapping my fist around her hair, not hard, just enough to elicit a moan from her throat. I bring her closer, running the tip along her lips. Her tongue dips out to lick the bead of precum at my tip, and I tighten my fist around her blonde strands. Gritting my teeth, I say, "Stop playing with it, Blake." She glares at me but takes me fully into her mouth in one fell swoop. An inaudible sound vibrates around me, and I hum.

"You're so much prettier with a cock stuffed down your throat. Who knew this is all it would take to shut you up?"

I use my hand to guide her head, and she moans around me again, louder this time. "You like that, huh?"

Her lashes flutter in agreement. "Tap my thigh if it gets to be too much." I release the fist of hair and switch it out to grab both sides of her head. I fuck her mouth. At first, I worry that it's too much, but she just matches each thrust with the bob of her head. It surprises me even more when she moves one of her hands that was resting on my thigh to position it between her legs. I bring her all the way down to my base and groan. So hot. So warm. So *wet*. I'm dying to be inside her at this point. I hold her there for a minute, only pulling her back when she gags, and tears begin to form at the corners of her eyes. Her mouth leaves me with a lewd *pop*, a line of spit connecting her mouth to me. I nearly finish at the sight. I pull away from her fully, and she whines at the loss of contact. I bend down and quickly kiss her before going to lay down on the bed. "Come ride me baby."

She doesn't hesitate in turning, and she crawls up the bed until she's straddling me. I reach behind her with one hand and unclasp her bra, letting it fall away. Her full and heavy breasts are finally on display. I trace her perfect pink nipples with one finger, devouring her with my gaze.

I'm gonna fuck those too.

And then I reach for her panties, ripping them in half with one harsh tug that causes her to gasp. "Those were expensive!" She gapes at me in shock, but I only smile wickedly in return and tug her forward until she's perfectly lined up with me.

"I'll buy you a new pair." After this? I'll buy a whole fucking lingerie store for her. Make her try on every single piece and fuck her in them too.

"Now put it in." I nod toward my cock. She braces one hand on my chest, and the other reaches down between us, wrapping her fingers around my throbbing length. We both moan in unison when my tip brushes against her entrance. She sinks down on me, and when she pushes herself a couple more inches, she cries out once she's seated to the hilt. "So fucking hot. So tight."

I meant what I said. She's *a fucking dream*. Tits bouncing, head tipped back with her mouth in an 'o' shape. The sounds she's making for me. It sends us both over the edge. And we spend the rest of the night like this. In a handful of different positions, with little to no breaks in between. I revel in eliciting every moan and whimper from her mouth. I just can't get enough. I may never get enough of Blake. And now that I've had a taste, I'm never letting her go.

Chapter 56

BLAKE

I wake to the smell of pancakes and the sound of something sizzling. I roll over and reach out my hand, only to pop an eye open and see that the bed is empty. I groan before rolling back over and slipping on a piece of clothing closest to me. One, I assume, is Wesley's shirt from how low it hangs on my legs. Legs that are so sore I flush at the mere memory of *why* they're so sore.

His hands are folded behind his head, and he lays sprawled across the mattress like a king as he watches me bounce up and down on him repeatedly. The moans that escape my lips are unlike any noise I've ever made before. He's huge, much bigger than I've ever had, and the filthy words he whispers to me are ones I'll no doubt blush over tomorrow—

I blink, stopping myself and padding out of the bedroom, indeed fighting a blush at the memory of him inside me, only to find Wesley's bare back turned to me. Muscles flexing as he flips breakfast in one of my cast-iron pans. I wasn't quite sure what I was going to wake up to, but it wasn't this. A great date, followed by multiple orgasms *and* waking up to a hot guy making breakfast? In *my* kitchen? *Shirtless?*

Yeah. *Yeah, I could get used to this.* He looks over his shoulder as he greets me, dimples, and all. "Morning."

"Morning." I smile and toy with the ends of his shirt. I peek over to where two mugs sit on the counter. My eyes light up, and I ask, "Did you make coffee?"

"Yup." He grabs one of them and spins around to place it on the counter in front of me. The look he gives me at the sight of what I'm wearing...*god*, I hope he takes me right here on the counter. I'd let him. I go to sit down at the barstool and blurt, "God, I think I love you," as he slides me a mug of hot coffee. Then my eyes widen, and I slap a hand over my mouth.

I stutter, "I- I didn't mean it like-"

He laughs, all deep and rich. His eyes crinkle, and he waves a hand at me as he turns back around to tend to our food. "Blake. Shut up and drink your coffee." I turn red, thankful he didn't take it that way and glad he understands I'm not liable for anything I say until a little caffeine finds its way into my system.

"Sleep, okay?" He asks over his shoulder as he plates the food.

"Better than I have in a long time," I answer truthfully.

"Good." He slides my plate towards me. "I've got to get to work. But I'll swing by later?" He drops a kiss on my forehead, steals a piece of bacon off my plate, and saunters to the bedroom to get dressed. I look down and see he painted a smiley face on my pancakes with whipped cream and fruit. I almost giggle at the sight. This is the same man who just said and did the dirtiest things imaginable to me less than 12 hours ago. I'm so shocked right now, I truly have no idea what to say. But as he comes back out, pulling a hoodie over his head, I realize I stole his shirt.

"I'm sorry." I stand, embarrassed. Maybe it was too much of a couple-y thing to do. Way out of line. "I'll go take this off."

I stop when he catches my wrist. "Don't." He smirks. "I like it." I'm dumbstruck as he places a kiss on my wrist and drops it. Just as he closes the door behind him, Elain opens it and walks right through. Her eyes are wide as she spots me, and the minute the door closes behind her, my best friend's text flashes on my phone that lies face up.

Viv:

> **Did you sleep with your hot neighbor yet?**

Elain screeches "You *totally* fucked the hot neighbor!"

I bury my face in my hands and flop back onto the stool.

Chapter 57

WESLEY

"I don't have time for you to be a pain in my ass today, man." Haden's head pops over the counter with a shit-eating grin right in the middle of it.

"I missed you too." He winks.

Harper called me to let me know the soda machine broke at the bar, so now I'm crouched down behind the counter trying to fix the issue *again*. It's really just time to replace the damn thing. Otherwise, I would have spent the morning with Blake. Having breakfast. Reliving the events of last night. Hell, probably the entire day if she'd let me. The memory of her walking out in my shirt, hair tousled, and a flush on her perfect cheeks makes me wish I would have fucked her once more before leaving. Even if it made me late. My brother's head pops up next to Haden's. I groan. "What do you two *want*?"

They look at each other. "He's so mean to us." Haden says.

"So, mean." Wyatt says, nodding in agreement.

"Sometimes I wonder if we should sign him up for anger management."

"You know I think that'd be a really good –"

"I'm right here." I cut them off.

These two aren't going to leave me alone, so I stand, place my wrench on the counter, and then brace my palms on the wood. I raise my eyebrows, growing impatient.

"I need an extra pair of hands for the festival." Wyatt says, taking the hint.

Haden shrugs, "I'm just bored."

I cock my head at Haden. "Go work with Wyatt, then."

"What?" Both practically shout the word.

I shrug. "Why not?" I turn to Wyatt. "You always need the extra hands." And then Haden. "And you–" I point a finger into his chest. "Need to get off your ass and do something. Rather than terrorizing everyone who comes through this bar."

Haden looks at Wyatt. "How much you gonna pay me?"

"Show up first, and then we'll talk."

"Deal."

"Start tomorrow?"

"As long as I get to wear a hat." He flicks the rim of my brother's cowboy hat, and Wyatt swats his hand away.

Bunch of children.

"Great. You figured it out. Now leave."

Haden thankfully listens, shit talking a bit more before he does leave, but Wyatt's the one who leans on the bar and makes himself comfortable. "A little birdie told me you stayed the night at Blake's."

Elain. Of course. She goes down to see the horses often, so I guess I shouldn't be surprised. And seeing me leave their house at the ass crack of dawn is enough to give it all away. "It's new," I say gruffly. He smiles. Genuinely smiles. A rare one, especially coming from him.

"It's about damn time. You know, Dad would be planning the wedding right about now." He adds. He's not wrong. My dad adored Blake, and he was hands down worse than our mother when it came to the two of us. The side of my lip pulls up at the thought of how he'd react if he was still here. As if he can see those thoughts, he leans forward and slaps me on the shoulder. About as sentimental as he'll ever get with me. "Now just make sure she sticks this time around, yeah?"

I shake him off. "Don't you have a ranch to run?"

"But bugging my little brother is just *so much* better."

Chapter 58

BLAKE

After answering a fire of questions from Elain this morning, I had an unyielding urge to see my mom. She was ecstatic to see me show up. She made us some coffee and stuffed me full of so much food I'm surprised I haven't puked. Granted, I've missed her cooking, so that part's on me just as much as it's on her. I haven't been avoiding her per se, but I know I've been distant. Trying to figure out where we stand, and what lies between us. Where I fit in this new world. But I've never questioned my mother's love for me, and I owe her a visit at least once or twice a week. Even if it's so she can show me my baby album for the millionth time. Or so that she can gossip about this week's town drama.

I was just leaving when I decided to share some of the new developments in my life with her. "I'm...seeing Wesley. Officially."

"I know."

My face scrunches, and a nervous laugh escapes. "What?"

"Oh, please. I've seen how that boy has watched you since you two were running around in the field and flinging mud at each other. It's about time." She then waves a finger up and down my body. "Plus, you've got that sex glow going on. And my new favorite daughter told me he stayed the night."

"Mom." I bury my face in my hands. This woman has no filter. And Elain has a big mouth.

When I look back up, she's smiling at me though, all trace of humor gone. Her eyes, a bit watery, but so full of love. "I'm happy for you, baby. You know that, right?"

"I know." I smile at her, and it's genuine. A survivor, just like myself, stands before me. And while we may have survived two different things, I know I got the strength to pull myself back together from her. The thought makes me stay just a moment longer.

"Mom?"

"Hmm?"

"I just want to thank you for getting Elain's mother help." Her eyes snap up to meet mine once she hears the shake in my voice. "And...and I just want to say that I'm not mad at you. I never was. I left because it's what I thought was best. And maybe it was for the best...or maybe it wasn't." I shrug.

"I don't know if I could have healed if I stayed." Tears threaten to burn the back of my eyes, but I blink them back, "The only thing I was sure of when I left was that I was not ready to face my monster. I was not ready for the entire world to know what he did to me. But I don't blame you for anything that happened. And I hope you don't blame yourself either."

She doesn't hide her watery smile as she comes forward to take my hands in hers. "I am so, so proud to be your mother, Blake. I'm sorry that I wasn't there. That you felt like you couldn't run to me. I can't change what happened, but I can promise that I'll be here for the rest of it if you'll let me. As your mother, it breaks my heart that this life has never been easy on you, but it made you the woman you are today. Not because of me or your father, but because in spite of us. You *choose* to be better. Do better." She hugs me, and for the first time in a long time, I feel the crack in our relationship begin to mend. One I'll make sure to keep filled for the rest of our lives. At the same time I go to bounce off the steps, a familiar sheriff's car pulls into my mother's driveway. I look over my shoulder; my mother's face is beet red as her eyes bounce from me to the car.

"You know you deserve to be happy, too, right?" I ask. Some of the color lessens from her face, and it softens when she realizes I'm not as oblivious as she hoped. "Just...no little siblings. Little late for that."

We laugh, and she rushes forward to kiss me on the cheek once more before I leave. I meet Sheriff Eaton halfway from where he exits his car, and he nods in acknowledgment. Swallowing nervously and looking from me to behind my shoulder at where my mom waits. "Blake."

"Mr. Eaton." I smile and cock my head at him. "You love her, don't you?" His eyes widen just enough for confirmation, so I land a hand on his shoulder and give it a shake. "Then what the hell are you doing?"

He nods, sucking in a breath and continuing the rest of the way to mom. That *look*. I don't need to stay around to know what happens next. My chest fills with a blinding happiness at my mom's happy ending.

Chapter 59

BLAKE

I hum along to the music blasting through my headphones as I finish wrapping up the last of the cookies.

Whitney hasn't been feeling her best now that the pregnancy is getting farther along, so I offered to help with some of the prep for the festival, hoping to take some weight off her shoulders. It's one of her family recipes. A cornbread cookie drizzled with honey and a delicious frosting. Something I've never had before but is now easily a favorite. Just as I tie the last orange bow around the plastic bag, a hand sneaks around my waist and hauls me from the ground. A shriek leaves my lips, first from fear and then excitement when I recognize the smell and warm hands. I turn around and slap Wesley's chest playfully as I pull an earbud out. "You scared me!"

"That was the point." He quirks a brow and then plants a quick kiss on my cheek. It causes the butterflies in my stomach to go haywire. He glances around the kitchen, a mess from all the baking I've been doing today. "Smells good."

I turn around, his arm still wrapped around my middle, and break off a piece from some of the extra cookies I made to keep. I pop it into his mouth, and he nods his head, moaning dramatically. "Yup. That's good."

"But I think I want something a little bit sweeter." He says on a breath, gaze slowly and deliberately dropping to my lips. Now I'm the one moaning as his fingers tangle in my hair, and he picks me up, placing me on the counter. His lips never leave mine. My mouth parts as his tongue darts out, both of us battling for dominance. He begins trailing one of his rough hands up my thigh until my skirt is bunched messily at my waist. And then he's yanking my head back and gripping the middle of my tank, pulling it down roughly until my breasts are pouring out over the fabric. I gasp at the sudden movement, and my palms land on the counter behind me to steady myself. His eyes darken as he takes in the sight of me sprawled on the counter, legs spread and chest on full display. My pussy aches with need as I watch him look at me. Look at me like he hasn't eaten in days, and I'm the only thing on the menu.

"No panties?" He murmurs, voice rough.

Those blue eyes are glazed over with pure lust, and I squirm beneath the heat of his stare. I shake my head, unable to give him a verbal answer. His grip tightens on my hair, eliciting a sharp moan from my lips. "I asked you a question, Blake."

"N-No."

He hums in approval. "You're dripping all over the counter, sweetheart. I haven't even touched you yet." His head cocks as his eyes roam over my wet heat. He brushes the pad of his thumb over my sensitive clit, teasing me with slow, lazy swirls. "You want me to play with this sweet cunt?"

"Yes."

"Say please, then."

He wants me to *beg*.

"*Please*, Wesley." I cry and buck my hips forward, desperate for even the slightest friction. "Touch me."

"That's a good girl." He takes the honey dipper from where it's discarded on the counter, rolling it around in the pot full of dense, dark syrup. Once he's satisfied with the amount he's collected, he pulls it up, the texture viscous and slowly dripping back into the pot.

"W-what are you doing?" I moan, tipping my head back. He doesn't give me a response, just brings it up to swirl it around my nipples until they're hardening painfully and I'm a panting mess, begging for more. He trails it down my stomach, honey sticking to my skin, until he's circling my clit with it. I gasp at the odd sensation, and he uses my surprise as an opportunity to plunge it in. Not deep, but just enough to coax a moan from me. The ridges of the stick and the thickness of the honey are unlike anything I've felt before, and I'm crying out his name in pure bliss.

It's erotic. So *wrong*. Something you'd probably only read about in a dirty book or see on a porn site. But it's also so fucking *intoxicating* that I never want it to end. He drops to his knees, still moving the honey stick in and out at a tantalizingly slow pace.

"Spread your legs, baby, that's it...*wider*." A growl breaks from his throat as I comply, and then he's quickly pulling the stick away before replacing it with his tongue in one swift motion. But he's not done with it just yet. He brings it up, looking at me from beneath thick lashes. The honey coating it almost completely gone, and he presses it against my parted lips before sliding it against my tongue. "Clean up your mess, Blake."

A whimper escapes my mouth as I grind back against his face and lick the stick clean. The familiar tang of honey mixed with my own arousal floods my taste buds. His head dips back, and he moans. "So fucking sweet." He murmurs against my mound, sending shivers down my spine. And then he's licking and sucking, nipping and biting, and it doesn't take long before him and his filthy words to cause an orgasm to crash into me in waves, making me dizzy and breathless. He pulls away, his lips glistening, mixed with my juices and the honey. The sight is likely to be forever engraved in my mind. I'm still coming down from my high, not even realizing he moved until he returns with a warm, wet washcloth. He drops a kiss to my inner thigh after wiping me off and helps fix my clothing before taking my hand and helping me down from the counter.

The sweet gestures make my face heat for an entirely different reason this time.

Curiosity gets the best of me, and I glance down at his jeans. The painfully large indent in the fabric tells me all that I need to know. But he sees the intent in my eyes before I can even reach for his belt. He shakes his head. "Why not?" I give him a pout. "I want to return the favor."

He only smirks and dips his head, breath fanning over my face. "It wasn't a favor, Blake. It wasn't even for you. That one was for me."

I narrow my eyes at him and pull away before I ask him to fuck me on the counter next. "Fine," I grumble. "I need to get dressed for the festival, anyways."

I turn to go towards my bedroom but hear a shuffle behind me. I whip around and see Wesley with his hands stuffed in his pockets and an oddly innocent-looking expression on his face. "Did you just stuff another one of those in your mouth?"

He shakes his head, then puffs his cheeks out. He mutters a muffled "No."

I roll my eyes, turning back in my original direction. "You're such a boy sometimes."

Chapter 60

BLAKE

I've just finished stringing up a sign above the coffee bar when I catch the tail end of Wyatt and Whitney's standoff. He dropped off lunch for us, and they've been bickering for the past half hour about God knows what. I just began listening in when his voice turned frustrated, and a tad louder than I'd ever heard. For someone so well-reserved, Whitney sure does get under his skin. I can't tell if they're about to start brawling...or make out?

"I think I, of all people, deserve to know-"

He's cut off when Ana pops up behind him, smacking him right upside the back of the head. "I know I didn't raise you to talk to a woman like that!"

"Mom!" Wyatt's hand flies to the back of his head, face lighting up. Despite whatever they may have been arguing about, and the fact that she's hysterically giggling into her hand, Whitney doesn't hesitate to come to his rescue with a teasing jab. "He's awfully broody, isn't he?"

"You think *that's* bad?" Ana scoffs. "You should've seen his dad after a long day."

"I'm right here." Wyatt grumbles, but they ignore him.

"I'm sorry for your loss." She places a hand on top of Ana's.

The way Ana smiles at her...it has me blinking in surprise. I know that look all too well. She gives her a meek smile, letting her eyes drop to Whitney's belly. "When are you due?"

"April." Whitney replies.

She reaches up, unclasping the chain dangling around her neck, the very one that holds her wedding band, and nods toward Whitney's bump. "Do you mind?"

At Whitney's confusion, Wyatt scratches the back of his head. "It's an old wives' tale. If the ring moves in circles, it's a girl. If it swings back and forth, it's a boy."

His mom nods along eagerly. "Worked on both of my pregnancies."

Whitney holds Wyatt's gaze for a moment longer than considered normal, then concedes with a nod. We watch as Ana holds the wedding ring over her belly. At first, it looks like it may just swing vertically, but then it slowly morphs into a circle and stays swinging. "That means it's a girl?" Whitney questions, biting her lip nervously.

Ana nods, beaming. Tears and what looks to be a little bit of hope fills Whitney's eyes. Maybe at the idea of repairing what she didn't have the gift of growing up. At getting a chance of being a loving, and present mom to a little girl, when she so desperately deserved one herself.

I jump as Wyatt abruptly stands from his seat and leaves without another word, swinging the door open rather aggressively and bidding none of us goodbye.

Ana sighs at her son's rude departure, and I intervene with an exaggerated groan, hoping to break some of the tension and heighten Whitney's spirits. "Dear god, I hope so. I already started buying pink outfits and bows."

We all giggle, both women giving me a thankful smile.

"But fair warning, they might be even sassier than boys. Blake was a menace from the day she was born," Ana adds. I roll my eyes, but the quip warms my heart. Ana has always been my mom just as much as my own.

"Were you scared?" Whitney asks, "When you found out?"

Ana widens her eyes comically. "Terrified."

"Really?"

She hums. "I was in denial for a few weeks. But I had an amazing support system. Something I suspect you do as well." Her eyes bounce to mine. "The first few weeks, hell, the first few years, will be hard. But you'll do just fine. You grow as they grow."

Whitney leans forward to squeeze her hand. "Thank you."

We all fall into random chatter about the boys and me as kids, the festival, and anything else that makes for good gossip. Ana is just leaving to 'go check on her asshole of a son' when the doors swing open again. "Got the cookies!" Elain shouts, stepping through the coffee shop doors. Wesley and Elain oversaw dropping the cookies off so that I could help Whitney setup. She's been ecstatic to help, even more so to check out her very first Clover-Hills festival. My mom's meeting her soon, so they can walk around together. The two have grown rather fond of each other.

"I like the scarecrow." Elain adds as she sets down the first tray. The scarecrow that Whitney and I put together has a skeleton head and hands. A witch's hat and a set of headphones adorn its skull. *And* it's holding a cardboard coffee cup. It's so stupid that it's adorable.

Whitney comes around from where she's at behind the counter, her face brightens when she sees the assortment of cookies. "They look great! Thank you again for helping out with them."

"It was no problem." I say with a wave of my hand.

She leans in to get a better look, laying a hand on her belly, "Awe, you even drizzled a little honey on top. How fancy!"

My skin involuntarily flushes at the word honey, which earns me an odd look from Elain, and another one from Whitney that says *you'll be telling me about that later.* I doubt it. That one's going into the deepest vault imaginable.

"Shit!" Whitney cries, slapping a hand over her face. "I forgot to grab more sugar since we ran out yesterday. This baby brain is going to be the *death* of me."

"You know what? I have some at the house from all the baking." I say, already turning toward the door. "I'll just run there and grab it. It'll take me like ten minutes."

"Really?" She sighs, letting her shoulders slump. "You're the best."

"I know." I sing. "Be back in a bit!"

Chapter 61

WESLEY

I always moan and bitch about these festivals before they happen, but even I know just how fun they are when it comes time. The entire town comes together, some people even travel from out of state for it. It's in full swing by the time I arrive at the bar, an extra bag of ice slung over my shoulder. Stilt walkers are roaming around, hayrides are full, and live music is already underway.

"That's pretty badass, Harper." I put her in charge of the scarecrow this year, and she killed it. It looks like a classic scarecrow, but it's wearing sunglasses and sporting a beer belly. The best part about it all is the basket full of beer that says, *Adults take one.*

"No way was I letting us lose to Clover's *again* this year." Clover's, the vet shop across the street. Last year, they had a dog scarecrow with a bunch of little puppy scarecrows. The locals went crazy for it, so they won. The town always gives a small donation to the winner, so I wasn't too shaken up over it. They needed it more. Harper is always one for a challenge, though, cute puppies aside.

Haden sits at the bar sipping on what looks like whiskey. I can't stop my gaping mouth when I see what he's wearing. "Cute costume."

He frowns as he looks down at his Spider-Man-clad body. "Harper told me you were dressing up as Iron Man."

His narrowed eyes slice to hers as she taps her chin in thought. "Did I? I don't recall."

Haden doesn't miss a beat, though, and doesn't even glare at her. His signature flirtatious smirk lights up his face. "If you wanted to play dress up with me, Harper, all you had to do was ask."

Her face morphs into one of disgust, but I don't miss the way she turns crimson red. I cut it off before Harper chooses to start throwing fists. "You two are going to be the death of me."

"Aren't you supposed to be with Wyatt?" I add. He always sets up and brings some of the animals for the kids to see. No other reason than he loves to watch a kid's face light up at the sight of a horse or pig. He may be a prickly bastard, but he's as soft-hearted as they come.

"I'm taking a break." Haden shrugs.

With whiskey? Sounds about right. "Well, no breaks here. Get off your ass and help me bring the rest of the ice in from the truck, Spider-Man."

Chapter 62

BLAKE

A creak sounds from somewhere in the house, but I don't pay it much mind. What once would have sent me running to my bedroom and hiding beneath the covers doesn't seem to bother me as much anymore. A house this old tends to be a bit noisy. "Ah, there it is." I mutter as I spot one of the large white bags of sugar tucked behind some other ingredients.

I reach forward, pulling one of the bags down and setting it on the counter. I move for another, but a voice causes me to jolt, and one of the bags tumbles from my hands. I curse as it breaks open, mounds of sugar pooling at my feet. It takes me a fraction of a second to register *whose* voice it is.

The very voice that's appeared too many times in my nightmares. It rings in the air around me like a ghost dragging its fingers down my spine, cold and unwelcome. Once I finally see him, he's raising his hands in a 'I *surrender*' motion. "Don't freak out, baby, I just want to talk."

His once-blond hair is entirely gray. He's as tall as I remember, but much thinner than the last time I saw him. His clothes don't fill out his frame, like they're two sizes too big. A round face with large green eyes and a slender nose. He's aged, and it somehow makes him more intimidating than before.

Fear consumes me. Fear, so intense I've only ever felt it once before. At the hands of the same man now standing before me. In *my* house. In *my* safe space. It's cruel how something that's become so comforting to me can become so tortuous in just a few seconds.

"You can't be here." I try to keep my voice steady, but it comes out so small and so frail, and I *hate* it. I've dreamed about this moment. What I would do and say. All the ways I'd scream at him and tear him apart for what he put me through. But with him standing here, right in front of me, it's as if my body is betraying my brain. As if I'm just that small, broken girl again, begging for her father to be as gentle with her as he used to be.

I'm so scared, so *petrified* that all the words I want to say don't come out. I'm sure that even if they could, only the wrong ones would. "You got so big." He whispers. Taking me in like a father who wasn't the sole reason his kid grew up without him.

"How are you here?" It's then that I look over his person. No sort of ankle monitor in sight. Whether he removed it or not, I have no clue. But I don't want to stick around to find out. "You're supposed to be on house arrest." My heart is beating erratically, and I'm trying my best to comb through all the ways to get *out* of this situation.

His eyes turned cold and calculating at my words, and he dropped the hands still raised in the air. "I tried seeing your mom first, but she wasn't home."

I close my eyes for just a moment. *She wasn't home.* That's one small blessing. God knows what would have happened if she was. I give myself just that brief moment of peace, and then I'm opening my lids again. Taking my eyes off this monster for more time than necessary isn't a mistake I can make twice.

"I missed my girl. I just wanted to see you. Jason told me you came back home." His tone is both pleading and full of unmistakable malice. All it does is send a sick feeling shivering up my spine.

"You need to leave." I say, my voice wavering. At that moment, my phone rings, and we both lock eyes before diving for it. I manage to grasp it first, but he still lunges for me once it's in my shaky hands.

"Dammit, Blake!"

I turn to bolt, but I trip on the rug beneath my feet and come crashing down. The pain of my fall vibrates through my body. Before I can flip onto my back, his weight comes crashing down on me. "Dad!" I scream. "Dad, stop! Please, please, stop!" I can't stop the cries that tear their way out of me. I'm too panicked at the position he's got me in. How vulnerable I am. I hope that just saying his name, calling him something I promised to *never* call him again, would pull him back to reality. To the fact that I'm *his daughter.* But it doesn't. It only adds fuel to the fire. He rolls me onto my back, face red and seething above me. He then lifts his hand and sends it flying, backhanding me so hard it sends my head swinging to the right. Involuntary tears begin to leak from the corner of my eyes.

My world slows down and speeds up at the same time. My body falls into fight-or-flight mode.

I reach out with the one loose arm he let go in his effort to strike me, and I wrap my fingers around a nearby object, bringing it back to slam it against his head. I know I've met my mark when he lets out a wild roar. It dazes him enough for me to scurry out from underneath him. I don't bother to search for my phone or see if he's gotten up yet. This familiar terror of him catching me and beating me within an inch of my life is what makes me successful in barreling through the front door.

***

A sharp throbbing ricochets in my head, and every single part of my body hurts in a way I've never experienced before. I slowly open my eyes, covering them as light pours in, causing them to sting. For just a moment, I have absolutely no idea where I am. But when I turn my head and see the broken glass shards and a large lamp sprawled on the floor, it dawns on me. The once-foggy images are becoming clearer as I take in the scene around me. The living room is torn to shreds. My chest rises faster and faster as I realize what's happened. As I recall the memories that have left my frail body broken and bloody on the floor. Dread sets in as I realize just how bad the situation is.

He beat me so badly I blacked out.

Pushing up, I wince as the glass all around digs into the palms of my hands. Tears spring to my eyes at how much noise I've made from just that little sound. I try my best to stay quiet, even going as far as to hold my breath. Not sure where he is, but knowing I need to get out as soon as possible. Rising to shaky feet, I take in my surroundings. Eyes darting all around the room. And they freeze as I take in my father sprawled on the large couch in the center of the room. His knuckles are bloody from my assault, and a bottle of rum hangs from his limp fingertips.

A warm trickle falls down my arm and past my fingertips. I let my eyes slowly track it before it lands on a piece of glass with a light plop. I bite my tongue to stop myself from crying out. A large gash runs up the middle of it, and it leaks a steady flow of blood. It's going to scar, and it needs stitches. Soon.

I force my eyes to stay glued to one of the larger glass shards covered in blood. It's as large as a kitchen knife, and I think about picking it up.

To do what? Who knows? But for just a second, all the young, broken girl inside me wants to do is make him hurt just as badly as he's hurt her. I begin to crouch and then stop dead. Because despite what's just happened, he's still my father. For just a second, I think it. Think about picking up the broken glass and using it on him. It's a horrendous thought. Something that will probably live in my head for the rest of my life. But I can't bring myself to feel an ounce of shame just yet.

Right then, a floorboard creaks beneath my weight, and the snoring stops. Panic and fear hit me like a train, and I don't wait to see if he's woken. I'm sprinting, barreling through the front door, and jumping the porch steps. I pump my arms and legs as fast as they can go, bare feet digging into gravel and dirt. I don't look back, too scared I'll turn and see him following. I run, and run, and run, until my lungs are sore and begging for mercy.

Chapter 63

WESLEY

"Hi Wesley!" Elain chirps, nursing a paper cup to her chest. It's probably the coldest day we've had in Clover-Hills this season, so she's bundled up in a large coat with matching gloves and a hat. For someone who just went through one hell of a traumatic experience, she seems to be holding herself together rather well. A part of me knows that it's because of Blake.

I ruffle her hair as I walk by. "What's up, kid? Is Blake here?"

She pats down her hair with a scowl, but her face stays playful and light. "I dunno, just got back from seeing the horses with Elise. Whitney might know, though. She's out back."

I nod, leaving her at the front of the shop. I find Whitney sitting behind her desk in the office, one hand raised to her mouth where she bites at her fingernail, and the other resting on her swollen belly. She's nervously glancing at the cell phone that lies sprawled on the hardwood before her. I lean against the doorframe and knock against the framework, causing her to look up. "Hey. Have you seen Blake?"

"She left like an hour ago to grab some sugar from the house. I've been calling her nonstop, but she won't answer."

"I'm sure she's alright, probably just got caught up." Or distracted. She probably saw a cute animal on the side of the road and stopped to take a picture of it. It wouldn't be out of the ordinary for her.

"She said she'd be back in ten." Her pinched expression tells me she's worried. I try to keep my expression neutral in hopes of not stressing her out any more than she already seems to be. It's the last thing a pregnant woman needs.

I reach into my front pocket and wave a hand in her direction. "I'll try her cell." It rings for a few seconds before I hear the line connect. "Hello?"

All I get in response is what sounds like a crash, followed by muffled screams. My heart rate surges, panic racing through me. Endless possibilities of what's happening run through my head. "Blake?" I pull the phone away from my ear to glance down at it, making sure I called the right number. Dread only turns to lead in my stomach when I see that I did. I don't hesitate in pivoting toward the front of the shop, fear motivating me to move faster than I've ever possibly moved. "Call the Sheriff!" I yell back at Whitney. I don't wait to see if she responds as I'm already sprinting out the front door, bells that suddenly seem far too loud chiming above me. Shouts come from what I can assume is Elain and everyone else standing by, but I don't stop. My pounding heart and the endless scenarios coursing through my thoughts were only pushing me faster.

***

I've tried her phone maybe a hundred times now, and every single one just rang, and rang, and rang.

I turn the corner that puts me onto our road, nearly skidding from the speed. I just pass my house when I have to slam on my breaks as a mop of blonde hair comes sprinting in front of my truck. I wrench it into park, the motion jolting me. But I don't let it slow me down as I whip open the driver-side door and rush to Blake. I immediately spot the small cut on the side of her face. Tears stream down her flushed cheeks. She's hysterical. I gently grab a hold on her biceps and quickly glance over her frame. Checking for any other injuries. "Are you okay? What happened? Tell me what happened."

"M–My father." She blurts between hiccups.

Two words. Two words that make me see *red*.

"You're okay?" I ask again, doing a third glance over her. She nods. Shocking me when she throws herself into my arms, wrapping herself around my middle. I wrap my own back around her, bringing a hand up to cup her head. I drop a quick kiss on it before pulling back. "Get in the truck, Blake. Lock the doors, and then call the police."

Whitney should have already called, but better safe than sorry. I walk calmly until I'm out of view of Blake, thankful that she listened to my directions instead of trying to fight me on it. I find the prick stumbling out of the front door, hand pressed to the side of his head. My heart clenches at the fact she even had to defend herself, but a ripple of pride follows at the fact that she was so capable. My girl's a fighter. Always has been.

My steps eat up the distance between us. The ground thundering beneath my boots. I can hear the sirens in the distance, the sound of a car already pulling into Blake's driveway, but my attention stays focused on Derek Warner. He opens his mouth, but I don't give him the chance to spew any bullshit my way. I cock my arm back, pitching it forward until it connects with his face. A satisfying crack rakes through the open air. I revel in the sting that shoots through my knuckles. I reach down and grab his collar, bringing his bloody face forward to meet mine. I bare my teeth at the pathetic asshole, but Blake's voice stops me cold. "Don't! Please."

I force myself to calm. He deserves for me to put him six feet in the ground. But not now, not with Blake watching. I settle for yanking him to his feet aggressively, accidentally slamming his face into one of the porch's wooden beams. He sobs once he sees Blake. "I'm sorry, baby. I just wanted to see you."

My grip tightens on his shoulder, so hard the knuckles turn white. I hiss in his ear. "Don't talk to her. Do you understand me? The *only* reason you're even breathing is because of the blood you share with that woman."

But Blake doesn't cower at his words. She keeps her body in a defensive position. Her chin wobbles, but she just tilts her head higher. Looking down her nose at the smallest man who ever lived. "No, you're not sorry. You never were."

The way she says it is a revelation, and it makes me so proud. She's the strongest woman I've ever met. She pushes past us and goes inside the house without another glance in his direction. I shove him down the porch once I see the cop car pull in. He opens his mouth as if to call after her, but his eyes slice to the figure who now stands where Blake was mere seconds ago. He snarls. "Elise."

Blake's mom doesn't take her eyes off Derek while she talks to the Sheriff, who's now joined her side. "Eaton, did you see Blake's new place? It's gorgeous, isn't it?"

The Sheriff takes his time turning and taking in the house. "I love what she did with the place." He squints his eyes as he evaluates the porch. "Is that the natural wood?"

Elise takes the Sheriff's "*distraction*" and runs with it, nailing her ex-husband right between the legs. He cries out, doubling over and falling to the floor in a pathetic heap. She spits at the dirt beside him. "Have fun rotting in prison, prick." Then, she storms after Blake.

Sheriff Eaton lets out a low whistle as he pretends like he has no idea what happened. Bending over and harshly yanking him from the ground. He may or may not so subtly bump Derek's head on the way into the cop car. He shoots me a wink over his shoulder. "Oops."

Chapter 64

BLAKE

Wesley toys with my hair as he lays behind me, snuggled up close and under the blankets with me. We haven't talked, just sat here, in this comfortable silence. The evening light streams in through the bedroom window, and the heat of his body makes me never want to leave this bed. My mom just left, having spent the majority of the day in Wesley's place. I know he was dying to see me after the whole ordeal, but he gave us our moment. Something I appreciate more than he could ever know. I turn my head over my shoulder, finding that he's already watching me. One hand is propped on his head. "Can I show you something?"

He nods, confused but refusing to question me. "I'll drive." He speaks.

***

"What is this?" Wesley asks as we pull into the driveway. "I've never been here."

I can feel his stare burning into the side of my face, but I just exit the truck and make my way to the front of the house. He follows, quiet and unquestioning. Once we step inside, I go to stand in the middle of the living room, toying with my hands. I take in a deep breath and let it loose.

"There." I point at the bottom of the staircase. "There was the first time he ever laid a hand on me."

My father's old house. It's empty now. No one ever did anything with it. All the old furniture is still here. Everything was dusty, dead, and untouched. When he realizes what this is, what I'm giving him, his brows furrow, and he steps towards me.

"Blake, you don't have to -"

"Yes, I do." He snaps his mouth shut and doesn't say anything more. Doesn't move. Just watches me. "He slapped me. Then he cried after it happened. Said it would never happen again. That it was a mistake. That he loved me and would never, *could* never do such a thing." I suck in another breath. "I believed him."

"And then there." I moved to the open dining room and pointed at the table. "I asked to go visit my mom, and he threw me down on it. Choked me until I nearly passed out. That time, he didn't apologize." I turn toward the kitchen. "I dropped the take-out box he made me pick up for him. He slammed my head into the counter because of it." My chin begins to wobble on that last word, but I keep going. I move around the house, pointing out different spots. Explaining what, when, and where the abuse happened. It hurt to share it, it hurt even more to see how broken Wesley looked as I continued. But it was also freeing. So, so freeing that I wish I had the courage to do this sooner. I come to a stop in the middle of the living, next to one of the only windows facing the front.

"And here? Here is where I got this." I stretch out my arm. I haven't even acknowledged the tears streaming down my face, not until he steps forward to wipe them away. A few of his own slipped down his. "I...he caught me sneaking in. After our night out. He beat me so badly that I passed out. So, when I woke up and found him asleep, I ran. I ran all the way to Whitney's, where she helped me get out."

"When I woke up, I knew what I had to do. I knew I had to leave. I...I knew I couldn't say goodbye to you because I knew you'd follow me." A sob escapes my lips. "And I would never be able to live with myself if I was the one who took you from your mother. From Wyatt. They needed you more than I needed you. I love you, Wesley. I love you more than I can even begin to explain. Everything, *everything* was a blur when I left, but that? That never was. I loved you then, and I love you now. And I will love you for as long as you'll let me."

He grasps my face, his blue eyes boring into mine, and I know with absolute clarity that the little blue house I stumbled upon isn't home. This town isn't home. New York isn't home. Wesley is home. My home. My salvation. And I will never run away from it. I'll fight for it in the same way he always fought for me. So, I lean my head against his, recalling those words he spoke to me so long ago. "Where you go, I go.".

Chapter 65

BLAKE

We're settled back in the truck, but before Wesley can turn the key, I lay my hand on his. "I think...I think I want to start a group. Somewhere, people can go to talk about these things. About life. Where they can ask for help."

He doesn't hesitate to take my hand. "Then that's what we'll do."

We. God, I love the sound of that. I lean forward and plant a kiss on his lips at the word. It's sweet, short, and tender. But soon it takes a hungry turn, and the need to feel him, all of him, becomes crucial. I crawl into his lap, keeping my lips locked on his. Once I'm fully seated in his lap, he grips the sides of my head, pulling me back so that we're eye to eye. "I love you." He whispers.

"I love you." I don't hesitate in my response because it's the truth. Wesley is the one, and deep down, I think I always knew he was the one. We may have been worlds apart for years, and we may have lived different lives for the majority of it, but my heart never left his. It never will. I reach between us to grasp the buckle of his jeans, but he's searching my eyes for any sort of hesitation. "Are you sure?"

I nod eagerly and breathlessly. "Yes. Yes, I'm sure."

A low groan rises from his throat as he jerks my head back down and into a searing kiss. He tastes like mint and smells like spice and looks entirely like he's *mine*. We get his jeans pulled down, with his boxers following suit. His hard member presses against the rough material of my jeans, and we both moan in unison at the friction. His hands slowly roam under my shirt, cold as they splay against my middle and creep up to the lacey underwire of my bra. He takes his time undressing me. Slipping my long sleeve over my head, freeing my breasts to the chilly air, and unbuttoning my jeans. Once I'm bare from the waist up, he's trailing small kisses all over my collarbone and up my neck. Kneading my ass and rolling my hips against his own. An elated giggle erupts from me as he hovers over a particularly sensitive spot, and he nips it in return.

He raises my hips so that we're perfectly lined up, and we both watch with heavy-lidded eyes as I sink onto him. We both stay there, still for a moment, until it turns frantic, and we're both chasing the release. The windows turn foggy, our handprints littering the glass. And while it's still a hurried moment full of lust, it's different than before. Sweeter. Slower. Softer. As if we're savoring each other. As if we finally understand that *this* is real and that it's not going anywhere.

Chapter 66

WESLEY

The beginning of November has finally found its way to Clover-Hills. Blake shivers and rubs her hands together after she places the last cardboard box inside the back of my truck.

She's moving in with me, officially. Both her and Elain, since her mother is still recovering in rehab. Elain was more than inviting to the idea, seemingly excited that she'd get her own room with the extra space in my house. We decided, soon after everything that's happened, that we weren't going anywhere. And it's much easier to just share the same bed versus going back and forth every night. Surprisingly, it was Blake who brought the idea up first. I had been dying to bring it up for quite some time but didn't want to push her. Her *only* stipulation is that we'd add another room for Vivienne for when she wants to stay the night. I didn't question that one. Better that she has her own room than kicks me out of my bed. To say we celebrated in more ways than one would be an understatement.

The first snow day is supposed to hit the end of this week, so we decided to move everything rather quickly. Thankfully, it's not a very far move. And she's not bringing much, just personal belongings. Most will stay to use for the health center she's creating with her mom.

"I'll go turn off the lights," I tell her. "Hop in the truck where it's warm." She doesn't protest, more than willing to get back into the truck. Later this week, we're going to go look at a new car for her at a dealership out of town. I haven't told her yet that I'll be looking for a new truck, too. With heated seats, since that seems to be the only thing she complains about when it comes to my dad's old truck. I'll still be keeping it, but there's nothing wrong with change. Not anymore.

As I get inside, I head to the kitchen to switch off the overhead lights above the island, but my eyes snag on what looks like a piece of paper that's tucked halfway under one of the cupboards. I bend down to pick it up, feeling the dust and grime that coats it dusting my fingertips. When I see that it's an old photograph, I wipe it on the front of my jeans. I pause as I finally look at it.

It's Ethel, the woman who lived next door to me before she passed. And...and an older man standing next to her, with his arm slung over her in a warm embrace. Their hands are on full display, showcasing the matching wedding bands the two bear. Of course, I knew she was married. She told me stories of her husband who passed nearly a decade ago, but I never saw any pictures. But that man...I recognize that man. The same one who sat next to me at the bar just a few months ago. The same one who told me about his wife.

I never asked her name, I didn't think to.

But now – now I know.

It was Ethel.

Tears prickle the back of my eyes as I realize why I truly saw myself in the older woman who lived next door. Why I looked at her and saw myself sitting in that rocker chair on the porch. She wasn't lonely. She *had* shared a home with someone. She had someone to call home, and she *was* content with the life she shared with him. She found her person and loved him until the very end. All because he let her go once and never made that mistake again.

A honk sounds from outside, signaling Blake's irritation at my dallying. But I only smile and holler that I'm coming, knowing exactly how this story ends. How *our* story ends.

Chapter 67

BLAKE

Elain and I were officially moved into Wesley's, the latter ecstatic at having her own room. Wesley even took her down to the department store to pick out a new paint color and some décor to make it her own. Moving in with him was an easy decision to make. Wesley was my home, and it didn't matter where we stayed or where we went. That wouldn't change. Plus, seeing how well he did with Elain and how easily their friendship formed was the selling point for me.

That little cottage I found when I moved here would now become Clover-Hills' very first Therapeutic Treatment Center.

It'll be a safe space for anyone who needs it. For anyone who needs a place to stay. For anyone who just needs someone to talk to. We'll hold weekly or daily therapy groups where everyone can share their stories.

Residents can come for counseling and advice, and it will be completely free for anyone who needs it. It'll be a cozy space, where you can come and just sit on a couch before the fireplace, drinking a coffee and reading a book. One where you can feel comfortable enough to not even talk, but to just be surrounded by people who you know *care*.

People will use it to heal. To find peace.

That's exactly why I've decided to visit my father today. To find my peace.

Wesley offered to come, but Elain was the one who insisted she tag along. He didn't fight her on that. We now sit at the front of the prison, having already gone through the gates and whatnot. Elain's going to stay in the car, but I'm beyond grateful that she's chosen to join me. That she'll be my support. Someone who understands what this is like. I can't help but wonder if when she's further along in her healing journey, I'll be the one to join her when she sees her father for the first time.

"You've got this." I don't respond, only nod before slamming the driver-side door before heading to the front.

***

I'm not as nervous as I was when I first stepped in here. I'm oddly calm, and somehow that's more nerve-racking. I wait on the other side of the glass that separates civilians from the inmates. A phone sits on a hook beside the cubby.

Soon, a buzzing fills the air, and my father comes into view. He's dressed in orange, shackles on his hands and feet. His face was bruised from what I can assume was a brawl within the prison. I'm not surprised, as I hear child abuse doesn't sit well with one's fellow inmates. I don't feel any pity for the man as he sits across from me. He picks up the phone, and I do, too. He goes to open his mouth, but I put my hand up to stop it. Surprisingly, he listens. "I'm not here for you. I'm here for me."

I lift my chin and meet his eyes. Refusing to cast my gaze downward. "What you did? I'll never forget. I *can't* forget. That you made sure of." His face scrunches, and he looks like he wants to speak, but I forge ahead. Not giving him the chance. "I love you because I unconditionally love the father you were to the little girl I was. But I don't understand you. I don't *know* you. How you can hurt the one person you're supposed to protect is beyond me. It hurts that you'd choose this," I wave my hand around us, "Over what you could have had. The *family* you could have had. That is a decision you will have to live with for the rest of your life." I shake my head. "You don't deserve my forgiveness, so you won't get it. But I do deserve to move on. So that is why I'm here."

I pull in a long breath, choosing to fight back that part of me that wants to scream and tear this entire room to shreds. The side that wants to lunge at this man and shake him for all the pain he's caused. "I hope you get help while you're in there. I hope you sit in there and you understand why what you did a few months ago was wrong, and why what you did *years* ago was wrong."

"I don't need you. I never did. And I hope you find peace in your life choices, the same way I've found peace in letting you go." I pull the phone away from my ear as he begins speaking, spewing an apology I don't want to hear. I lay it down before me and stand. I turn away from him without another glance, not even having to fight tears because I've already shed more for this monster than I'll ever shed again. It hurts, but it's better to feel this kind of pain than nothing at all.

I leave, content in that this is the last moment I ever see my father again.

***

I barrel into my car seat again when Elain turns her body toward mine. "You, okay?"

Worry is etched onto her features. Not pity, not sadness, but worry. Knowing what kind of toll this kind of situation can take. But I just reach forward and squeeze her hands. "I will be." She smiles at me, and that smile tells me that I really will be okay. That we both will be. Because while we both need to heal, we'll get there. And we'll be stronger because of it. If she can smile after everything, so can I.

She squeezes my hand back. "Let's go home, then."

Chapter 68

BLAKE

"**I**'m gonna go read." Elain declares as we reach the front steps to the house.

We watch as she goes inside, and Wesley stands from the rocker chair to come stand in front of me. He cups the side of my face and lands a quick kiss on my forehead. "How'd it go?" He asks.

"As good as you think it would." I shrug.

He just looks at me, brows slowly rising in question. "It was...good. For me, it was. It hurt, but it was freeing. I think I needed it."

He nods, not pushing me any further. And I'm thankful for it. He cranes his head to look behind me. "Want to go for a walk?"

I nod, turning my head to follow his gaze, knowing exactly where he wants to go. I gracefully take the coat he's handing me and place my hand in his awaiting one.

***

We walk for just a few minutes before we're standing at the pond nestled next to my previous home. Our hands, still interlocked. It's frozen over now due to how harshly cold the weather has become, but it's our pond all the same. I breathe out, watching as my breath fogs in the air before me. "It's crazy what time can do to a place like this."

He nods along, bringing our hands up to place a tender kiss on top of mine. His lips are hot against our cold hands. "It's crazy how much a place like this can do for *us*." A little smile graces my lips at that comment, and his grin mirrors my own as he turns fully to face me, dropping our hands and wrapping his arms around my middle to pull me in.

"What now, Miss. Warner?"

"What now?" I repeat, leaning my head against his chest. "Now, I'll share my story."

And I will. Now, I will write that book that Whitney reminded me of when I first quit my job in the city. I'll write for me. For Elain. For the next little girl who feels like the bruises were her fault. For the woman she'll become, the trauma that will shape her for the rest of her life. For the daughter she'll have that will only ever know love and gentle hands. Because there will be someone else, in a world like this, there always is. But I'll do my best to help heal even one.

Epilogue

BLAKE

"Now, remember, Hun." Ana takes my face in her hands. "It's my son, but I'll still kick his ass if you ask me to. And I'm afraid there's no return policy on this one."

I tip my head back and laugh at my soon-to-be mother-in-law. "Thanks, Ana."

I turn back toward the large oval mirror before me and finally take in my appearance. My blonde hair is pinned up in a beautiful bun, a few curls falling to frame my face, with a veil flowing over my back. My stark white wedding dress starts with a sweetheart neckline, where it falls into a classic ball gown that allows me to live out my Cinderella-esque dreams. Lace, pearls, and diamonds are scattered all over the material in a beautiful pattern, and it's so breathtakingly gorgeous that I can't help the tears that spring to my eyes at the sight.

I'm marrying Wesley. *Today.*

This is it.

"You look beautiful." Ana whispers from my side, taking in my look from the mirror as well.

"That, she does." My mom's voice flutters to us as she walks into the bridal suite, her smile wide as she meets my watery gaze in the mirror. "Our girl is all grown up." She adds as she approaches, reaching out to take Ana's hand. My heart squeezes at the sight.

The two have been blubbering messes since they found out about the proposal, and were more than happy to help plan the wedding. I wanted something small, but unsurprisingly, it ended up being the biggest event this town has ever seen.

It doesn't matter if Wesley and I got married in a courthouse or in the prettiest view this town has to offer. What matters is that I get to marry *him.*

Soon, Vivienne, Harper, Whitney, and Elain are all piling into the room to get a look at me in my dress. Whitney and Vivienne almost look like twins in the similar green bridesmaid gowns we picked out. Elain's wearing a darker shade of green, with a matching crown of flowers adoring her dark locks. She's my flower girl. I was more than shocked that she had agreed to it so easily, but I think Wesley may have bribed her with cash to even make that one possible.

"Are you ready?" Vivienne asks.

I smile. "Almost. I just need to do this one last thing."

***

The one last thing required the girls to fetch Wesley for me and to find us a spot where I could give him his wedding gift without him seeing me.

We both stand back-to-back in a room with no one else around. I wanted privacy for this moment, but I don't want us to see each other just yet. The minute the door clicks, signaling we're alone, he doesn't wait to tease me about requesting a last-minute audience before our wedding.

"Miss me so much that you couldn't wait until the altar, Mrs. Conway?"

I roll my eyes. "I'm not a Conway just yet."

He just lets out a breathy laugh in return, one that sounds like it's full of pure excitement and nerves. I can't imagine I sound much different. We fall into a comfortable silence, so I use that as a moment to crane my arm around and hand him the small book I've been hiding the past few weeks. This is something I've been dying to show him since I first sent it off to the editor.

My very first completed book.

"What is this?"

"My story. *Our* story."

The idea of being a published author...it's unfathomable. A dream. One I've been so excited to share with Wesley. It releases the day after we get back from our honeymoon. He doesn't say anything for a few moments, but a small sniffle echo's in the silence around us.

"Are you crying?" I blurt out in question. He only scoffs.

"No." Another sniffle. "I think someone's cutting onions."

I reach back and grab the hand that's dangling at his side. He squeezes it immediately and sighs in frustration. "I want to kiss you so bad right now."

I laugh. "Catch me at the altar then, Conway."

Bonus Chapter

BLAKE

I flip the page of my book, face burning as I read a rather steamy scene. The enemies just turned lovers, and I'm practically foaming at the mouth for the long-awaited end to this slow burn. Wesley and I have plans after he closes the bar. Currently, it's just the two of us.

"What are you reading?"

My eyes shoot to his, but I slam the book shut and tuck it into my chest. "Nothing!"

He raises a brow, chucking the rag he'd been using to wipe the counters to the side and placing a hand on either side of me. Leaning in so close that his nose brushes against mine. "I think it's adorable how flustered you are over a book."

His small distraction has me loosening my grip on my book and leaning forward in my chair. He uses this as a chance to sweep the book from my hands, giving me a peck on the cheek as my protests ring out. It takes him all but a second to flip open to where I've placed my bookmark. I bury my face in my hands as he reads the text, getting cockier and cockier as his eyes skim each line.

"This sounds fun." He smirked, eyes looking me up and down before turning back to the page.

"As if you could get me off that many times."

His eyes spark with a challenge as he leans back in. "You baiting me, sweetheart?"

"I think you're giving yourself too much credit." I tilt my head, making a show of fluttering my eyes and pulling my bottom lip between my teeth. His hand shoots between us, wrapping his hands around the bottom of my chin, letting his fingers dig into my throat. It's gentle but rough and full of enough promises to shoot a pool of warmth between my legs.

"You weren't saying that the last time I had you *begging* for me to stop."

Just then, the sound of the bar doors swings open, but Wesley doesn't let me go. Doesn't break our staring contest to even throw the newcomer a look. "We're closed."

"But-"

I swear I hear Haden's voice cut through our little game, but I don't care. Wesley holds eye contact with me and tightens his grip just a fraction to ensure I don't move. He grits a "Get. Out." at Haden, and my core feels like molten lava beneath his heated stare. I instantly rub my thighs together and whimper.

Haden doesn't question it any further, only turns right back around and closes the door.

Smart man.

He lets go so that he can point at the pool table towards the end of the bar. "Take everything off and get on all fours."

I don't protest, only push from my stool and stand on shaky legs, but he tuts when I move away. "You're forgetting something." I turn to find him holding my book. The very book that started this to begin with.

I flush, taking it gingerly from his hands and treading to the pool table. While I undress, he locks the door. And by the time I'm where he wanted me, he's whistling at the sight of me laid bare. "Fuck." He mutters as he comes up behind me, spreading my thighs farther apart. "I bet you like this, don't you? Sprawled out on all fours, begging, and waiting for me to use you like a little whore. Right where anyone could walk by and see you."

He's right. They'd have to cup their hands and press their faces against the glass to see, but if someone truly wanted to, they could see *everything*. The idea only makes me hotter, and I'm practically panting by the time Wesley finally touches me. I look over my shoulder at the same time a line of spit drips from his mouth and lands on my skin. We both watch as it slides down from my ass to my entrance. Wesley wastes no time in spreading the wet, hot substance before plunging his fingers into me.

I moan at the contact, instinctively pushing back into his touch. God, whatever he's doing with his fingers... I don't want it to stop.

"Should I make you read me that little scene from your book?"

I nod, opening my mouth, but words fail me as his fingers curl and hit just the right spot. I reach forward and palm the book, open the pages to where I left off. Trying and nearly failing to focus on the words while Wesley's hands roam over my ass. "H–he leans forward, taking her wet, heat into his mouth. Sucking and licking until she's a moaning, withering mess beneath him. His cock is in his hands as-"

I gasp as Wesley does just that. His mouth is on me in an instant, and the sound of a buckle coming undone lets me know he plans on acting this out word for *word*. A sharp smack lands on my ass when my words falter, and I jolt from the sting. "Did I tell you to stop?"

"N–no."

I read on, earning more smacks anytime I stutter or stop. Orgasm after orgasm racks my body as his mouth, fingers, and cock take turns worshipping me. He spends the rest of the night proving me very, very *wrong*.

Book 2 Sneak Peak

WHITNEY

I stare down at the bottle of pills clutched in my hand, and when I let my gaze flicker to the picture of Brinley on the dash, my eyes begin to burn for what must be the fourth or fifth time today. It's a picture of her the day after she turned six months old. It was the first time she sat up on her own, and she was wearing the best kind of gummy smile on her face. My heart clenches at the sight, remembering how excited I was to catch the moment on camera.

How is time such a thief? How did she get so big, so fast? It's like you blink, and all time does is slip through your fingers like water. I would have done anything to get through those first few newborn nights, but God, it hurts to know she's growing up. It hurts to know that I wasn't all there the first few months–that I missed out on some of the best days of my life. That I let myself become a shell of who I used to be. That, in some ways, I still am a shell of the woman I was.

It's the very reason I went to the doctor today. Postpartum hit me harder than I could have ever imagined. It's impossible to prepare for the things that people tell you to prepare yourself for, because you can't prepare for something you've never experienced before. There were days when I couldn't even pull myself out of bed. Days I'd cry and beg for her to calm down. When I'd get frustrated and scream, and then wallow in guilt and shame over the tears I had caused. When I'd look in the mirror and not recognize the woman staring back at me. Messy hair, puke-covered T-shirt, and eye bags so dark they seemed never-ending. I was in denial for months, because I grew up in a family that taught me mental health wasn't something you ran to pills for. But Brinley deserves a mom who's present. Who wants to wake up energized and ready to play with her. Who's excited to start the day–not one who breaks down at the slightest inconvenience.

She doesn't deserve a mom like the one I had.

About the author

Kelsee Warrick is an American author, making her literary mark in 2025 with her first novel. At 21-years-old, Kelsee has a deep passion for romance, crafting stories that capture the complexity of love and relationships. She's passionate about creating vivid scenes that feel like they jump off the page, drawing readers into the heart of each moment. When she's not writing, Kelsee lives in New York with her fiancé, two dogs, and her child. She draws inspiration from her bustling surroundings and the quiet moments spent at home. Her writing reflects a deep love for characters who navigate day-to-day challenges and the emotions that make them human. Her debut novel marks the beginning of what promises to be an exciting journey as a writer.

Acknowledgements

To my Husband and Daughter,

Jacob, thank you for being my Wesley when I'd only known Marshalls. Your unyielding love and support are what made this dream possible, and I'm grateful to spend forever with you by my side. You and Oakley are the reason I choose to wake up every day and become a better version of myself than I was the day before. I love you two more than life.

To Viviana,

My lifelong friend and soulmate. None of this would have been possible without you. Before I even began writing this story, you were there, cheering me on when I needed it most. I never would have finished this story if it weren't for you.

To Hayley,

My unauthorized editor, bonus sister, and biggest cheerleader. I love you so deeply, and I'm forever thankful for your kindness. You've shown me that family is just as easily created as it is made.

To Dad and Pacee,

You two are my light. For as long as I could talk, I've wanted to write, and neither of you ever doubted me. Thank you for creating a space that let me believe I could and would accomplish anything.

To Kristie, Geoff, Maddy, and Grant,

Thank you for being my bonus family. Thank you for loving my daughter so completely. Your love and support mean the world to me, and I'm so thankful to know and love each of you. I may not have been in your lives from the start, but you are every bit my home and heart.

To Jen, Jason, Brittany, and Rebecca,

I'm so grateful to be a part of your family. I found my best friend and life-long partner in your son and brother, and in turn, became part of a beautiful family who loves me as their own. Thank you so much for your unwavering support, and for the warmth and care you show my family.

To Morgan,

My bonus sister. I would have never gotten my spark back if it weren't for you. Thank you for showing me there's always light at the end of the tunnel. I am forever proud of what a strong woman you are.

To Brianna,

Thank you for everything that you do-from the marketing and editing to the encouragement and dedication. Your positive nature and support are so deeply appreciated. I am so, so happy that you created Silver Editing & Co. – you make smaller authors like me possible. Thank you for making my life so much easier!

To my readers,

Thank you for taking a chance on me and reading my debut novel. I hope you've learned it's okay to break a little before you heal and that the journey is just as rewarding as the end. I hope you all find your Wesley in your pursuit of happiness. Go chase those dreams. I promise they're not as impossible as they seem.